Pennine Adventure

Richard Stoll

Copyright © 2015 Richard Stoll

ISBN 978 – 1 – 326 – 47882 – 7

When young schoolteacher Hannah set out on a spur-of-the-moment walking holiday in the Derbyshire Peak District she had no idea that it was part of God's plan for her life. If she had, she might, like Jonah of old, have run in the opposite direction. The next few days would turn out to be a puzzling time. Why did a relatively minor mishap, for which she was by no means responsible, result in so much anger and venom being directed at her by an extremely unpleasant character? And what were the motives of the helpful young man who befriended her on the train? It did not take long to find out. Even greater surprises were to follow, however, and her life would never be the same again.

Note
The Derbyshire Peak District National Park has long been known as an area of extreme natural beauty and a magnet for holiday makers and serious walkers, but it was only fifty years ago that the construction of the less well-known Pennine Way was completed. Its route winds for 268 miles from the village of Edale in the northern Peaks to Kirk Yetholm on the Scottish border. In Northumberland, the Way joins a short section of the walking trail along the remains of the ancient Roman wall near Haltwhistle in Northumberland, built by soldiers during the reign of Emperor Hadrian to guard England from the Picts who lived in what is now eastern and northern Scotland. The wall originally ran all the way from the River Tyne near the North Sea to the shore of the Solway Firth on the Irish Sea.

Acknowledgement
The author is indebted to Steve Rabone for his inspiring set of photographs taken on a series of walks up the Pennine Way. They can be viewed on steverabone.com/PennineWay

CHAPTER 1

The thief opened the small wrought-iron gate and closed it carefully behind him before creeping down the basement staircase to the shadowy darkness outside the scullery door. He was thankful his surreptitious and tortuous journey to this large Victorian terraced house in Wimbledon had been uneventful. Pulling a black balaclava over his head, he waited quietly and listened.

Footsteps passing along the pavement above caused him to shrink down into the corner of the stairwell. The steps faded and he gave a small sigh of relief; it was sometimes advantageous to be small and insignificant. The dial of his wristwatch was only just discernible in the faint light; it was 4:35 and high time he tackled the lock on the scullery door. The five-lever mortice lock with a single dead bolt should pose no problem: he had yet to come across a lock that could defeat him. He was loath to tackle the simpler spring-lock on the front door because it was exposed to the light of a nearby streetlamp. There was also the risk that the door might be bolted.

At least he knew there was no alarm system. Late the previous afternoon, endeavouring to put on a friendly expression – not easy on a face wearing an habitual scowl – he had called at the basement door with an empty sugar bowl. Pretending to be a neighbour, he had spun a yarn about two sweet-toothed friends unexpectedly dropping in for a cup of tea. A young woman, who looked like an au-pair, had nodded understandingly and taken the bowl through to the kitchen beyond the scullery, leaving him standing at the open door.

Quick as a flash, he had inspected the lock and any sign of a magnetic alarm trigger on the door jamb or additional bolting system. To his relief, the lock was the only security on the sturdy door.

A couple of minutes later, he walked home happily – at least the closest he ever got to happiness – after emptying the sugar over a neighbouring hedge.

The lock yielded to his sensitive manipulation within two minutes. He put his small set of lock picks safely in his pocket and replaced his gloves. Entering silently, he crept through the kitchen and up the narrow staircase to the main hallway. The first door turned out to be the dining room but the second was the study. His objective was an attaché case tucked neatly beside the desk. How his boss knew that it would be there was a mystery to him, but he supposed the shadowy person who was employing their services had some inside knowledge of the house and the habits of the owner.

His boss owned a slightly dubious antiques business in south London and was not averse to accepting lucrative orders to steal any item if the price was right. Indeed, out of the four members of staff, one was an expert on locks and safes, one provided the necessary security, and only two knew anything about antiques.

The thief had been ordered to take the case intact; without delay if locked, but otherwise to open it and check that it contained a laptop computer and a small object similar to a USB flash drive.

Within twenty minutes of arriving, he was slinking back along the quiet street. He had been told to lie low on Wimbledon Common for a couple of hours and then make his way to the Starbucks café in Southfields soon after opening time. The "protection" would arrive at about eight-thirty to escort him back to the shop in Mitcham via a roundabout route.

The rather shabby jeans he was wearing did not go well with the business-like attaché case, although, thankfully, he had had the sense to wear a shirt and tie under his black anorak.

As the thief slipped into edge of the Common, he grumbled to himself about having to wait so long before he could get a decent breakfast. The others would still be asleep: it was all right for some people.

At least it looked as if it would be a fine and sunny day.

CHAPTER 2

Hannah locked the door of her small studio flat, carefully stowed the key in an inside pocket of her anorak and headed down the long staircase. A physical-education teacher, she normally took the stairs at a trot, but greater care was needed this morning because she was wearing stout hiking boots and carrying a rucksack for a hill-walking holiday in the Derbyshire Peak District National Park.

Her slender frame belied unusual strength for a girl. At the beginning of her probationary year, only just completed, her modest stature had caused some sniggers and smirks amongst the older boys. They had soon found out to their cost, however, that their new PE teacher was considerably tougher and fitter than they were.

A Dorset girl born and breed, she loved the country; her parents ran a small farm in a village two miles south of the market town of Sherborne. Working in a south London school for the past year had been quite a strain; in fact, she sometimes felt almost suffocated. This was compensated, to some extent at least, by the pleasure of seeing the beneficial effect of her enthusiastic teaching on the health and wellbeing of children who hardly ever experienced the pleasure of activities in the countryside.

It was now Monday morning. Hannah's secondary school had broken up for the summer holiday only the previous Friday. She could not wait to breathe some clean fresh air and blow away the cobwebs. She had been saving up for a holiday for months, but her limited budget might not last very long; even modest bed-and-breakfast places would be expensive in the peak holiday season and she could not always rely on finding a convenient youth hostel.

To leave immediately had been a sudden impulse the previous afternoon, reinforced by the fact that Sunday had seen the start of what the forecasters predicted would be a long spell of sunny weather after a very disappointing spring and early summer. She had recently spotted some enticing pictures of the Peak District in a magazine: hence the train journey to Sheffield, only a few miles east of that delightful area of Derbyshire. The sudden decision also meant that it had not been possible to book a ticket in advance. Regretfully, she would have to buy a full-price one at St Pancras station.

Hannah consulted her wristwatch as she reached the street: she was cutting it rather fine to reach the station in time to catch the 10:58 train. Although the London Underground station on Tooting Broadway was only a short walk away, it would be just her luck if the first train turned out to be taking the western branch of the Northern line; for St Pancras she needed the eastern branch going via the City and Moorgate.

She was approaching Tooting High Street when two men hurried around the corner towards her. One was very tall with long blond hair tied back in a ponytail. The other was considerably shorter and thinner with dark hair and an unpleasant face that bore an angry scowl. He carried a smart attaché case.

In fact, to describe their motion as "hurrying" was an understatement: such an extremely abrupt change of direction caused the lid of the case to spring open and deposit the contents on the pavement, including a small laptop computer in a protective slipcase.

The two men jumped in shock and dark-haired one let out a loud expletive. He hastily retrieved the laptop, while his companion rushed into the road and struggled to gather up some sheets of paper that had escaped from a folder. Two of these floated down the pavement towards Hannah. She deftly intercepted them and handed them to the small man who snatched them with an ugly look that suggested she had no right to touch anything so precious.

Hannah hurried on past the men, determined to put the unfortunate episode out of her mind. This was not to be, however, because, as she reached the corner, there was an unpleasant scrunch under one of her boots. Looking down, she was surprised to see what appeared to be a memory stick or flash drive. She stooped cautiously to pick it up and stood gazing at the small object lying forlornly in the palm of her hand. It was in a sorry state with a cracked casing and an even worse split in the small cap that protected the USB plug.

"Help!" she thought guiltily. "It probably belongs to the laptop in that attaché case." She glanced back down the narrow road.

The small man was standing about fifty yards away searching anxiously in the attaché case. Finding the flash drive missing, he glanced back towards the corner and saw Hannah standing there. It did not take a genius to guess what she was holding. He started to run towards her, his blond companion not far behind.

"That belongs to me! Give it back at once; at once, do you understand?" he bellowed furiously.

"I'm so sorry! I stepped on it by accident. It looks completely broken!" Hannah called apologetically.

The man scowled even more fiercely and shouted again, "Let me have it now – immediately, or you'll be very sorry!"

He was now quite close. Hannah had never seen such a threatening expression on a human face. She turned and fled, leaving the man still shouting behind her and ordering his tall companion to catch her and get his property back.

"Be careful. Don't draw attention to yourself!" were the last words left ringing in her ears.

Fortunately, the entrance to the underground station was only a few yards away. She looked back as she darting inside; the blond man had just rounded the corner and was running swiftly along the broad pavement. She rushed across the vestibule, at the same time feeling in her anorak pocket for her Oyster card to swipe over the detector beside the turnstile. It was only then she realized she was still clutching the memory stick.

"I should've dropped it back at the corner," she thought. "I'm in a pickle now! They're obviously determined to have it back!"

She hurried precariously down the last of the steps to the platform, hoping her pursuer did not have an Oyster card and would be delayed by the turnstile.

While she was racing up the platform seeking to get as far from the bottom of the steps as possible, a north-bound train roared into the station. She climbed aboard with considerable relief, regardless of its intended route. Settling thankfully into a seat, she determined to stay on the train even if it took the western branch. If necessary, she reasoned, she could get out at Euston station and run the short distance to St Pancras.

As it happened, Hannah was on the right train and she began to relax. The flash drive was still in her pocket. Perhaps she should take it to a police station. This would seriously delay her, however, and fast trains to Sheffield only departed every two hours. Missing the 10:58 would mean having to go to King's Cross for a train to Doncaster and then taking another train for the short journey due west to Sheffield. It would be more sensible to find a police station in central Sheffield and explain her predicament there.

Her thoughts now turned to the underground station shared by both St Pancras and King's Cross; she remembered that the two mainline stations were about a quarter of a mile apart and there was consequently a warren of subterranean passages to negotiate. She needed time to purchase a ticket to Sheffield and so could not afford to make a mistake and get lost; otherwise she might have the awkward problem of buying a ticket from the inspector on the train.

A few minutes later, somewhat recovered from her ordeal, she looked up at the map of the Northern Line above the window opposite her seat and saw that the train would shortly arrive at Angel, the stop immediately before her destination.

Glancing sideways towards the end of the carriage, she froze. To her absolute horror, the blond man was gazing at her intently through the windows in the locked doors at the ends of their adjoining carriages.

It took her at least two seconds to recover her ability to think and plan what to do. The man obviously possessed an Oyster card and had been able to reach one of the rear carriages before the doors closed. Therefore, she reasoned, it would be easy for him to follow her through any exit turnstile.

Her carriage had become considerably more crowded as the journey progressed and now contained a number of standing passengers. She got up quickly and threaded her way down the carriage away from her pursuer's gaze to the far end. Standing near to an exit door, she desperately hoped that the man would assume she was leaving the train at Angel and alight there as well. If there was a sufficiently large crowd on the platform to obscure his view, she reasoned, he might fail to get back on the train.

As the doors began to close again, she risked looking out very quickly. To her great disappointment there was no sign of him; no doubt he was still on the train and her ploy had failed.

At King's Cross, she shot out on to the platform, only to see that he had done the same. Unfortunately, he was blocking her route to St Pancras and so she ran in the opposite direction down the long network of passages towards the King's Cross escalators. Her pursuer followed at a rapid rate.

Arriving at the surface, she made as if she was aiming for the mainline platforms of the large station. However, passing close to a side exit, she suddenly darted out into the open air. Running to the broad pavement on the Euston Road, she turned right towards St Pancras. Her strength and stamina were such that she was able to keep up a fast pace even with the rucksack on her back. By the time she reached the entrance of St Pancras, her pursuer was about fifty yards behind.

Once inside, she looked quickly at the departure board and noted the platform number. The roundabout route she had been forced to take meant that the time was now 10:57 according to the station clock. The platform gate began to close just as she sprinted through the opening and up the platform to the nearest carriage door. She was greatly relieved when it slid smoothly open at the press of a button.

Glancing back as she entered the carriage, she saw the man standing outside the gate breathing very heavily and trying to make a call on his mobile 'phone.

She breathed a long sigh of relief as the train drew smoothly away from the platform. There was no way the man could find her now, even though he would be able to see where the train was calling: Leicester, Derby, and Chesterfield before Sheffield, where it terminated.

Hannah carried her rucksack carefully through the first-class carriages and into the buffet car. The serving counter was still closed. She decided to find a toilet and then return for a much-needed coffee; a seat in one of the second-class carriages further forward would have to wait.

In the privacy of the WC, it occurred to her that there was something very strange about the whole experience. Why had her pursuer not moved from one carriage to the next at each stop until he found her and politely asked for the return of his damaged property? It would have been an entirely reasonable request even in the presence of other passengers. After all, he had only had to chase her in the first place because of the appalling behaviour of his dreadful companion.

But then she remembered that the latter had warned her pursuer not to draw attention to himself. This almost made her smile; chasing a fleeing girl was anything but discrete and the small man himself had probably been heard over most of Tooting!

As she unlocked the door and made her way back to the buffet car, she felt a quiver of excitement mixed with apprehension: perhaps the next few days would turn out to be more than just a straight-forward walking holiday.

CHAPTER 3

Paul settled into a forward-facing seat on the 10:58 Monday morning train from St Pancras to Sheffield with a sigh of relief. Arriving at the station with only a few minutes to spare, he had had to hurry past the queue at the coffee shop on the concourse. He was annoyed to have misjudged the time it would take to walk across the centre of London from Waterloo to St Pancras because he would now have to buy an inferior cup of coffee on the train. Perhaps he was less fit than he thought, although he had been carrying a sizeable rucksack. The latter would be his companion for many miles, so he had better get used to it!

He had lived in Sheffield all his life, including the three years spent studying physics at Sheffield University, until leaving to do an accelerated teacher-training course in Winchester. His parents had moved to their present house five years ago after the death of his grandparents who had owned the property. He was going to spend a night with them in his old bedroom before catching a train early tomorrow to the village of Edale in the Peak District, the southern terminus of the famous walking route, the Pennine Way, running all the way up the spine of England to the Scottish border.

The plan was to walk up the Way for about 180 miles as far as the town of Haltwhistle, just south of the ancient Roman Wall (usually referred to as Hadrian's Wall), to spend two nights with his older sister Sue and her husband Ian, a pharmacist, and their small toddler Toby.

Very conveniently, his younger brother Mark had recently moved to a small-terraced house in Skipton, two days hard walking from Edale, and he was planning to stay there on Wednesday night before trekking onwards.

Leaving Haltwhistle, he anticipated following the same route back, with a few detours, arriving in Sheffield in time to spend at least two nights with his parents before returning to London.

He was really looking forward to seeing a total of six members of his family again and energetic walking in fresh air surrounded by wild and beautiful scenery. With the exception of Skipton, nights on the Pennine Way would be spent at bed-and-breakfast establishments, or a youth hostel if one happened to be in a convenient location.

Thoughts of the long trek ahead made him glance sadly at the empty seat beside him: it should have been filled with John's substantial, albeit fairly muscular, bulk. John was a mathematics teacher at the Sixth-Form College in the Basingstoke, Hampshire, where Paul had just completed his first two terms teaching A-level physics.

Paul was only one week past his twenty-second birthday and a mere NQT (newly-qualified teacher), whereas twenty-five-year-old John was head of the mathematics department – the youngest head of department the school had ever had. Perhaps unusually, the two men had become instant friends after Paul had volunteered to help out with some mathematics teaching when a member of staff had fallen ill.

John was almost as keen a walker as Paul, but, what with a large mortgage, wife and young child, he had little time or money to spare for his hobby. Paul, however, had recently come in for a totally unexpected windfall.

At the beginning of the summer term, he had gone down with a short bout of 'flu. Alone in his flat and feeling quite poorly, he had tried to cheer himself up by watching a couple of afternoon episodes of the ITV antiques programme "Dickinson's Real Deal". Out of sheer boredom, he had submitted a web-entry for the simple, almost trivial, competition. Some days later, he had been astonished to learn that he had won £3,640. As a result, he had offered to pay a substantial part of John's expenses on a trip up the Pennine Way, while the latter's wife and small son stayed with her parents.

All this was shattered on the day before leaving for Sheffield when John's wife telephoned to say that he had been rushed into hospital with acute peritonitis and was scheduled to have his appendix removed that afternoon.

Thus Paul now sat on the train with two sets of tickets to Sheffield and back. Having been bought three weeks in advance at less than half the standard fare, they could only be used on the dates specified and on a given train. He was not worried about the cost of the unusable tickets but extremely sad for his friend.

Fortunately, the news from the hospital late on Sunday evening had been good: the operation had been a success. John, however, would be out of action for some days and certainly not fit for arduous walking that summer.

The train pulled away from the platform and Paul almost immediately moved down the train towards the buffet car, having left a book on his seat and a newspaper propped against the arm rest in the hope that it might deter a late comer from taking the aisle seat. After all, there were still a few other seats available and so it was not being entirely selfish.

The serving counter had only just opened and it was not long before he was sitting at one of the tables reserved for passengers consuming items purchased at the buffet. He did not intend to stay long, but wanted to reduce the level of the hot liquid before making the rather unsteady journey back to his seat.

As he sat gazing down at the coffee on the table, a soft voice spoke just above his head.

"May I?" it asked.

CHAPTER 4

Paul looked up in surprise. A slim girl stood beside him clutching a sizeable rucksack in one hand and a cup of coffee in the other. She was not beautiful, but her small elfin face with hazel eyes and wide mouth had a strange sort of charm and portrayed the faint hint of a mischievous nature.

"Yes, of course, I'll move up," Paul said, rising as far as the table edge would allow.

Even so, there was a "tut, tut" from the plump lady directly across the table as her drink wobbled alarmingly.

The girl smiled with relief and began to squeeze her rucksack under the table between them, still only using one hand. Paul reached out to give her a hand, but it was not needed.

"She's stronger than she looks!" he thought as he sat down again and the girl joined him.

"I'm sorry my luggage is getting in the way. It'll be less heavy when I've eaten my tins of food. I'm going to the Peak District to do some serious walking – at least twenty-five miles a day." she said and then added an afterthought: "I've not yet looked for a seat and must keep an eye out for the ticket inspector because I need to buy a single to Sheffield."

Her hands trembled as she removed the lid from her cup.

"It looks as if you need that," said Paul, nodding towards her drink and wondering why she had volunteered so much information.

The girl looked at him for a moment; it was quite a searching gaze. Then she seemed to come to a decision.

"You can say that again! I've just been chased across London – all the way from Tooting where I have a studio flat. It's only because I'm a PE teacher that I managed to move fast enough to escape," she said quietly.

Paul hoped his mouth had not fallen open in surprise, but it still took him a couple of seconds to recover.

"I'm not sure if that's frightening, exciting, mysterious, or all three. It depends on who or what it was!"

He did not like to press her to explain, although it was obvious that she needed to unwind, and so he concentrated on sipping his coffee. The girl did the same.

"I do, however, have an easy solution to your ticket problem," he said suddenly. "I have a spare ticket to Sheffield that can only be used today on this train."

The girl looked at him with an expression that combined interest and apprehension.

Suddenly realizing that his offer could be construed as a novel way of trying to pick her up, Paul hastened to explain further.

"I was meant to be travelling with a colleague from the college where I teach A-level physics. John and I were intending to walk up the Pennine Way as far as Hadrian's Wall and back. Very unfortunately, he had to have an emergency operation yesterday to remove his appendix. I bought our tickets two weeks ago at considerably reduced cost. It's not possible to get a refund with this type of ticket and so you're very welcome to have it."

The girl relaxed and smiled. "That's very kind of you," she said quietly, putting a hand inside her anorak as she searched for her purse. "How much do I owe you?"

Paul looked at her. Although her anorak was spotlessly clean it had seen better days and her rucksack was also extremely shabby. On sudden impulse he said: "Let's call it payment in advance for today's exciting story!"

For a moment the girl looked doubtful, but then grinned and nodded. "OK, but this isn't a good place. Also, I insist on giving you a small contribution." She put £10 on the table.

Paul took the banknote reluctantly in exchange for the ticket.

"The next coffee, or any other drink you fancy, is on me," he said firmly. "I have a seat two coaches up the train. There was a spare one beside me; hopefully it's still vacant."

She smiled again and stood up, dragging her rucksack with her. Paul took both cups of coffee and led the way. As they threaded their way forward, he spoke over his shoulder, "I'm Paul, by the way."

"And I'm Hannah," came the reply.

The double seat was still empty. Paul quickly pushed his own rucksack as far as possible along the luggage rack and turned to take the girl's, intending to lift it into the space created. To his surprise, she was already stowing it neatly with effortless ease and so he courteously removed his book and newspaper from his seat and stood back to offer her the window position.

She seemed reluctant to accept for a moment but then gave him a smile that lit up her face. "Thank you. That's very kind," she said quietly as she sat down.

Then she realized she was still wearing her anorak and struggled briefly to remove it; although the garment was a summer-weight one, the day was quite hot. She carefully buttoned up the inside pockets before handing it to Paul, who folded it as neatly as possible and managed, with some difficulty, to add it to the rest of their luggage.

As he sat down, he took in the fact that she looked trim and businesslike in a neat but rather faded short-sleeved olive-green shirt. Her slim forearms were lightly tanned and firmly muscled. She is probably a very competent, no nonsense, PE teacher, he surmised.

It suddenly occurred to him that she might also make a good walking partner, but this was not the time to mention it. He merely turned to her and said quietly, "What about your story?"

They both glanced over at the opposite seat. The single occupant seemed to be fast asleep.

Hannah spoke quietly for not more than five minutes while Paul listened with increasing amazement. He was also impressed by her ability to state the facts simply and clearly without unnecessary elaboration. He only wished his students could be as precise and objective. Rather than hurry him for a reaction, she sat looking out of the window in silence.

"It's clear those men are crooks," Paul said after a short pause. "They probably stole the attaché case and its contents, either for their own use or on behalf of somebody else. Otherwise, there's no adequate reason for the dark-haired man to be so furiously angry and threatening: it was hardly your fault that you stepped on the wretched thing. Even more convincing is the fact that his large companion wanted to avoid being seen in public trying to get it back and was looking for an opportunity to corner you alone! By the way, may I see it?"

Hannah looked across at the seat opposite; its occupant was still asleep. She delved carefully into the breast pocket of her army-style shirt and withdrew a small object carefully wrapped in a paper handkerchief. Paul gingerly unfolded the wrapping and looked at the device with interest.

"Despite the crack in the main body, I think the memory chip has probably survived," he said. "But it remains to be seen if the plug is too damaged fit into a USB port."

He very gingerly removed the badly split cap, but, even so, it fell to pieces in his hand. Holding the plug in the bright light coming through the window, they examined it closely. Finally, he wrapped everything up in the handkerchief and handed the tiny parcel back to the girl.

"The good news, if that's the right phrase, is that the distortion of the plug is very slight. The protective cap has obviously done a good job," he said. "But there's something else: I suspect the device may not be a flash drive after all."

Hannah looked surprised and he hastened to explain his reasoning. "It's unusually stubby for a flash drive and not made by any of the well-known manufacturers. Another thing, the size of the memory in gigabytes is always printed on the casing. This device gives no such information, which leads me to suspect it may be a dongle."

"What on earth is that?" Hannah asked, now totally confused.

"Dongles can have more than one application," Paul replied. "But the only type I've come across makes it impossible for an unauthorized person to gain access to commercially sensitive software or its associated files unless the dongle is plugged in, although the computer can still be used for other work. It's a rather old-fashioned method of software security. One obvious disadvantage, of course, is that the dongle may get lost."

Then he delivered his bombshell, although he was speaking as softly as the noise in the train would allow. "I believe your crooks are completely stymied. They have stolen a laptop but have lost the way of gaining access to the contents they really want. No wonder they were so anxious to get the dongle back!" He sat back in triumph.

Hannah looked at him in admiration. "You're right; you must be right! But how can we be really sure?"

Paul looked at his watch. "We should be arriving in Leicester soon. I need to think as well as pay a quick call. Suppose I walk down the train and get us both another drink. I may have a possible solution by the time I get back."

He disappeared quickly, anxious to return before the train reached its first stop. It was not very long before he reappeared with two cups of tea.

"I have two suggestions. First, I have an old desktop PC using Windows XP at my parents' home about three miles from the centre of Sheffield. I used it during my final years at grammar school and all three years at Sheffield University. It's not connected to the internet any longer and so we could try plugging your device into one of its USB ports without risking any harm. If the device turns out to be a flash drive, it may be possible to see what's on it. If it turns out to be protected a password request will appear on the screen. A dongle, on the other hand, will probably announce that it can't find its software or just sit there completely dumb! If the latter happens, we'll still be in the dark, because the chip may be broken after all."

Paul paused for a moment before ploughing on. "This is my second idea. John and I were going to start our walk early tomorrow after spending tonight at my parents' house. My mother has already made up our spare bedroom for him, and, what with all the chaos yesterday and the rush to get the train this morning, I haven't yet let her know he's not coming. If you're willing to come with me to test your device and have something to eat, you could also stay on with us for the night before catching the train from Sheffield into the Peak District. I'm sure my mother would be happy for you to take John's place – I'll warn her in advance of course. What do you think? I'm quite harmless and my parents are lovely down-to-earth folk. My father's a taxi driver."

Paul stopped abruptly and looked at Hannah enquiringly. For a second or two she gazed at him thoughtfully but then smiled rather charmingly.

"Thank you. That's a very kind and generous offer if you're sure your mother won't mind, although perhaps we shouldn't mention all this excitement unless it becomes necessary. We could simply say we met very recently and found we were aiming for similar holiday destinations?"

"Excellent!" Paul replied. "It'll be mid-afternoon anyway by the time we've tried the experiment and you've had something to eat. Also, of course, depending what we find, you may feel you need to report all this to the police, which will waste another hour or so of your holiday. By the way, how long are you planning to be away?"

"About two weeks, depending on how quickly the money goes! I hope to be lucky enough to find a reasonable number of youth hostels and not to have to use too many more expensive bed-and-breakfast places."

Paul looked at her again, hoping he was not being too forward.

"If you can last for eighteen nights, you're welcome to have – and I mean have – John's ticket for the journey back to London," he said. "It's dated for two weeks on Friday using a midday train. I wanted to stay away for three weeks but John was worried about leaving his family for so long."

Hannah looked rather doubtful. "Again that's very kind of you, but I doubt the money will last that long!" she said sadly.

Again, Paul hesitated. He had been looking forward to going with John. The Pennine Way could be very lonely in places, even with other walkers around. Hannah might make an excellent walking companion. He took the plunge.

"What about coming with me up the Pennine Way to Haltwhistle and back? Even if we make a small detour or two at places of interest on the return leg, we could also see some more of the Peak District; John and I were hoping to have about two days there."

He waited for her reaction, hoping it would be positive.

Hannah now looked very uncertain. "Can we leave that decision until tomorrow morning?" she said quietly.

"Of course," he said, feeling he had overstepped the mark. "I'm sorry to be so hasty. It was totally thoughtless of me because you couldn't possibly decide without knowing more about the Pennine Way, not to mention me!"

She waved away his apology with a shake of the head and a small smile that seemed to forgive him.

Paul, however, was appalled that he had been so premature. After all, they knew very little about each other. Suppose they got on each other's nerves; he could hardly leave her to walk any distance back down the Pennine Way alone. Nevertheless, he felt strangely attracted to her and intrigued by the mysterious dongle.

CHAPTER 5

At Sheffield, Paul 'phoned his mother to announce his arrival and tell her about John's sudden operation. He hoped she would not mind, he said, if he brought a girl called Hannah instead, who was going on a walking holiday in the Peak District for a couple of weeks.

He ended the call and returned to the waiting girl. He would have to tell his mother not to read too much into this new acquaintanceship as soon as possible, he thought.

"My mother is sorry about John, but will be delighted to welcome you," he reported cheerfully. "It'll probably take us about thirty-five minutes to get there if the bus comes fairly quickly."

"We could walk after sitting for two hours on the train," Hannah suggested. "We can cover three miles quite easily in forty-five minutes."

"I'm game if you are," Paul replied, and they set off. He was pleased to see that she was happy to walk at his normal pace; in fact, her motion was amazingly free and easy, given her heavy backpack.

His mother opened the door with a beaming smile and hugged her son before turning to Hannah with outstretched hand.

"You must be Hannah. I'm so please to meet you!" she said as they shook hands. "It's nearly two o'clock. You must be hungry and thirsty by now. I've made a few sandwiches and the kettle is on the boil for tea or coffee. There's water and orange squash on the kitchen table already. Paul can take you up to the spare bedroom and show you the bathroom. There's no rush; just come down when you're ready. I'll be getting a chicken ready for the oven. We usually have our evening meal at about six-thirty, or whenever my husband gets home if it's not too late: it all depends on his taxi bookings. By the way, please call me Sarah. Paul's father is Jack."

Paul's mother stopped abruptly. It was as if a switch had been turned off.

Hannah was finally able to speak. "It's very kind of you to have me, especially as I've only just met Paul. I'm a PE teacher and love cross-country walking. Staying here for a night will enable me to afford an extra night in the Peak District. I've not been before but pictures of it look lovely!"

"It's certainly a beautiful area," Sarah agreed. "You should get Paul to show you some of the special places, especially those not so well-known to tourists. He's got some ridiculous idea about trekking for miles and miles up the Pennine Way to visit his elder sister and her husband in the town of Haltwhistle. He's even planning to walk back. Would you believe it?"

Although Paul's mother pretended to be shocked at the thought, she knew her son only too well and gave him a loving smile as she disappeared towards the kitchen.

"But mum, you know I promised Sue I'd visit her this summer!" Paul called after her. "It would also be good to see how Mark's getting on in his new home and job in Skipton."

"You could always take the train after walking in the Peak District!" a muffled voice replied.

Paul had detected a faint glint in his mother's eyes. He must put her straight before wedding bells began ringing in her head. He had already alarmed Hannah by making too many suggestions at once and must prevent his mother making matters worse.

He took Hannah upstairs, gestured to the bathroom in passing, and opened the door of the spare room. It had been beautifully prepared with no sign of clutter anywhere. There was a small vase of flowers on the dressing table, clearly from the garden. Two towels of different size had been neatly folded and stacked precisely in the centre of the foot of the bed. The window overlooked a small back garden from which a pleasant faintly-scented breeze wafted into the welcoming room.

"This is really lovely and looks so comfortable!" Hannah exclaimed. "Your mother has gone to such a lot of trouble."

Paul smiled. "It was all ready for John but I suspect the flowers from the garden are in your honour. You won't be surprised to learn that she was a chambermaid in one of the large hotels in Sheffield for a long time, especially when you see the bathroom! Anyway, I'll leave you now and switch on my computer; it takes about two minutes to sort itself out. Bring your flash-drive-cum-dongle along when you're ready. My room's on the other side of the bathroom.

He disappeared quickly, pushing the bathroom door slightly open as he passed, not that it was possible to get lost in such a small house. He was glad his parents had had the kitchen extended a couple of years ago to make the ground floor slightly more spacious; they could now eat at a table in the homely room.

Three minutes later, Hannah tapped on his door and entered with the small dongle in her hand. Paul very cautiously inserted it into one of the USB sockets and pushed as firmly as he dared. The small object resisted slightly but then slid in reluctantly. There was a brief period of rather noisy activity on the hard disk before it died down to the hum of the internal fan.

"My hard disk's been noisy for ages!" Paul explained. "I was holding my breath during my last year at university, hoping it would not fail on me! The brief noise just now may indicate that your device is alive and the computer is trying to communicate with it. If it was broken, its presence would not even be noticed."

They waited for a few seconds, but nothing more happened.

"If your device was a flash drive, this XP machine should have displayed a notice announcing that a new storage device has been detected and offering a list of possible actions," he said. "So it's probably a dongle as we suspected."

He opened Windows Explorer to see if a new device had been registered, but only the hard-disk partitions were listed. The PC and new device had obviously been unable to communicate.

Paul gingerly extracted the dongle and carefully wrapped it up before returning it to Hanna.

"We must go down the kitchen. Mum will be wondering what we're up to!" He shut the desktop down as Hannah descended the stairs.

The chicken now sat in the roasting dish ready for the oven and Sarah was just washing her hands carefully.

"Would you mind pouring tea for all of us, dear?" she said. "I hope Paul won't be long. It's in danger of getting stewed!"

Hannah smiled inwardly with pleasure: to be addressed as "dear" reminded her so much of her own mother.

"Paul's just coming. He was quickly showing me his old computer. He says it's almost out of the Ark!" she responded, doing as she was asked.

"Well, seven years is really old for a PC these days" Paul said with a chuckle as he entered the room.

He went over and kissed his mother before sitting down. The latter looked delighted, and, once again, Hannah felt quite moved. She began to relax further as they spent a short but happy time sitting around the table enjoying Sarah's excellent sandwiches.

It was not long before Paul looked at Hannah enquiringly. She nodded almost imperceptibly in response. He turned to his mother to give a much watered-down explanation of what had happened to Hannah on her way across London, saying that, after discussion, they felt they should make a brief report to the police and leave the small strange device with them.

"I'm sorry to go out so soon after arriving," he ended. "We promise to be back well before six o'clock and spend the evening with you and dad."

His mother looked rather shocked at Hannah's experience and disappointed at their need to go out again. She reluctantly agreed, however, that it was the right thing to do.

"Your dad 'phoned while you were upstairs," she said. "Partly to find out if you'd arrived safely and then to say that he'll be dropping off his last passenger not far from here and will be home a few minutes before seven. But please, you two, come back just as soon as you can. You're not here long and I expect you'll want to leave early tomorrow to make the best of this fine walking weather!"

Hannah and Paul left the house almost immediately and walked to a nearby bus stop.

"To save time, it's better to take the bus now. We can walk back during the rush hour when the bus will be crowded and slow," he said sensibly.

The desk sergeant looked at Paul and Hannah enquiringly over his high counter. "How can I be of help?" he asked.

Paul explained that he and Hannah had met on the train from London and discussed a rather alarming thing that had happened to her on the way to St Pancras. He then paused for Hannah to take up the tale.

Her description was briefer than it had been to Paul on the train because she could abbreviate some of the zigzagging she had had to do to escape her pursuer. She then looked at Paul to explain why he had deduced that the small sorry-looking object now lying on the counter was almost certainly a computer dongle.

After first taking their names, addresses, and mobile numbers, the sergeant had begun to write brief notes, but stopped after two or three minutes in some confusion; he looked even more flummoxed when a dongle was mentioned. Paul made a vain attempt to explain but the man interrupted half way through.

"I'll take you to see the detective sergeant and then get the office to check with London to see if any laptop thefts have been reported," he said.

He let them in through the security gate and escorted them down a short corridor before knocking on a door.

"Come!" a gruff voice called out impatiently and they were ushered inside. A tall man in civilian clothes looked up wearily from a cluttered desk and the sergeant explained their presence.

"I suppose you'd better sit down," the tall man said, waving a hand at two uncomfortable-looking chairs. The two young people repeated everything again, but this time Paul was able to finish explaining the use of a computer dongle.

"So you see," Paul concluded. "If those two men are criminals, the laptop is now useless to them. Hence, their desperation to get the dongle back; Hannah told them it was broken but they must be hoping that it's not a total write-off!"

"I called out when the dark-haired man was some distance away, but I'm sure he heard me," Hannah expanded. "He was shouting angrily and looked so threatening that I'd fled by the time he was within speaking distance! Of course, with hindsight, I should have flung the wretched thing at him, but I was too frightened to think straight."

"Actually, holding on to it was a sensible thing to do if he was a thief," the detective remarked, smiling slightly for the first time. "The legitimate owner can presumably get a replacement from the manufacturer quite easily. The trouble and expense will serve him right for being so unpleasant!"

Just as Paul was thinking they were speaking to a capable person at last, the desk sergeant poked his head round the door apologetically.

"All but one report of laptop thefts in London during the last 24 hours have been large expensive ones or completely new, some still in their cartons, Sir," he said. "The exception is an eleven-inch Sony notebook stolen yesterday afternoon from the table of a Costa café in Whetstone in the extreme north. I'm sorry Sir – I should have checked before troubling you."

The detective looked a little peeved. "Yes, it would have saved time," he muttered crossly. The sergeant withdrew his head quickly before he was further humiliated in front of strangers. The detective sat back in his chair and put his hands behind his head.

"Well, I think that's it," he said. "I'll get a short summary of your information put on our system just in case it rings a bell with the London people at a later date. In the meantime, enjoy your holiday. We have your parent's address and 'phone number here in Sheffield and both your mobile numbers in the very unlikely event that we need to contact you. We're so busy that I don't want to spend time and effort on bagging, recording and storing that dongle. I'll take a 'photo to add to the report, however, because most of my colleagues won't know what a dongle looks like."

The man took a digital camera from a drawer of his desk and quickly snapped a close up of the small object lying in a forlorn state on a sheet of white paper in front of him. Then he stood up to indicate that the interview was over.

When Hannah had difficulty wrapping the dongle up in a now extremely tatty paper handkerchief, he produced a small transparent plastic bag from yet another drawer. She found this far more convenient; it could even be closed by pressing the edges of the opening firmly together.

As the two young people walked home, Hannah asked Paul about something that had surprised her. "Why did one sergeant call the other one Sir?"

"Because the man in the office is a detective sergeant, which is one rank up the scale; uniformed sergeants have the same rank as detective constables," he explained.

Just then, they passed a florist and she insisted on going in to buy a bunch of flowers for Paul's mother. He, however, did not allow her to take many steps outside in the street before he had persuaded her to let him contribute half the cost.

Paul's mother was delighted when they arrived home just after five-thirty and beamed with pleasure when presented with the bouquet. After Hannah had arranged the flowers in a vase and helped to lay up the table for the evening meal, they relaxed in the kitchen chatting over cups of tea while Sarah continued with the cooking.

At ten to seven, Jack entered through the back door and hugged his son with delight before shaking Hannah warmly by the hand and kissing his wife, who pointed to the flowers in the centre of the table.

"Look at the lovely flowers Hannah and Paul have brought! We can admire them while we eat, before I put them on display in the parlour."

Hannah's heart warmed at the sight of Jack's obvious love for his wife and son, and also the homely reference to a parlour. But then all this reminded her of home in Dorset and a shadow of sadness crossed her expressive face.

She was surprised at Paul's quickness to notice. When he asked, in a whisper, if she was all right, she explained aloud that the sight of all of them as a happy family, plus the homely reference to the parlour, had brought on a pang of homesickness.

Sarah beamed at her with understanding and sympathy, privately thinking what a good daughter-in-law Hannah would make: not exactly beautiful, but sweet, caring and competent. Then she stopped herself; she was not sure if Hannah was a Christian.

She, her husband, daughter Sue and son-in-law were all regular churchgoers. Sadly, Paul and his younger brother had not yet come to faith and she had hoped Christian girlfriends might be the incentive needed for them to begin to take God seriously. The rest of the family had been praying for the two boys for years; she must include Hannah from now on. She would telephone Sue in Haltwhistle before Paul got there, just in case Hannah decided to go with him, although Sarah was in two minds about her doing so because it was a long arduous walk for a woman, even a PE teacher.

After a good meal in a delightful family atmosphere, Hannah and Paul insisted on washing up while his mother made hot drinks. They then retired to the parlour, where Jack had been reading the newspaper, and over an hour passed in pleasant conversation. Hannah became almost animated when she was asked about life on the farm and work as a school teacher in Tooting.

A little later, Sarah asked her son whether he had completed his plans for the Pennine trek.

"Only in outline," he replied. "My hope is to get to Sue's by next Monday, at an average of nearly thirty miles a day, spend two nights there and then take a little longer on the return journey. But John and I only planned the first four days in any detail."

He went on to explain that tomorrow's walk would be 27 miles to the northern edge of the Peak District, some of it on steep gradients, finishing at a small guest house where he had stayed about two years ago while on a weekend trip with two fellow university students. In fact, the accommodation had already been booked on-line and paid for at a good discount.

The following day was the rather less interesting and more level walk to Mark's home in Skipton on the southern edge of the Yorkshire Dales National Park, but this would mean a journey of about 37 miles. The third day would only be 25 miles to Horton-in-Ribblesdale where he had booked another small guesthouse. On Google Map the place appeared to be delightfully quiet, overlooking a small tributary of the River Ribble.

"If Hannah decides to come with me, she may feel the 37-mile leg is too much. I can always 'phone Mark to see if we could drop in on the way back instead," he concluded.

"You mustn't do that on my account!" Hannah said quickly. "I'd be delighted to accept the challenge of what sounds like a real hike. I think you'll find PE teachers can be quite tough!"

Both Sarah and Jack looked quite surprised at her confidence; Paul gave her an encouraging smile.

After Sarah mentioned that there was plenty of hot water for a shower, Hannah excused herself to go upstairs. Bidding everyone goodnight, she turned to Paul and promised to be quick.

Although some years old, the cubicle was spotless and provided a far better spray than the apology for a shower in Hannah's studio flat. She delighted in the opportunity to have a really adequate wash. As she towelled herself down, standing on a freshly laundered bath mat, she saw herself in the mirror on the wall opposite.

Somewhat thinner than she would have preferred, she had come to accept that her particular metabolism probably meant having to stay that way. On the other hand, her supple limbs looked firm and strong, with excellent tone and muscle definition, thanks to a very active occupation. She was sure she could rise to the challenge of a long trek up the Pennine Way.

Paul had given her a clear invitation, but she was still undecided. She liked him, found him easy to talk to, and his advice and support today had proved invaluable. On top of all that, his parents could not have been more welcoming.

Her earlier concern, towards the end of train journey, that he was being a little too pushy had now dissolved; his mother had effectively confirmed that the trek up the Pennine Way had been long planned and that Paul would genuinely welcome a walking companion to replace the missing John. Although he obviously liked her, it was in no way a ploy to get a convenient girlfriend. Hannah smiled at the thought: not many girlfriends would put up with the rigors of a 180-mile trek over rough and hilly terrain within seven days! On the other hand, she herself would relish the challenge.

In the end, her hesitancy boiled down to the fact that she could not anticipate what being in Paul's company for a long time would be like, or to what it might lead. Whilst she would be quite happy to do a circular tour of the Peak District on her own, she did not fancy having to walk back down the Pennine Way alone if the need arose.

She left the bathroom and tapped on Paul's door to let him know the bathroom was free. "Thanks – sleep well!" he called back.

As she thankfully settled into the comfortable bed, she determined to stop mulling over her options and leave the decision until tomorrow. She was conscious of the faint sounds of Paul in the bathroom next door but it was not long before she was fast asleep.

The household stirred just before six-thirty the following morning because Jack had an early booking. Hannah and Paul needed to get started anyway; slow trains that stopped at Edale, the starting point of the Pennine Way, were infrequent.

At breakfast, Sarah generously offered to put Hannah up again when she returned to Sheffield on her way back to London.

"To encourage you to come, I'll leave your bedding untouched," she said. "Of course, if you walk up to Haltwhistle with Paul, then I also expect you to come back here with him. You'll be very welcome whatever you decide!"

Jack had smiled in agreement with her words as he hurriedly departed just before eight o'clock. When Paul and Hannah left shortly after, Sarah hugged Hannah just as warmly as she did her son.

"Have a good time whatever you decide to do," she whispered softly.

At 8:50, they boarded the slow train to Manchester at the suburban station of Dore and Totley, not far from Paul's home. Once in Edale, less than twelve miles away, Hannah would have to make a choice: either to walk south into the central area of the National Park or join Paul on his journey north. He had even thoughtfully brought his map of the central and southern Peak District for her to borrow if she decided to walk alone. He had also persuaded her to leave half her small selection of provisions in Sheffield, because, he told her, most of the walking would involve steep gradients and an over-heavy rucksack would be a liability.

During the short journey, Paul told her about his younger brother Mark. "He's twenty-one and recently completed his degree in electronics before joining a small company specializing in computer software in Skipton. He's even bought a two-bed terraced house on a hill overlooking the town. If you come, you can have the small spare bedroom and I'll sleep downstairs on a fold-out settee."

"I should be the one to have that!" Hannah declared.

"John would have had the proper bed and so shall you," he replied firmly.

No more was said for a few minutes, but, as she looked out of the window still pondering her decision, the train stopped at the small village of Hathersage. The delightful landscape of the Peak District had now really begun and she turned to Paul, unable to contain herself.

"It's so lovely here!" she exclaimed.

A smile lit up his whole face as he responded: "Just wait until we get further in!"

By nine-thirty, they were sitting with a cup of coffee at a table in the small rear garden of a café overlooking the forecourt of Edale station. They were not enjoying it particularly: Hannah had just set herself a four-minute deadline to reach a decision. Paul waited anxiously, determined not to influence her choice.

He tried to lighten the situation. "It's a pity we don't have a four-minute egg timer and could watch the sand gradually filling the lower glass bulb!" he chuckled, hoping it was not making matters worse.

Somehow, his words helped Hannah arrive at a decision – she could not believe it had taken her so long. A compromise was the obvious solution. She could still spend a good deal of time in the beautiful Peak District that now surrounded her if she walked up the famous Pennine Way with Paul for one day and then doubled back, perhaps even by a different route.

She was so relieved that she smiled quietly to herself as she lifted her cup to take the last mouthful of coffee. But she was not to drink it: her hand remained poised halfway to her lips.

CHAPTER 6

Hannah's cup remained frozen in her hand for several seconds.

From her vantage point at the café table there was a good view of the station entrance. A large black car had just drawn up. A man was getting out of the front passenger seat, clearly intending to go inside. His body was partly hidden by the vehicle, but she could see that he was tall and had long blond hair tied back in a ponytail. Even worse, the driver on her side of the car was clearly visible – he was short and dark!

She shook her head in disbelief and put her cup down. "I'm imagining things!" she thought. "It can't possibly be *them*; there's no way they can know where I am!"

But her mind was now made up. Turning back to Paul, she made a single brief statement.

"I'm coming all the way to Haltwhistle with you. No more dithering! I'm sorry I've selfishly taken so long to decide."

She stood up and put her rucksack on.

Paul relaxed and beamed at her.

"It doesn't matter in the least; I'm delighted to have a walking companion!" he said as he followed her back to the road.

"This girl certainly gets going once she's made up her mind," he thought. "It's a good job I've already paid for the coffee!"

The small station cul-de-sac led to a lane going north across the railway line and on towards the centre of Edale. Even without a map it would have been obvious where to go because a steady stream of tourists was leaving a nearby car park and moving in the same direction.

Hannah set up a good pace, but, a quarter of a mile later, as they approached the Visitor Centre, Paul took her elbow and was about to guide her inside.

"I know this immediate area quite well and I've got an excellent guidebook for the whole walk containing 1:25,000 scale extracts from Ordinance Survey maps and other useful information," he said, patting a small satchel hanging at his waist. "But a larger-scale map of the area of the Peak District north of here might be useful if we decide to do a little more exploring on our way back."

Then he noticed Hannah looking anxiously back down the road. Making no comment, he pretended to change his mind.

"On second thoughts, the morning's going fast. We'd better keep going," he said.

As they moved on, Hannah glanced back again. The black car was slowly nosing its way around a bend about a hundred yards away.

She gave a tiny gasp and hurried up the road followed by a worried Paul. To her relief, she heard the chatter of a large group of tourists coming out of the Visitor Centre just behind them.

"They'll act as a screen," she thought, as she moved up to mingle with other walkers going in the same direction.

After passing an attractive church, they arrived in the centre of the village. The fields and scattered houses had now been replaced by closely-spaced buildings of pleasant honey-coloured stone.

"We've reached the start of the Pennine Way," Paul said, guiding her sharp left into a track running almost due west. It was directly opposite an attractive pub, The Old Nag's Head.

Hannah increased her pace even more and he looked at her in alarm. "Are you worried about something?" he asked, unable to restrain himself any longer.

So she described what she had seen at Edale station when they were finishing their coffee and her second sighting of the same black car.

"My head says it's impossible but deep down I can't help feeling worried. You didn't see the look on the dark-haired man's face in London!" she concluded, upon which Paul touched her arm in sympathy.

"It was a nasty frightening experience for you," he admitted. "However, I can't see how these criminals could possibly have kept track of you. You're just a nameless young woman to them. The only thing you have on you that could be traced is your mobile 'phone, but they don't know its details, even if they were able to access a tracking service. Anyway, if they're so very clever, why didn't they find you in Sheffield late yesterday?"

Hannah had to concur. "It just doesn't make sense," she said. "In fact, it's spooky!"

Paul turned to grin at her. "Remember, I'm a physicist: we deal with facts and supportable theories!"

They hurried on, although it would now be difficult for a car to follow – assuming she had been spotted turning off at the Old Nag's Head, which was unlikely given the large number of people in the village. Fortunately, there were some popular paths that wound up the slopes above Edale and could be reached by continuing on up the village street to the end of the road. Paul had noticed quite a lot of tourists going that way and surmised that it might be a more popular option for visitors only in Edale for a few hours.

The Pennine Way tended to be for more serious walkers, of which there were quite a few in view of the time of year and sunny weather. They would add camouflage should anyone be trying to watch the path from the edge of the village.

They found themselves on a lovely stretch of open land and following a narrow path of carefully-laid paving stones. Hannah looked at the low hill a short distance ahead and the blue sky above; it was all so peaceful, even with the walkers spread out in single file ahead of them. She noticed thankfully that Paul was walking close behind her to act as a screen. She began to relax slightly but still kept up an impressive pace.

"All this is so lovely after London!" she exclaimed, giving a small happy sigh. "It reminds me of a short holiday I once had in the Shropshire hills when I was sixteen. My aunt and uncle – my mother's brother – took me to stay in a small hotel as a reward for doing well in my GCSE exams. They were keen walkers in those days and we had an energetic week. They had no children and so, after my aunt died of cancer six months ago, my uncle lives alone in Sherborne." She lapsed into silence again to concentrate on walking.

After commenting that he would like to visit Shropshire some time, Paul told her that the present route of the Pennine Way starts off by going almost due west from Edale to skirt the southern edge of an area of high ground known as Kinder.

"The original path went right over the highest part of the Kinder plateau – known as Kinder Scout – but the ground got badly worn," he explained. "So the path was moved further west to follow the edge of the plateau to reach Kinder Downfall, the tallest waterfall in the Peaks. We'll be going up the spectacular Jacob's Ladder – you'll understand the reason for the name when you see it – to reach a high point of about 630m at Kinder Low, presumably so named because it's slightly lower than the Scout!"

As they crossed a tiny stream, Paul explained that it was one of a network of tributaries feeding the River Noe, a small river that runs east past Edale to join the River Derwent as it winds its way southward.

"In fact, the Derwent passes close to the famous Chatsworth House; we can visit there during our time in the south of the Peaks," he said.

Hannah gave him a happy smile of anticipation.

After they had negotiated several gates and stiles in the dry stone walls separating the fields, the scenery became even better. The path widened into a track and they passed several farm buildings before veering in a more northerly direction.

Hannah spotted a narrow meandering river a short distance to their left with an ancient-looking wood beyond.

Paul noticed her interest. "That's the Noe again and all that remains of the woods that used to cover these slopes."

"This is extraordinary!" Hannah said, turning briefly to look back the way they had come. Bathed in bright sunshine, the view down into the valley was really beautiful.

"I'm so glad I came!" she added, beginning to climb again.

Soon the path began to descend, revealing a small attractive valley with a few buildings nestling in a hollow surrounded by small trees. The lower slopes of the surrounding hills were covered with grass and what appeared to be heather higher up. A broad track through the valley gradually led them up towards a ridge at the end.

The gradient increased and they came to a long curved path climbing steeply upwards, at the foot of which a small notice announced, "Jacob's Ladder". It was composed of densely packed flat slabs of rock that resembled the treads of a staircase.

A beautiful view confronted them when they turned to look back shortly before reaching the top. The valley up which they had come curved out of sight behind a hill to the left of them and a series of rolling hills guarded the opposite side. Everything looked so tranquil, even the diminutive figures who were moving slowly up and down the lower path.

From the top of the Ladder there was a relatively short climb to the edge of the Kinder Low plateau where the path became largely paved again to avoid damaging the peaty surface of the moorland. It seemed no time at all before they were standing beside the trig point on the summit gazing at the view in the company of several other tourists. The surroundings, however, were dominated by a rather ugly foreground of rocks and patches of bare peat.

"It's rather like pictures of the surface of the moon!" Hannah exclaimed sadly.

"Most of the heights in the Pennines are rather barren due to two hundred years of pollution from the mills of Lancashire," Paul told her. "The soil is now very acidic."

But something about her obvious disappointment had suddenly caused him to remember something else. He took her arm to encourage her to move on down the path so that they would have more privacy.

"In all the uncertainty about your choice and then my pleasure when you decided to come, I've completely forgotten to 'phone ahead to the guesthouse to see if it's possible to swap the twin-bedded room I originally booked for two single rooms," he confessed. "The place has four small singles sharing a bathroom, one en-suite double and one en-suite twin. I may be lucky; otherwise there's another guesthouse a short distance away."

Hannah looked at him with a quizzical smile that was difficult to interpret.

"But then you'd lose the money you've already paid!" she said with a shake of the head. "I'm happy to share if you are. We're both adults and I trust you completely. If not, I wouldn't have agreed to come with you. I suggest you don't even 'phone; the en-suite sounds a wonderful luxury to me!"

Paul looked at her. "Are you really sure?" he asked. Hannah nodded. "Then tonight's accommodation is on me, including the meal, assuming we can find one somewhere! The guesthouse only supplies an evening drink and biscuits. I'll be most displeased if you try to pay for anything. Anyway, the room was quite a bargain because I booked and paid well in advance."

"Then I accept with many thanks!" Hannah responded with friendly smile. "Now we'd better get moving! Our average speed so far hasn't been very good!"

With that she speeded up and set a cracking pace, although the path was now dropping slightly. They quickly approached the far side of the plateau and followed the path as it meandered along the edge. Their earlier disappointment was now compensated by beautiful views of the lower ground to the west.

They spent a few moments inspecting the impressive drop of Downfall. Although there was only a trickle of water at this time of year, it still sent up quite a spray as it splashed down the rocky escarpment and was caught by the strong breeze.

They had only moved on a short distance before Paul said: "Turn round and look behind you."

Hannah did as bidden; the large expanse of the Kinder Scout and its plateau lay bathed in the hot sunshine. "It's barren, but somehow beautiful at this distance!" she exclaimed.

The path descended gradually, crossed a narrow valley and climbed again to the flat summit of Mill Hill. The path was now paved again as it descended and ran over boggy moorland, fed by a series of tiny streams that flowed off the higher ground. A long low ridge faced them in the distance as they traversed the final stretch of moor to reach a wicket gate that guarded a road running east-west.

"This is the so-called Snake Pass road between Manchester and Sheffield," Paul informed her.

They crossed quickly, looking rather anxiously in both directions for a black car, but there was only a silver one approaching from the east and a small red Volkswagen parked beside the road, obviously belonging to some people out for a stroll. In fact, Hannah could see a couple who were probably the occupants walking some distance ahead of them.

"It may surprise you, but we're still about 500 metres above sea level," Paul said. "Even though we've dropped down slightly from Kinder, we're still on a ridge joining it to the Bleaklow plateau that has similar areas of thick peat and strange outcrops of rock."

He was following Hannah's rapid pace and they quickly caught up and passed the walking couple with a polite exchange of greetings.

The Pennine Way continued to wind its way through various gullies and beside narrow streams before climbing up over Bleaklow Head – the highest point of the Bleaklow plateau – where they gazed appreciatively at the sweeping panorama of blue sky dotted with small fluffy white clouds.

Eventually, they dropped down to the attractive little valley of Crowden Beck and on into the Longendale valley towards a string of small reservoirs along the A628 Manchester to Barnsley road.

Just to the south of one of these reservoirs, Paul led Hannah towards a café that he remembered from two years ago – the Old House Tea Room – for a much needed drink.

They had been walking for just over five hours and only stopped briefly for some of his mother's generous supply of sandwiches.

"Sarah's given us enough food for two lunches!" Hannah had exclaimed as they were putting everything back in their rucksacks.

"Just like my mother!" had been the reply. "It's a good job you suggested saving the cheese ones, because there's a faint chance that they'll survive until tomorrow; the ham ones would've been a write-off!"

Tea and cake in the pleasant café made an excellent short break and the friendly waitress even re-filled their water bottles. It was a much refreshed couple who set off on the final leg of the day's journey.

"I guess we can make our guesthouse in about three and a half hours of hard walking," said Paul. "There's less hill work than earlier, although we'll be climbing to the broad top of Black Hill at a height of about 580 metres."

Hannah turned to grin at him, delighted with the challenge ahead.

They passed the Torside Reservoir before crossing the A628 to a lay-by on the opposite side. Making their way past a group of walkers standing in a huddle consulting a map, Paul was opening the gate marking the entrance to the north-bound Pennine Way when something made him glance back down the road. To his horror a large black car was approaching slowly from the west.

CHAPTER 7

Paul grabbed Hannah's hand and hurried her on to a broad path that ran parallel to the road for a short distance, thankfully separated from it by a low stone wall and verge covered with bushes and trees.

Hannah realized something must have alarmed him. She did not object as he kept hold of her hand and steered her along the far edge of the path, trying to use his body to shield her from an observer passing along the road. Fortunately, the walkers who had been standing at the gate were following close behind, chattering excitedly, and he hoped all this would provide sufficient camouflage. It would be a different matter if one of the men decided to get out in the lay-by and followed on foot.

A couple of hoots came from the road but Paul did not risk looking in that direction until Hannah was safely through a second gate and the path had turned north away from the road so that he could walk behind her. The reason for the hooting now became clear: the black car had been travelling so slowly that it was causing congestion on the narrow road. It was still in sight and he could just glimpse the blond hair of the front passenger. Fortunately, there were enough walkers behind them to severely limit the view of someone sitting in a car.

"That was a close escape!" he exclaimed. "The fact that the car slowed to a crawl, much to the annoyance of the other traffic, means they suspect we're very near. But how on earth do they know?"

Hannah was looking quite pale with shock. "They must have spotted us entering the Pennine Way in Edale and managed to judge how far we'd be able to walk in five hours or so!" she said. "But why on earth don't they park somewhere and find a place where we can be intercepted easily?"

"It baffles me!" Paul replied. "They're bound to try again and probably do what you suggest further up."

They were now heading towards a valley. She looked at him enquiringly as he fumbled to find the correct page in his guidebook.

"The valley up there has been formed by a stream called the Crowden Great Brook," he said, nodding up the track. "The path runs up the valley a short distance west of the stream. We're aiming for a rather barren and soggy peat plateau appropriately named Black Hill, except there'll be a detour before then to Laddow Rocks that form part of the western side of the valley."

It was a pleasant level path and Hannah was taking the opportunity to move at over four miles per hour. Paul did not mind how fast they travelled; not only were some determined criminals following them but they still had about nine miles to go and would soon come to some more steep gradients.

"This girl's a real trooper!" he thought. "I know we've only covered just over two-thirds of today's hike but she's not showing the slightest sign of weariness!"

He could not resist giving her a compliment. "You're an amazingly good walker; not only athletic and fit, but also light on your feet despite wearing boots. In fact, I'm surprised you came down hard enough to do the dongle so much damage!"

Hannah grinned at him. "Well, I was on a hard pavement and just changing direction at the sharp turn into Tooting Broadway," she said, "but I'm really glad I'm not delaying you!"

"Far from it! I think you could give me a run for my money," he replied.

"I don't believe that; we're very well matched," she asserted generously, although she was privately rather pleased he thought so highly of her. His opinion of her seemed to matter somehow.

Eventually, the path began to climb up the side of the valley away from the stream. Hannah barely slowed, except when they paused briefly to look back at the rather barren but strangely attractive landscape they were leaving far behind. Now visible ahead was a ridge that marked the edge of the Black Hill plateau, and, slightly to the left, the nearer rocky promontory of Laddow that seemed to point directly towards it.

The narrow path wound between coarse grass and small clumps of heather and dipped briefly to follow a narrow ravine down which a small stream cascaded in a series of tiny waterfalls.

"I suppose that stream must be flowing down to join the Great Brook," Hannah remarked, giving no sign of being out of breath.

At last, the edge of Laddow Rocks stretched out before them: a mixture of steep slopes and a sheer rock face from which small lumps of rock had fallen into the valley below. The path became quite steep for a short distance and then they were winding along the edge of the promontory. It was essential to go single-file and David followed Hannah as she moved smoothly along.

After a short distance, the path ran gently down to merge with the upper end of the valley of the Great Brook. The latter had now shrunk to a shallow trickle that they followed for half a mile or so as the path took them gradually up on to what appeared to be a rather soggy moor. A few small pools of water were all that remained of the stream.

The path was now carefully paved with stone slabs and continued to rise slowly until they reached a white-painted trig point, strangely mounted on a slightly tapered platform built of neatly-fitting grey stones.

"The guidebook refers to this as Soldier's Lump!" Paul announced. "Apparently it was originally built by army engineers to mark the highest point of the Black Hill, although, for something called a hill it has a remarkably large flat top!"

The paved path continued to take them roughly north-east until beginning to descend from the barren plateau. An attractive panorama confronted them as the path widened into a gravel track and continued to drop down, with a few undulations, for another mile to the A635 Greenfield to Holmfirth road. They had to follow the latter for a short distance before turning north again and took it at the trot: they were determined not to be caught by the black car again.

A wide track led them across Wessenden Moor to Wessenden Head Reservoir – Paul announcing each landmark as they passed – before dropping down rapidly towards an attractive valley with the much larger Wessenden Reservoir in the middle distance.

After following the edge of the reservoir, the track twisted and turned its way past a strange confluence of very small valleys; it looked almost as if a giant had carelessly tossed down a piece of heavy rather drab velvet. The sight left Hannah quite intrigued and Paul rather surprised because he could not recall seeing them on his trip two years ago.

Nevertheless, the guidebook seemed to indicate that they were on the right route as the path led them down into a narrow valley, across a bridge over a stream and up the other side. Passing a smaller reservoir, they found themselves out on Black Moss moor and heading towards Swellands Reservoir and the Standedge cutting on the A62 road between Manchester and Huddersfield. A small car park on the southern side of the road still contained two or three cars.

"They probably belong to tourists wanting to walk beside the reservoirs on such a pleasant evening," Paul surmised.

He guided Hannah straight across the road and up a short stretch of fairly steep path on to yet another moor.

"Just under a mile to the guesthouse now!" he said encouragingly.

Hannah glanced at her watch: it was almost seven o'clock. "It's later than I thought!" she said. "Yes, we do need to get there before they give our room to someone else!"

Very soon the path merged with a narrow lane. "We must stay on this lane," Paul said, taking her arm. "The place is about half a mile on the right. It has a lovely view back towards the Peak District. It's so peaceful that it's hard to believe there's a long railway tunnel buried beneath the A62 and that small reservoir beside it!"

They passed a junction from which a short road ran down the slope to link the lane with the main road they had crossed earlier, rounded a wide bend and found their guesthouse on the right-hand side. As Paul had promised, the outlook from the front of the building was delightful on such a beautiful evening.

A few minutes later, they were comfortably installed in a twin-bedded room at the front of the house overlooking the expanse of the Black Moss moor and the hills of the Peak District in the distance. From this vantage point, Hannah realized that the area was not quite as isolated as it had first appeared: she could see a few scattered houses and farm buildings.

The bedroom was rather cramped but everything in the en-suite shower room worked well, and so they were able to have very welcome showers before getting ready to go out to find a pub for an evening meal.

"It's nice to be able to go out without a rucksack and walking boots!" Hannah said as they descended the stairs at about eight o'clock.

She was now wearing trainers and Paul was astonished when she showed no surprise at being told that the nearest place for a decent meal was the Great Western Inn roughly a mile away. Was there no end to her stamina?

One of the two women running the guesthouse happened to see them just as they were opening the front door.

"When you arrived, I forgot to ask if you would like a hot drink at ten o'clock or just after – coffee, tea or hot chocolate?" she queried. They selected chocolate.

At that moment, a middle-aged couple passed them on the way out to their car. Hearing the conversation, the man kindly offered to give the young people a lift.

"We're going into Marsden. It's about three miles east of here," he said. "Can we drop you off somewhere?"

Paul immediately accepted thankfully; not only would it save time and energy, but he had noticed earlier that the main road had no pavements and the verges were very narrow, especially in the Standedge cutting itself.

As a result, less than ten minutes after leaving the guesthouse, they were comfortably seated at a table in the Great Western's pleasant restaurant consulting the menu.

When he noticed Hannah searching for the cheaper items, he insisted that she ignore the prices and choose something she really fancied. When she showed some reluctance, he reminded her that he was not paying for this holiday out of his teacher's salary but using his competition winnings. As a result, they both ordered soup followed by lamb steaks with a selection of fresh vegetables and sat back to enjoy a refreshingly cold drink.

"I've spent less than £20 since meeting you on the Sheffield train yesterday!" Hannah exclaimed in dismay and began listing all that Paul had done for her, not to mention his parent's hospitality.

However, he interrupted her flow of words. "You've made what would have been a lonely trek much nicer," he said. "Just image what parts of the Pennine Way would feel like if you were on your own, especially in less pleasant weather!"

She gave one of her rare smiles that made her elfin face look really beautiful; it was a smile that seemed to convey a mixture of surprise, gratitude, and delight.

For a few minutes, they continued to sip their drinks in silence.

The soup was accompanied by crisp rolls and proved to be just what two hungry walkers needed. The main course appeared soon afterwards. The vegetables were generous and nicely cooked, but the lamb steaks, although tasty, were slightly tough. Hannah chewed slowly with such obvious enjoyment, however, that Paul relaxed and followed suit. Quite a contrast to John, he thought, who would have almost certainly complained.

When he looked over at Hannah again, giving total attention to her food, he was surprised to feel a surge of tenderness for her. He realized for the first time that it must have been quite hard to be a farmer's daughter, especially whilst still a schoolgirl.

He imagined her coming home from senior school – presumably two or more miles away in Sherborne – and having to cope with GCSE or A-level homework as well as jobs around the farm. She had then probably left home to train as a teacher, unless there was a suitable college somewhere nearby, and now existed in a London suburb paying an exorbitant rent for a tiny flat and trying to make ends meet on a relatively low salary.

There and then, he determined to do all in his power to ensure she had a happy holiday and really enjoyed her time on the Pennine Way. Without appearing to do so, he would always let her set the pace and try to pay for as much as she would let him.

Hannah suddenly became aware of his gaze and looked up. He simply gave her a friendly smile, however, and concentrated on his meal again, conscious that she continued to look at him for several seconds. Just as he was wondering what was going through her mind, she spoke.

"Do you know something? I feel remarkably comfortable in your company: more than with anyone I can remember, apart from my mother, uncle and aunt, when she was still alive. Even my father, bless him, is disappointed that I wasn't a boy who could help him with the running of our small farm and take over eventually."

She reflected for a moment. "The problem is that, as an only child, I've grown up accustomed to being a loner. It takes a lot to thaw me out and you're doing it by being so kind and understanding." She stopped abruptly, rather embarrassed she had revealed so much.

"I don't think of you as a loner, but as quiet, thoughtful and considerate," Paul said softly. "Perhaps it's because I'm rather a loner myself that we get on so well!"

Another delightful smile lit up Hannah's face.

She declined a desert and opted instead to enjoy the late evening light with a cup of coffee at one of the tables at the front of the building. Although terrace overlooked the A62, it was not busy at this time of day and there was an attractive view over a small reservoir on the opposite side of the road.

Paul paid the bill before taking their coffee outside. At the time, he did not realize how important this simple act would turn out to be.

They slowly sipped the hot liquid in quiet companionship, enjoying the glow as the sun set almost directly over the Standedge cutting to the east of them. There was a slight breeze and the last of the reddish-golden rays were catching the ripples on the surface of the water not far away.

Just after nine-thirty, Paul suggested returning to the guesthouse before it got too dark and also to be in time for a hot chocolate.

The table area was protected from the road by a low wrought-iron fence that almost completely enclosed the front of the building. In order to walk back along the road the way they had come, it was necessary to go through a small gate at the far corner of the building into the adjacent car park.

Just as Hannah reached the open gate with Paul immediately behind her, the squeal of car brakes not far away made him glance over his shoulder. A large car coming from the direction of Marsden had just crossed the carriageway to their side of the road and pulled up sharply in a bus lay-by at the far end of the building.

He felt as if he had received an electric shock: the car was black and the light was just sufficient to glimpse the blond hair of the man sitting in the front passenger seat.

CHAPTER 8

Paul turned back to Hannah and almost thrust her bodily through the gate and round the corner into the relative safety of the side of the restaurant. She was just about to complain at her rough treatment, when he whispered two words, "Black car!"

He held her safely behind him with one arm while he cautiously peered back to the far end of the building. To his surprise, the blond-headed man was gazing intently at something in his hand. He then handed whatever it was to the driver, got out of the car and entered the inn.

"What on earth's going on?" Hannah asked rather sharply, rather annoyed at being held firmly against the wall.

"The large black car has not only appeared again, but this time they seem certain we're here, even though they can't possibly have seen us! The blond one has just gone inside," Paul whispered back, still horrified that the criminals seemed to possess a sixth sense.

Immediately he said these words, something clicked in his brain as if a light had been switched on; everything fell into place and he suddenly became a man of action.

"Do you have the dongle on you?" he said quickly. Hannah nodded. "Give it to me!"

She looked surprised but fished the little plastic envelop out of her pocket. He took it from her and issued some brief instructions.

"You must trust me. There's no time to explain. I'll be back in two minutes. Meanwhile, you go straight to the last of the cars over there at the back of the car park and crouch behind it. Keep out of sight of the road and the front of the building. The black car is just beyond the main entrance and the driver is facing in this direction."

While he was speaking, he put the small object out of sight behind a convenient fragment of brick lying close to the wall. Giving her arm a reassuring squeeze, he slipped to the back of the building and down a path that he hoped led to the kitchen. To his relief, one of the kitchen staff was enjoying the evening air.

"Excuse me," he said with a friendly smile. "My friend and I have just enjoyed a meal in the restaurant. I've now got a small problem in the car park. Is it possible to have a strip of aluminium cooking foil about four or five inches wide?"

The man looked surprised but did not stop to ask any awkward questions. In less than a minute he was back again with the foil in his hand. Paul gratefully took it in exchange for a £1 coin, blurting a relieved "Good night" as he hurried back the way he had come. The man looked at the coin in his hand with a happy smile.

Paul retrieved the dongle and hastily wrapped it several times in the foil strip before making his way cautiously back to Hannah's hiding place.

Crouching down beside the relieved-looking girl, he gave her a reassuring smile before creeping further forward to the shelter of another vehicle to get a better view. Although dusk was developing fast, the front of the black car was clearly visible in the light shed by a lantern above the door of the inn.

The blond man was back in the passenger seat; Paul could just make out the fact that he seemed to be arguing with the driver. A few seconds later, the engine roared into life and he only just made it back to Hannah before the car shot past them and down the road.

Taking somewhat of a risk, he led her quickly in the same direction, keeping as close as possible to the side and ready to step on to the verge whenever a car approached.

"I don't think they're likely to come back until they've looked along the road for a couple of miles at least," he called over his shoulder and began to quickly explain what he had deduced.

"It suddenly dawned on me that the only way the crooks could have been tracking you is for the dongle to be "alive" and sending out some sort of radio signal at regular intervals. They don't need to see you while you're carrying the dongle – although they may have done so as you disappeared up the Pennine Way in Edale, giving them the clue where to begin searching again. There must have been a detector in that attaché case able to pick up the signal from the dongle if it gets lost. Of course, they may also have seen me with you in Edale."

"However," he continued, "the detector probably has a fairly short range and is really intended to be used to trace the dongle if it gets mislaid in a factory or office complex. Thus, lacking a more powerful detector, the men are reduced to zigzagging backwards and forwards on roads that cross the path of the Pennine Way trying to pick up the signal again. It's also a good job their device is not very accurate, otherwise they might have come direct to that little café and not Edale station!"

He gave a little laugh of triumph. "Anyway, I've foxed them now. I got some aluminium foil from the restaurant kitchen and wrapped the dongle in it. There's no chance of a radio signal getting through several layers of conducting foil!"

Hannah laughed delightedly. "I think you're a genius! I'm so glad I'm with you!" She gave him a friendly pat on the back.

Just then they arrived opposite the small Pennine Way car park. Paul decided it would be safer to turn right off the road and follow the rough path.

"This route is both shorter and safer if that car comes back again," he said cheerfully. He produced a pencil-torch from his pocket.

"You think of everything," Hannah said admiringly as she slipped her arm through his.

"Well, I knew it would be dark by the time we came back!" he replied, rather liking the comforting feel of her arm. He reflected sadly on the fact that he had not had a steady girlfriend since his second year at university.

They managed the fairly short distance up the path surprisingly easily with the aid of the narrow beam from the torch and were soon on the lane that led to their destination. So much had happened in a short space of time that Paul was quite surprised when he opened the front door with his key and found they were only a few minutes late for a hot drink.

"I'll go straight to the breakfast room while you nip upstairs and put the dongle somewhere safe," Hannah said.

Upstairs, Paul quickly re-wrapped the dongle more carefully in the foil strip and washed the dirt off his hands. Returning downstairs, he found Hannah sitting with their two mugs of chocolate at a long communal table.

"I refused extra sugar," she said with a grin. "It's probably too sweet already!"

Paul nodded his thanks as he sat beside her. A party of three lads in their mid-teens looked rather disappointed at his appearance, but he gave them a friendly smile and asked if they were hiking together on the Pennine Way.

"My father dropped us off here in his car and will pick us up at Edale in two days time," one responded. He winced slightly at what was almost certainly a kick under the table: his companions were obviously annoyed that he had inadvertently revealed that they were still dependent on parental transport.

Paul merely remarked that it looked as if they would have good weather for the journey, but Hannah chipped in: "You'll really enjoy the walk. We've just done it today!"

"In one day?" the first lad gasped. Hannah nodded. The threesome looked both impressed and rather deflated: how could this slip of a girl walk that far in one day they were obviously thinking.

Fortunately, they were saved from further embarrassment by the sudden appearance of the friendly landlady as she bustled in with a plate of mixed biscuits.

"I'm sorry. I forgot to put these out earlier!" she apologized.

She offered first choice to Hannah and Paul. After taking one biscuit each, they both nodded in the direction of the boys who were looking hungrily at the plate. "Let them have the rest," Hannah whispered, and watched with a smile as they eagerly shared them out.

As the woman retrieved the empty plate, she reminded them that breakfast would be served from seven o'clock until eight-thirty and asked if everyone would like the full English breakfast. Upon receiving an affirmative answer, she informed them that a slice of black pudding would be included tomorrow unless anyone preferred a spoonful of baked beans?

The boys looked puzzled and Paul had to explain that black pudding was a type of sausage made of pork, dried blood, suet and oatmeal. Willing to try anything new, the hungry lads agreed, but Hannah and Paul opted for the baked beans as they got up to go to bed.

"It's been a long day," Paul explained as they bade everyone goodnight.

Hannah had no sooner entered their bedroom than she went across to her rucksack and extracted a small bar of chocolate.

"It has got a little soft but is still edible. I'll take it downstairs to the boys – assuming they're still there – as a small apology for rather unkindly taking them down a peg by letting on that we did the journey from Edale in one day! You have the bathroom first."

When she returned, Paul was almost ready for bed and came out of the bathroom rather apologetically because he had only brought pyjama trousers with him to save space and weight.

Hannah grinned rather mischievously. "No problem!" she chuckled. "It's good to know my walking companion is not only clever but also tough and strong!"

She did not mention aloud that it was particularly comforting if, by any chance, the crooks had not given up the pursuit after their setback.

Paul was in bed and already quite drowsy when Hannah emerged from the bathroom clutching her discarded clothes and respectably clad in rather faded blue pyjamas. She put her clothes tidily away and slipped quickly into the bed by the window; Paul had deliberately taken the one nearer the door because he was uncertain about the lock and felt it would be the more chivalrous position. She was asleep within a minute or two of exchanging a whispered goodnight.

In fact, they both slept so soundly that neither roused until Paul's small alarm clock sounded discretely at ten past six. They had agreed to be down to breakfast at seven o'clock so that they could be off early for the day's long hike. They also thought it sensible to have a quick shower before leaving, even if the water was tepid, because Paul was not sure how adequate his brother's hot-water supply would be in Skipton.

"You have a shower while I shave out here," Paul said. "I can charge the battery while we're having breakfast."

Hannah was out of the bathroom within fifteen minutes. "All yours! The water's still tepid and so I had a very bracing cold shower instead. I'm now ready for anything!"

She certainly looked totally refreshed.

They were greeted cheerfully by the same woman who had been there the previous day. She seemed to be in sole charge of contact with guests. As if in answer to their unspoken question, she informed them that her sister did all the cooking, laundry, and shopping, while she handled the front of house, including the accounts and getting the six rooms ready for the next guests.

"Most people are walkers on the Pennine Way and only here for one night, so there's a lot of housekeeping and laundry!" she said. "The couple in the double room are here for three nights, which is very unusual for us and a nice change!"

An excellent cooked breakfast arrived almost as soon as Paul and Hannah had finished their cereal and they were leaving the room by the time the three lads appeared rather sleepily for their meal.

CHAPTER 9

Just before eight o'clock, the young couple were striding back up the lane towards the Pennine Way. Hannah looked full of energy and enthusiasm in shorts and T-shirt; Paul could not help reflecting how fortunate he was with his walking companion.

The entrance to the northbound Pennine Way appeared on their left as they walked along the track leading down to the main road; Hannah had not noticed it the previous evening. They turned north and began climbing the narrow winding path towards the heights of Standedge Moor.

Suddenly, Paul had a thought. "Keep on walking slowly," he said. "I'm just going to double back a short distance until I can see the main road, then I'll hurry to catch you up."

Hannah looked rather surprised but just nodded her understanding and slowed to a casual pace. About five minutes later, Paul returned and they reverted to their normal stride.

"There's no cause for alarm; I thought this might happen," he said. "The black car is in the small car park on the other side of the A62 with two men standing on a bank behind it. One is your blond friend and the other is much smaller: probably the dark-haired one who threatened you. They're scanning the Pennine Way south of the road with binoculars, having presumably gazed as far as they can in this direction. Fortunately, only a short length of this path is visible. It's obvious they can't detect the signal from the dongle any more and are having to rely on sight and guesswork."

He was pleased to see that Hannah was undisturbed by the news. She merely looked at him with a confident smile. "I'm glad I'm with you!" was all she said, seemingly happy to leave him to handle the situation.

It was several minutes before he spoke again. "After being delighted to pick up the signal a short time earlier, the men must have been shocked when it disappeared soon after they pulled up at the Great Western, especially if the waitress confirmed that someone answering your description had just been in for a meal. Having failed to find us further along the road, they probably deduced that we were staying somewhere nearby and so came back early this morning to see if they could spot us re-joining the Pennine Way. Eventually, they'll give up waiting and probably start zigzagging up the Way again."

Paul paused to smile with some satisfaction. "They've wasted two days already, not to mention driving for miles, all because darkie could not control his temper back in Tooting! His boss must be hopping mad: the laptop is worth far less without the dongle because it'll cost their paymaster a fortune to get an expert to hack into the software somehow."

He stopped suddenly. "No! I believe it's even worse than that! In addition to allowing access to the software, the dongle probably has some form of cipher key that enables the encryption and deciphering of the software and its associated files. It may also be unique; one designed for the same software on another computer might have a different encryption key. Wow! This dongle must be protecting some extremely secret information."

Hannah was impressed by his reasoning but had been thinking as well. "Surely the sensible thing, depending on how big the gang is, would be to send two men up the Way from here and have a couple more walk down from somewhere further north?"

"Maybe they're not keen on hard walking and hoping the dongle may recover and start emitting a signal again. After all, they only missed us by a whisker at the Great Western!" Paul replied.

"All thanks to your quick thinking!" Hannah muttered under her breath.

They hurried on in friendly companionship, both conscious that the events of the previous evening had introduced a new element of warmth into their relationship. Hannah now trusted Paul completely and had begun to rely on him more than she would probably have admitted if questioned.

As they walked higher, they glimpsed the village of Diggle nestling down in the valley from which they had come, and then, a few minutes later, a splendid panorama was spread out before them. Paul's guide book informed them that the trig point they were approaching marked the highest point of the Standedge moor at 448m above sea level and that the adjacent outcrops of rock were formed of millstone grit.

"The name comes from the fact that it was used to make millstones for water-powered flour mills. It originates from sandstone that has been heated to very high temperature by volcanic action," Paul said.

"A geologist would love this trip!" Hannah commented.

The path was winding over level ground now and he reckoned that they must be walking at over four miles an hour, so eagerly was she moving forward. Although barren, the surrounding hills and ridges, interspersed with occasional small reservoirs lying in the deep folds of the land, were strangely attractive under an almost cloudless pale blue sky.

The Pennine Way swung northeast at a stone marker, helpfully placed to redirect walkers, and began to drop down to the A640 Oldham to Huddersfield road.

They approached the small car park beside the road cautiously, although Paul was sure the crooks would not have had time to drive the miles needed to arrive before them.

It was necessary to turn left and follow the road for a few yards before the path continued again up on to the moor and the White Hill trig point. They passed close to an unsightly communications mast and straight across the A672 from Oldham to Halifax.

The roar of traffic sounded in the near distance and it was not long before Hannah was surprised to find herself on an elegant concrete footbridge crossing the busy M62 motorway connecting Liverpool on the west coast to Hull on the east coast.

After another stretch of rather barren moor, they walked along the crest of Blackstone Edge with a panoramic view to the southwest that included the large town of Rochdale. There were a multitude of rocks scattered about, so much so that the path was quite difficult to follow as they descended towards what almost appeared to be a plain after the hilly terrain they were leaving behind.

Their route took them down an old Roman Road for about a quarter of a mile before Paul guided Hannah right on to a track that led down to the A58 Rochdale to Halifax road close to the White House pub. They entered the road without hesitation because they had had a good view in both directions while on higher ground.

"Would you like a cup of coffee?" he asked.

"Love some!" Hannah replied. "But it's on me this time."

About thirty minutes later they were back on the Pennine Way that now ran along a wide track below the embankment of the Blackstone Edge reservoir and then beside several smaller reservoirs.

"All rather flat and uninteresting, but at least we can put on some speed," Hannah chuckled.

Paul looked at her in admiration. "You're doing well. I think we'll make my brother's house in Skipton before seven o'clock," he said.

"You bet!" she replied determinedly.

Two and a half miles later they were crossing rough moorland again when Paul pointed out a tall monument in the distance.

"That's Stoodley Pike, according to the guidebook," he said. "The originally was built in 1815 to commemorate the defeat of Napoleon. It was destroyed by lightning and had to be replaced in 1856."

Glimpses of the valley below appeared every so often before the path reached the edge of the moor and revealed a really spectacular panorama before swinging back to climb up to the monument.

Stoodley Pike was disappointingly ugly at close quarters.

"There's something unpleasant about it!" Hannah remarked.

"I agree," Paul responded. "But the view over the valley is amazing!"

The Pennine Way now descended into cultivated land and a pleasant wood where they stopped briefly to sit on a grassy bank to eat the remainder of the cheese and pickle sandwiches that Paul's mother had made, finishing up with a banana.

"They've just survived from yesterday; probably because they were wrapped in greaseproof paper and foil," Paul said thankfully.

A surprising number of walkers passed during the short time they were there. "Presumably most are going up to Stoodley Pike and back," Hannah surmised.

After walking down a gravel lane to the bank of the Rochdale Canal at Charlestown, about a mile west of Hebden Bridge on the A646, they crossed a bridge controlled by traffic lights and cautiously came out on the narrow main road.

Paul looked at the guidebook. "We must turn right along this road and then take the first turning on the left to go under a railway line where the Pennine Way should start again," he announced.

Leaving the railway, a paved path flanked by low stone walls ran gently up to join a track that wound its way past small cottages and fields to give a lovely view of the valley they were leaving behind.

"It's a strange thing," Hannah remarked. "Sometimes it's only when you leave a place that you appreciate its beauty!"

At one point, the side of the valley became very steep and they found themselves climbing some steps beside a small waterfall.

Eventually, however, they were back on a mixture of moor and farmland.

There were a surprising number of other people around; a few were clearly determined hikers tackling sections of the Pennine Way in earnest, but others were more casual walkers who probably preferred this softer landscape to the more barren Stoodley Pike plateau.

Still walking fast, Hannah and Paul had just caught up a party of five when the group reached a small road and streamed across the carriageway and through the narrow gap on the other side. Once on the path again, Hannah glanced behind her. To her surprise, the Pike was still visible in the far distance on the other side of the valley.

Fortunately, Paul had been paying more attention to their immediate surroundings. He suddenly took her by the hand to hurry her up the slope, simply muttering: "Black car coming from the left".

Fortunately, there were several walkers still with them and they were partly sheltered by a stone wall. He did not let go of her hand until they had reached the brow of the hill and slipped behind a bush. Peering out cautiously, they saw that the black car had just driven very slowly past the Pennine Way crossing; its occupants would have had quite a good view of the path, particularly to the south of the road.

"We're very fortunate that there were a number of other people around, otherwise we'd have been spotted for sure," Paul said. "The crooks have done surprisingly well to guess how far up the Pennine Way we'd be by now, six hours after leaving Sandedge, especially as they don't know exactly when we left. All the roads around here are narrow and it must be difficult to find a place to stop where the view of the crossing point is good and they're not causing an obstruction."

"I suggest we confuse them by speeding up. We could jog on the downhill and flat sections and only walk when going uphill or the route gets complicated," Hannah suggested.

"You lead then and set the pace," Paul told her. "I'll keep an eye on my map and call out a warning when there's a change of direction. Unfortunately the Way twists and turns all over the place! It also crosses several small roads and sometimes uses the road for a short distance."

Hannah's stamina was amazing. She jogged steadily over the pleasant farmland, only slowing down to cross a road just east of the village of Colden with great caution. It was only as the Pennine Way began to climb towards Heptonstall Moor that she reverted to walking pace.

Eventually the path began to drop down gradually and it was possible to speed up again. They were soon jogging along in single file beside an attractive stream.

"Graining Water!" Paul called out rather breathlessly.

The path suddenly turned away from the stream and arrived at a narrow lane where Hannah stopped and turned to ask for directions. Paul caught up with her.

"The Pennine Way goes left along this road for a short distance, so we must take great care. But, first, I expect you'd like a long cold drink and something to eat; there's an inn 200 yards up the lane on the right," he said.

"Just lead me to it!" she said, walking briskly up the lane beside him. "Something with protein in it would probably be wise," she added as an after thought.

The Packhorse Inn was an isolated white building standing out in the lonely landscape. There were only two vehicles outside. Inside, however, there were several walkers in addition to those who had been travelling by car. To save precious time, they chose homemade steak and mushroom pies that could be quickly heated in the microwave, but, while they were waiting for the food, Paul took the opportunity to refill their empty water flasks.

About forty minutes later they were walking back past the point where they had entered the lane. After a short distance they came to a small service road going north and bearing a notice that stated it led to the Walshaw Dean reservoirs.

"The Pennine Way runs up this road and then becomes a path running close to no less than three reservoirs," Paul announced. "At one point the path even runs along the top of a dam forming the end of one of the reservoirs."

At Hannah's splendid pace it did not take long before the reservoirs were behind them and they were back on bleak moorland, only made more welcoming by the warm afternoon sunshine.

The partly-reconstructed ruins of a building appeared a few hundred yards ahead and the young couple were surprised to see several small groups of tourists coming towards it from the other direction. Paul consulted the guidebook.

"Those must be the remains of a farm called Top Withins. It's said to be the location that inspired Emily Brontë to write her famous novel, Wuthering Heights," he informed Hannah.

"Apparently a visit here is a popular walk for literary fans from the village of Haworth – where the Brontë family lived. However, in view of the time, I suggest we don't stop."

The landscape began to improve considerably as they dropped down from the higher ground to cross Stanbury Moor and approach Ponden Reservoir lying in a shallow fold in the undulating landscape surrounded by peaceful fields. The route led them along the southern edge of the reservoir, over a bridge at its head, and then out on to a road that skirted the northern edge of the water.

"Haworth is about three miles along this road to the east," Paul stated, looking at his map. "But we need to turn west for about one hundred yards and look for a path on our right."

As they walked the short distance, Hannah could not help remarking on the beauty of the shallow valley. Sheep were grazing peacefully in the fields on either side, protected from the road by low grey-stone walls. In fact, they had to climb two stone steps set into the wall before they were able to reach the path that ran up the slope towards the higher ground.

Soon they found themselves walking beside a small wooded ravine – Dean Clough – to emerge on a narrow lane. After following this for a short distance, the path branched off to the north again and led them for nearly five miles over an attractive moor.

"This is all much softer and friendlier than the higher moors we've left behind," Hannah said. Paul nodded, pleased at her reaction.

They suddenly dropped down a short slope and emerged on a road that almost seemed to be clinging to the side of the ridge.

"This is the A6068 between Colne and Keighley," Paul said. "The village of Cowling is just below and to the east of us. We need to turn left and then almost immediately down a steep path on the right to a small road that runs towards the church over there." He pointed to a square tower not far below them.

Shortly before reaching the church, he guided her left up an even narrower lane that led them about half a mile across really delightful farmland to Gill Beck. On the other side, a discrete Pennine Way sign pointed up a wooded slope towards the top of Cowling Hill almost a mile away. From this vantage point, there turned out to be a splendid view of the shallow valley from which they had come.

They crossed a lane and the path continued for another mile or more across farmland, past Surgill Beck, and on to Lothersdale village where it joined another lane. Here they had to turn right for a short distance before the path appeared again on their left to continue its northbound journey.

A short distance up the path, Paul pulled out his mobile 'phone. "It's nearly six o'clock and Mark should be home from work by now. I'll let him know where we are," he said, as he selected his brother's number and gave Hannah a thumbs-up when it was quickly answered.

"Hi Mark, we're not too far away now – about four miles from Thornton-in-Craven. I notice from the map that the Pennine Way crosses a lane about two miles south of Thornton. It goes directly north-east towards Skipton. Would it be better for us to turn off there rather than go all the way to Thornton and then east along the A56?"

Hannah was aware of Mark giving directions but could not hear enough to make sense of the instructions. When Paul signed off, however, he turned to her with a big grin.

"Guess what!" he exclaimed. "Mark bought a small second-hand car last week. He knows the road I mean – it's called West Road – and he's going to drive out and meet us at the point where the path crosses the road before carrying on towards Thornton as a narrow tarmac lane. He'll park in a small lay-by close to the junction and wait for us. The car is metallic-blue and will be facing back towards Skipton. The other good news is that we've covered about 33 miles already today and there are only two more to go!"

He glanced at Hannah in admiration. "You've been brilliant; John would probably have jibbed at covering 35 miles in one day and most certainly would have refused to jog wearing a backpack!"

"I enjoyed the challenge," she replied courageously, privately quite relieved there was not much further to go. "Anyway it's my fault we're being chased all over the country by a couple of crooks!"

After two miles of rather bleak moorland, they came within sight of the West Road junction and spotted a fairly old blue Ford Ka in the process of turning to face back towards Skipton. Although the crossing was in a shallow dip in the moor, there was a good view of over 100 yards in all directions. After looking around cautiously, they hurried to join Mark.

The brothers greeted one another with obvious affection and Hannah was introduced. Mark greeted her warmly but with a rather enigmatic look. Although his brother had told him the previous evening that Hannah was merely replacing John, he was clearly wondering if there was more to this female companion than met the eye.

He managed to stow Paul's rucksack in the luggage compartment while the latter pushed Hannah's slightly smaller one to the far side of the compact rear seat so that she could squeeze in beside it.

Paul sat in the front seat and immediately asked how Mark's job was going. The latter launched into an enthusiastic progress report as he coaxed the heavily loaded car up the slope towards the brow of the hill.

Hannah began to relax in the confined space at the back ("A good job I'm small!" she thought) just happy to allow the brothers to enjoy each other's company.

As the car crested the hill, she casually looked out of the window beside her and noticed that they were passing several cars parked on a strip of gravel. It was clearly placed so that the occupants could admire the view down towards Thornton-in-Craven or take a short walk along the Pennine Way.

She caught her breath in shock, unable to breathe for a couple of seconds.

A large black car had just arrived and its two occupants were stepping out: one was tall and blond, one short and dark. Their backs were turned to Hannah, but the dark one appeared to be arguing with his companion.

CHAPTER 10

Paul heard Hannah's gasp just behind him and twisted round to see what was wrong. She had sunk down as low as possible in the rear seat.

"It's the black car again!" she exclaimed. "It's just parked at the top of the hill and both the men from Tooting have got out."

Paul strained his head to look in the rear view mirror on the door beside him. Sure enough, two men were walking towards the brow of the hill. The tall blond one was carrying a pair of binoculars, obviously intending to scan the Pennine Way in both directions.

"If Mark hadn't picked us up, we'd have walked straight into them!" Hannah reflected in horror. "Or, if we'd been walking on towards Thornton, they could have spotted us quite easily from the top of the hill."

Paul reached behind him and managed to give her hand a squeeze. "I wouldn't have let them harm you," he said gently.

Mark had no idea what was going on. "What men from Tooting are trying to harm you?" he asked, in complete bewilderment.

"It's a long story," his brother replied. "Perhaps it had better wait until we take you out for a meal tonight. We need to start at the beginning, which was early last Monday morning. Meanwhile, perhaps you can think of a good restaurant in the centre of Skipton."

Mark managed to restrain his curiosity and answer the question. "There's a very good and quite reasonable Italian restaurant about a quarter of a mile from my house. I know you like Italian food but what about Hannah?"

"I love it!" Hannah replied, glad to have something else to think about.

She was slightly disconcerted by the fact that she had not only found Paul's hand comforting but was also vaguely conscious of something else.

"But I'm contributing to the cost of the meal. After all, I'm benefiting from a free bed tonight!" she concluded.

"No," said Paul firmly. "I would've paid if John was here, so tonight's on me."

"We'll argue about that tomorrow!" Hannah warned.

Ten minutes later, Mark was squeezing the car into a small space in front of a terraced house in a cul-de-sac a short distance up a hill on the north side of the town centre.

"Welcome to my humble abode!" Mark said, although there was an element of pride in his tone. "There're only two bedrooms and the single is tiny, but it suits me fine. By the way, I've made sure there's plenty of hot water. I expect you'd both like a shower before we go out: after a pot of tea, of course! Paul, take Hannah upstairs while I put the kettle on. Her room is the one at the back with the bathroom beside it."

Paul insisted on carrying Hannah's rucksack upstairs. The rear bedroom was indeed small but had a splendid view over the town.

"You go in the bathroom first," he said. "I'll come up again in a couple of minutes."

A few minutes later they were having tea in the dining area of the open-plan kitchen.

"The previous occupants had the wall between this room and the original tiny kitchen removed," Mark explained. "It's made quite a decent room, especially with the fairly new kitchen fittings. The front room – the traditional parlour – is not a bad size either. Of course, I've got some decorating to do!"

Soon after eight o'clock, the three of them walked down the hill to the Italian restaurant Mark had recommended. It was quite popular and they were lucky to get a table without waiting.

"The menu changes almost daily and has a very limited choice so that the chef can concentrate on fresh good-quality food," Mark explained. "I think you'll find the service is quite speedy because they don't have to mess about getting all sorts of things out of the freezer!"

He was right. They had an excellent two-course meal and were drinking coffee well before nine-thirty. During the meal, Hannah had explained the saga of the dongle with Paul's help and Mark now made a suggestion.

"You know I'm into electronics as a hobby, don't you?" he said to Paul. "I have a work bench in the front bedroom squeezed in beside my bed and wardrobe. I'd be happy to test that dongle for you. I should be able to display any signal on my oscilloscope."

When they arrived back at the house, Mark ushered them upstairs to his bedroom. Hannah was surprised to see how much space the neat and tidy workbench took up in the modest double room. While she went to retrieve the dongle from her rucksack, Mark assembled the necessary items of equipment and switched everything on. A flat-line trace soon appeared on the oscilloscope screen.

He was just setting up some sort of small antenna when Hannah laid the dongle, still carefully wrapped in its aluminium foil, on the bench.

"Do you want me to unwrap it?" she asked.

Mark nodded. "Take the foil away completely," he said as he lifted the small object carefully and began to move it around the antenna. About twenty seconds later a sharp pulse appeared on the screen and stayed there.

"I've set the 'scope in storage mode," he explained. "Otherwise it would all happen too fast for us to see it properly. Paul, please hold the dongle in this position while I adjust the frequency scale and amplification."

The trace returned to an almost flat line and they waited expectantly. After a long pause, it sprang to life again.

"Excellent!" Mark exclaimed. "You can put the dongle down; in fact, it would be best to wrap it up again in case your friends have taken it into their heads to explore Skipton, although it's over three miles from the Pennine Way."

He fiddled with some knobs and the screen became clearer. "Lady and gentleman, may I present to you the signature of the mystery dongle!" he said as he stood proudly to one side and gestured with his hand.

"In addition to its circuitry for acting as a conventional dongle, it contains a radio-frequency transmitter powered by a miniature battery."

Paul put his arm around his brother's shoulders and looked at Hannah.

"My brother's an experimental genius, isn't he?" he said fondly.

"He certainly is! I'm sorry he wasn't there to advise us earlier," Hannah agreed.

"You two did all the deduction! I only demonstrated it working," Mark replied. "It's a very unusual feature and means the dongle must be particularly important, although this is an old system; most modern tracking devices are based on GPS."

Just then the doorbell rang. Hannah looked at the two men in alarm and Paul took her hand.

"Who on earth can that be? It's nearly half past ten!" Mark exclaimed as he hurried downstairs.

The young couple could hear a man's voice at the front door, followed by Mark replying, and then heavy footsteps entered the kitchen.

CHAPTER 11

Hannah stood in bedroom looking extremely perturbed. Paul tried not to show his concern but kept hold of her hand.

"Don't worry! It can't possibly be the crooks: the dongle was only exposed for about three minutes," he whispered. "Anyway, there are two of us to keep you safe. My brother's pretty tough and so am I when I get angry!"

"Can you come done?" Mark called up the stairs. "Two plain-clothed policemen are asking to see you!"

Paul gave Hannah a reassuring smile and they went down to the kitchen. The two men sitting at the kitchen table stood up politely. The older one was wearing a dark suit; his younger companion was more casually dressed. The former flashed his warrant card rather briefly and gestured to his colleague.

"We're from Special Branch in London and this is Detective Sergeant…on second thoughts it would be better if you just know him as Tony. I'm hoping you'll agree to help us," he said. "I apologize for coming at such a late hour but we've only just arrived from London and left our bags at a small hotel in the town."

He paused and it occurred to Paul that he had carefully avoided giving his own rank and name.

"By the way, may we have a cup of coffee, if it's not too much trouble? It's been a long day," the man continued.

"Of course," said Mark and put the kettle on. Everyone else sat at the table and the senior detective began to explain.

"The theft of a valuable laptop was reported last night to the head of security at the Ministry of Defence by one of their boffins who had broken all regulations by taking it home while he was on a few days' leave. Even worse, he had taken the small dongle – a clever encryption device – that is the only means by which some of the contents of the laptop can be accessed. The whole affair is an appalling failure of security because the dongle is meant to be returned to a secure storage location every evening and failure to do so should have been reported immediately!"

"In the event," he went on, "the theft was not discovered until the man tried to do some work yesterday evening and found that the small attaché case had been removed from the side of his desk. The police investigation found that one of the door locks had been very professionally picked, leaving almost no trace of entry. The theft probably occurred early on Monday morning, judging by your report to the Sheffield police; fortunately it was entered on the national computer soon after your visit on Monday afternoon."

The man looked at Hannah and Paul and nodded appreciatively.

"We're extremely grateful that you took the trouble to report what had happened," he said, "because the photograph of the dongle was recognized immediately. The laptop contains information that would be of great interest to a hostile country. We think it was stolen to order – possibly by the men you described – and the gang are probably desperate to get the dongle back so that they can pass everything to their employer and get paid!"

The man paused to sip his coffee and nodded to his companion to continue the tale. Tony did so with some enthusiasm.

"At first, we were annoyed with Sheffield for not keeping the dongle. However, it may turn out to be a blessing in disguise," he said, looking pleased when Hannah carefully laid the small object on the table in its foil wrapping.

"I see you've discovered it contains a radio-frequency transmitter. We've been trying to contact you all day to warn you, but your mobiles have been switched off." He looked at them rather accusingly before turning to Paul.

"It meant I had to 'phone your mother, Sir. I was careful not to alarm her, merely saying we needed to clarify something in your report. All she could tell me was that you were walking up the

Pennine Way and due here this evening. She gave me this 'phone number, but, once again, there's been no answer."

"I was at work all day and we've just been out for dinner," Mark explained.

Paul now decided it was time for him to interrupt: "Hannah and I only realized the dongle must be transmitting an intermittent signal after the crooks nearly caught us on three occasions. The first time, to our absolute astonishment, was in Edale yesterday morning; then again near the A628; finally, late last night, just as we were about to leaving a pub in Standedge after having a meal. I'm fairly certain they don't know we spotted them."

"That's good!" Tony said with some relief.

"Paul suddenly realized what must be happening and got a piece of aluminium foil from the cook at the pub to wrap the dongle in," Hannah contributed proudly. "They then lost the signal and we were able to slip away to our guesthouse without being seen."

"Even so, they know we're walking up the Pennine Way," Paul continued. "They've been zigzagging backwards and forwards by car on the roads that intersect the Way. Since last night, they've been very close to us three times to our knowledge. In fact, they were two miles south of Thornton-in-Craven three hours ago!"

Tony looked delighted at this further revelation, but it was his senior who took over again.

"That was rather distressing for you but very useful for us. We're hoping to lay a trap them. I have a man – let's call him Tim – who has spent a large part of today at the small company in Canterbury who make these dongles. They've been preparing a dummy one – suitably damaged I hope – that will be of no use whatsoever to the criminals but will transmit the same signal as the real device. I'm hoping you'll agree to take this with you tomorrow and let them have it the next time they find you. We don't think you're in danger; they merely want to get the thing back as soon as possible without arousing too much suspicion!"

The man looked at Paul and Hannah, trying to judge their reaction.

"We want to follow this gang back to their employer and pick up several culprits in one swoop," he explained. "Of course, we're also anxious to find the insider in the Ministry who tipped somebody off about the importance of the attaché case in the first place."

"You would be doing a great service to this country," Tony put in. "Although we're already in your debt for hanging on to the dongle and not throwing it away or letting these men have it."

"I'd be happy to take part if I was on my own," Paul said, "but I don't want Hannah put in danger."

Hannah looked at him in surprise. Before she could say anything, however, the senior detective interrupted.

"The deception won't work without the young lady," he said firmly. "The criminals may already be suspicious about the renewal of transmissions after losing it so suddenly when they were very close to you last night. If the young lady is not the one to hand the dongle over, the plan is sure to fail."

Finally Hannah had her say. "I'm quite prepared to help," she said with a hint of annoyance. "Not only will Paul be with me, but I assume you have some way of keeping track of us and taking over when the bait is swallowed!"

Tony reached into his pocket and took out two objects about the size of a small mobile 'phone.

"You're quite correct. If you each carry one of these, we'll know where you are all the time: within a distance of a few metres anyway! It's a small GPS tracking device. Two of us will be keeping quite close to you, but, if you're in difficulty, there are tiny "panic" buttons: if pressed we'll know you need help. I'll also give you our mobile numbers."

"We'll also be tracking the dummy dongle using detectors capable of receiving its signal within a fifty mile radius, depending on the terrain," he continued. "They're far more powerful than the one that's been tracking you so far. Please 'phone me as soon as possible after the hand-over and we'll begin the chase!"

His superior took over again. "Tim is flying up to Leeds early tomorrow morning with the fake dongle. Tony will pick him up at the airport at 7:50 and the two of them will rendezvous with you at 9:00 or soon after. Is there somewhere a short distance further up the Pennine Way that would be a good meeting place?"

"I can drop them at Gargrave before going to work," Mark said. "It's about four miles north-east of Thornton and the same distance west of here on the A65. There's a café called The Dalesman in the centre of the village where Hannah and Paul could meet them. The Pennine Way runs north from there up a narrow road beside the shop."

"By the way, the crooks are driving a black Ford Mondeo," Paul said as he searched in his wallet. "I did my best to memorize the registration number when I saw it outside the pub last night and wrote it down as soon as we got back to our guesthouse." He handed over the scrap of paper.

For the first time that evening, the senior detective looked really pleased. "Excellent! That'll be of great assistance," he said as he got up to leave.

His companion muttered, "You deserve a medal!" under his breath before saying cheerfully that he looked forward to seeing them in Gargrave at nine o'clock the following morning.

As they all walked to the front door, Paul had one last suggestion. "I've an idea to get over the problem of the temporary loss of dongle signal if anyone queries it; I could say my brother picked us up from the pub last night and took us to stay with him some distance away before dropping us back on the Pennine Way."

"A bit of good acting might come in helpful if they're suspicious, but don't volunteer the misinformation otherwise," the older detective said as he bade them goodnight.

It was now ten past eleven and Hannah and Paul were more than ready for bed.

"I'm sorry we haven't had much time to talk," Mark said. "How about coming here again on your way home? You can fill me in on all the exciting details!"

"We certainly will if Hannah agrees," Paul replied, looking at her.

"I'd be very happy to come again and you two need more time together," she said, "but, hopefully, the dongle affair will be over by the time we get to Haltwhistle. We'll 'phone you from there to let you know how things have gone."

She then bade them goodnight and went upstairs. It had been such an eventful day that it was not long before she was asleep.

Meanwhile, Mark opened out the settee in the front room to make a bed for Paul, who was asleep almost before his head touched the pillow. So much so that it seemed no time at all before his alarm clock sounded at 7:10.

Mark had just come downstairs and could be heard in the kitchen beginning to get the breakfast.

"Breakfast will be ready in about twenty minutes!" he said when Paul looked in. "I hope boiled eggs will be enough for you. I'm not much of a cook. You'd better go and wake your girl!"

"Hannah's not my girl! We just happened to meet when I was already missing John and I found out that she's a keen walker."

Mark did not look convinced. "I bet things have changed by the time you return," was all he said.

CHAPTER 12

Mark drove Hannah and Paul nearly four miles west along the A65 and dropped them on the outskirts of Gargrave shortly before nine o'clock. He bade them a warm farewell and turned the car round to go back to work in Skipton. They followed the main road a little further and found The Dalesman in the village centre exactly where Mark had described, with a narrow road called West Street running north beside it.

"This is where the Pennine Way leaves Gargrave," Paul remarked as they entered the café.

Tony and another young man, presumably Tim, were already sitting at a table.

"I've ordered coffees for all of us," he said, making the introductions.

Tim grinned when his name was announced. "I must remember who I am for the next day or two!" he chuckled.

Tony pretended to look shocked at this flippancy. "Now down to business," he said, producing the dummy dongle in its protective foil wrapping.

Paul was relieved to see that the damage inflicted on the casing looked convincing enough to make it reasonable to assume that it would no longer be in working order. It was quickly wrapped up again while Tony started to explain the observation strategy that had been worked out.

"Both of us can locate you via GPS, but we've only been able to borrow two of these powerful detectors from the company making the dongles. Tim has one of them and our boss the other; so Tim will be the one following you with two methods of keeping track of you, apart from occasional visual contact."

Tim patted a small satchel hanging at his side while Tony continued: "Tim will wait here until you've gone up the Pennine Way for a hundred yards or so and taken the dongle out of the foil.

As soon as he detects a signal, he'll 'phone you to confirm. You then carry on walking and he'll follow you at a discrete distance. Stop whenever you like for lunch etc. and forget about him.

"Meanwhile, I'll take the car north to Malham; it's about seven miles from here and the first large village you'll pass. I'll park somewhere and look around. If I come across the black car, I'll either 'phone you or warn you in person. If nothing happens near Malham, I'll drive up to Horton-in-Ribblesdale, leaving Tim to follow you again. I think you said you plan to stay in Horton tonight?"

"Yes," Paul said. "Although it's only about 21 miles up the Pennine Way from here, the last part contains some steep gradients and is one of the highlights of the Way. I booked a small highly-recommended place a few days ago – I'll give you the address and 'phone number." He searched in his wallet for a piece of paper.

As he was making a copy of the address, he thought of something else.

"Tomorrow, we've got a longer walk of about 32 miles to Tan Hill, a few miles south of the A66, where there's an isolated pub offering accommodation. I provisionally booked a twin-bedded room with shower a few days ago that must be confirmed by eight o'clock tonight. I'll give you this address as well."

"Fine," said Tony. "Our boss has instructed me to pay for your accommodation for the next two nights as a token of our thanks for acting as decoys. When I get to Horton, I'll check out the guesthouse and pay your bill in advance. I'll also 'phone the Tan Hill pub to confirm and pay."

Paul and Hannah looked quite astonished.

"That's very kind of you," Paul said. "But we didn't expect any reward for being public-spirited!"

"No," Hannah echoed.

The two detectives smiled. "It's not everyone who would be prepared to disrupt their holiday and put themselves to considerable inconvenience," Tim assured them. "It's the least we can do – anyway we must do what the boss orders!"

"That's settled then," Tony said with satisfaction. "Don't forget, I can track you via GPS. So I'll keep out of sight on the whole and only speak to you if urgent. Tim and I will end up in Horton, where we'll wander around like innocent tourists. Of course, if the bait has already been taken by then, we'll have disappeared on the chase! Please don't forget to 'phone me after the handover!"

He then produced a final piece of information. "The boss is being joined by another man who'll pick him up by car in Skipton later this morning. They'll position themselves further east near the A1 – the most likely route the crooks will take back to London."

"You won't forget to let us know the outcome of all this, will you?" Hannah requested.

"If our boss is too secretive to do it, I'll break all rules and do it myself," Tony promised, standing up and shaking hands with them. "Tim will wait until you go and then check that the dongle signal is being received. All the best!" With that he left.

As Paul and Hannah were shouldering their rucksacks, Tim made a helpful suggestion.

"If nothing's happened by the time we all leave Malham and Tony drives on to Horton, I could suggest to him that he take your rucksacks in the car and drops them off at your guesthouse – he's going there first anyway. It would make the longer part of the hike more enjoyable for you, but please keep the precious dongle with you!"

"That would be a great help, if it's not inconvenient for him," Paul answered, having first checked Hannah's reaction.

"He's senior to me and so I must check with him in Malham first. I'll 'phone you in the unlikely event that he doesn't want to do it," Tim replied.

Just as they left him in the café, he shook hands in a very friendly manner and said one word, "Godspeed!"

The young couple walked up West Street in silence for a minute before Hannah asked a question: "I like Tim – he's got a sense of humour – but why did he say goodbye in such a strange way? Is he a Christian do you think?"

"Quite possibly," Paul replied. "It's a rather old-fashioned way of expressing good wishes for a safe journey and the sort of thing my parents might say. It means something like, "May God prosper you". Anyway, it's good to know that Tim cares about our safety and is not just interested in catching the criminals!"

After a short distance, they crossed the bridge over the Liverpool to Leeds canal. Hannah looked down with interest; a holiday barge was in process of passing through a narrow lock and two people were heaving on a stout wooden beam to open the gate at one end.

Meanwhile, Paul removed the dongle from its foil protection. "Now we really are in the decoy business!" he joked.

A minute later his mobile sounded: it was Tim. "You're coming through loud and clear," he said. "You'll see me in Malham, but as a stranger. I'll be very discrete if I'm allowed to take your rucksacks to the car."

The morning walk was only seven miles through an attractive agricultural landscape, over a small moor, and then beside the River Aire for the rest of the way. After crossing the river several times, the path climbed to higher ground before dropping down into the picturesque village of Malham.

"We're now well into the Yorkshire Dales National Park and this village is a popular tourist spot," Paul said. "The Pennine Way turns right here and then sharp left beside that hotel a few yards up there on the corner."

Hannah looked in the direction he was pointing and could see a sign proudly advertising the Lister Arms Hotel.

"Although it's only 11:40," he continued, "we should probably have another drink and something to eat because there may not be much opportunity on the longer wilder trek up to Horton. Apparently there's a more down-to-earth pub, called the Buck Inn, near the centre of the village if we go left over the river."

They entered the saloon bar, already surprisingly busy, and found a table where Hannah insisted that Paul find a table and mind their rucksacks while she went to the bar to buy the drinks and choose some sandwiches.

After a few minutes, she returned with a tray and an excellent selection to eat.

"These are good!" Paul said appreciatively as he munched a beef and pickle sandwich.

"I'm glad; it's high time I treated you!" Hannah replied. "There was even more choice for those prepared to wait for them to be made to order, but I thought it better not to delay."

They were chatting away happily, not taking much notice of their surroundings, when Paul heard a familiar voice coming from the table behind him. He glanced surreptitiously over his shoulder: Tony and Tim had perched themselves on two small stools at a very low table in the corner of the room. They were taking the opportunity to have a drink and eating what appeared to be sausage rolls.

Tony raised his voice very slightly. "Yes," he said to Tim, "I've searched the village twice this morning, the last time only fifteen minutes ago, but still no sign of my parents. In about ten minutes, I'll park the car at the Lister Arms and wait."

"I'll join you if I may?" Tim replied. "I can spare a short time before needing to get going again."

Paul looked at Hannah who grinned at him. "They've been there for about five minutes," she whispered. "I assumed I should pretend not to notice." Paul nodded and smiled.

After another five minutes, Tony and Tim left and Hannah and Paul prepared to go.

"Just in case one of them discretely takes our rucksacks as we pass the hotel, we better take a water bottle each and clip it to our belts," Paul warned her. "I'll also put a couple of these fruit and nut bars in my shoulder bag with the guide book. Is the dongle safely tucked in one of your pockets?" Hannah nodded.

As they walked up the busy road, now even busier with tourists looking for somewhere to eat, Paul thought of something else as he glanced at Hannah's nicely tanned face.

"Did you renew your sun cream back in the pub: the sun is really hot when not covered by one of these small clouds?"

"You bet!" Hannah replied. "One thing I don't want to do is blister. Sunburn is very uncomfortable, as I found out a couple of years ago."

The car park of the Lister Arms was down towards the back of the hotel. Fortunately, however, Tim was standing beside the entrance appearing to consult a map.

Suddenly satisfied, he tucked it neatly under his arm. Paul and Hannah took off their rucksacks just before they reached him. The handover went smoothly and as they entered the narrow road on the far side of the hotel, they could see Tim just disappearing up the drive on the other side carrying their luggage.

"Now for the real walk of the day!" Paul said. "Although it's barely fifteen miles, there are some pretty steep gradients, particularly getting to the 649m top of Pen-y-Ghent shortly before our destination. I'm sure you'd like to go up there, although there is a short-cut to Horton that avoids it?"

"I'm game for any amount of climbing, especially without our packs," Hannah exclaimed, metaphorically rubbing her hands. "I love a real challenge!" They marched on happily.

Paul looked across at his companion. "I couldn't wish for a better walking companion," he thought.

He began to wonder in what way the crooks would try to waylay them. Just driving or sitting waiting in a car had now failed so often that they would surely start walking down the Pennine Way for short distances from possible parking places. Unfortunately, the limited maps in his guide book did not always indicate the presence of a small car park at places where the Way crossed a road, so he would have to take particular care shortly before each intersection.

Tony reached Horton-in-Ribblesdale and drove through the village on a quick reconnoitre before making his way to the address Paul had given him. It was in a secluded lane that seemed to be going nowhere in particular, but his map indicated that it looped back to join the road a little further east.

He parked in the small car park and rang the doorbell. It was answered by a pleasant-looking young woman who looked at him enquiringly.

"Good afternoon. May I help you? Although I'm afraid we're almost full for tonight," she said.

"Good afternoon," Tony responded with his most charming smile. "I was coming to Horton and offered to drop off my friends' luggage while they walk up from Malham."

He gave Paul's name and said that he had already booked a twin-bedded room for the night.

"In fact, I'd like to pay his bill in advance if I may. He and his friend have done me a really good turn and this is my way of thanking them. By the way, did he book an en-suite twin room – if you have one that is?"

The woman had been looking in her book for Paul's name while Tony was speaking.

"No, it was just a twin with washbasin. However, the booking for our only en-suite twin was cancelled a couple of hours ago. You can have that for them if you like? It's fairly small but nice and quiet."

"Yes please," Tony said, producing a Visa card. "I'll 'phone my friends and tell them."

After the bill had been paid, Tony said: "Would you like me to carry their luggage upstairs for you?"

"Yes please," the woman replied gratefully as she selected a key from the rack. "My husband won't be back until mid-afternoon and they look heavy!"

Tony had a quick look out of the window as he put the rucksacks on the floor of the bedroom. It was at the back of the building and certainly secluded, but his charges should be quite safe in here even if the criminals tracked down the location of the dongle during the night. Anyway, they would not risk a break-in because they did not want to draw attention to themselves.

With an expression of thanks, Tony left the guesthouse, parked his car a little nearer the centre and began to search the village again on foot.

Although he spotted a black car, it was not a Ford and had the wrong number plate anyway. It occurred to him yet again that Tim and he, not to mention his boss, were really fortunate that they not only had a sensible and obliging couple to help in this investigation but also someone alert enough to record the make and number of a car under stressful circumstances. He hoped that by now his boss had had the car – almost certainly hired – traced to its registered address and would let him know anything useful when he next reported in.

He looked at his watch; it was 13:56. In a few minutes, he must contact Tim and then make a decision about where the two of them should spend the night. Although not nearly as touristy as Malham, Horton would be popular at this time of year and they might have to go further afield to find accommodation.

By this time, he had reached the railway station on the northern edge of the village and decided to turn back. He passed the Crown Hotel, near the point at which the Pennine Way departed again to the north. The place looked attractive. On sudden impulse, he went inside for a cup of coffee. It occurred to him that it might be worth risking booking a room if one was available.

CHAPTER 13

Not long after leaving Malham, the path began to follow a narrow stream. "Malham Beck," said Paul, reading from the guidebook. He was about to say more when Hannah interrupted. She had seen a strange feature of the landscape directly ahead of them: a concave cliff of solid rock seemed to rise abruptly from the valley floor.

"Look up there!" she exclaimed. "It's like a cove on a rocky coastline: the sort of place where you'd find a secluded sandy beach lapped by the waves."

"You've got it in one!" Paul replied. "It's called Malham Cove. Apparently it was gouged out into that curved shape by water, although nowadays almost none comes that way even during a very wet season. Malham Beck must once have been a substantial river."

They had passed a few people on the Pennine Way since leaving Malham, but now several more appeared to be walking to and from the Cove on a smooth gravel path on the opposite side of the beck.

"There's a road that passes not far away from here and tourists can visit this popular spot by parking and walking a short distance," he explained.

The beck was extremely shallow and Pennine Way crossed some stepping stones to join the main path. At close quarters, the cliff face was imposingly tall and rather threatening in a strange kind of way, although a fringe of trees at its base softened the effect.

Hannah was still intrigued by the unusual sight when Paul eventually took her hand – an action that seemed to come very naturally – and led her along a path leading to a long flight of roughly-laid steps that climbed up to the plateau above.

As they climbed, she looked at him rather quizzically but made no attempt to withdraw her hand. She was somewhat surprised that she was enjoying this feeling of being looked after.

"Surely I'm not losing my ingrained sense of independence!" she thought.

However, she was totally distracted by what they found at the top; the plateau looked as if it was composed of huge rocks laid out to form an enormous area of giant crazy-paving.

"All this would have been solid limestone at one time," Paul informed her. "It was split up by the action of water, frost and ice, probably assisted by the sort of acidic pollution we saw earlier."

Further on, the path wound its way across coarse turf scattered with a profusion of small rocks and then down into a curious valley of rocks. Here, great care had been taken to lay a gravel path snaking past sizeable lumps of rock at ankle level.

Eventually, out on open moor again, they sighted Malham Tarn in the distance.

"We're approaching a narrow road," Paul warned. "I think I've spotted what looks like a car park on the other side of the road, so we need to keep our eyes open."

In fact, the Pennine Way exited northbound through the car park and would have been an ideal place for the black car to lie in wait. They were now heading directly towards the tarn about a mile away. The path joined a broad gravel track, clearly made for the benefit of farm vehicles, with a rocky hillside on the right and the tarn to the left. Then the track entered an attractive wood as it circled close to the northern shore with a pleasant view over the water.

"It seems a surprisingly large lake to be called a tarn!" Paul muttered.

Leaving the tarn and wood, the Way ran north again for well over a mile before reaching an isolated farm.

"I suppose this must be a sheep farm," Hannah remarked. "The soil here could not be cultivated successfully or produce good enough pasture for dairy farming."

The meagre grass soon became even more scrub-like and they were back on a long stretch of moorland that rose gradually towards a broad rocky upland. Then, in the distance, on the far side of a valley, she saw an almost flat ridge with a steep edge at its western tip.

"I think that's Pen-y-Ghent, the highest point of our route today," Paul said. "Apparently, it's quite a scramble to the top!"

"Good!" Hannah said with enthusiasm. Paul grinned at her delightedly, their immediate problem completely forgotten.

Down in the valley, they turned sharp right down a narrow winding road for about a mile before a small sign directed them up a farm track on the left. Hannah's earlier comment about sheep was now demonstrated by the presence of sheep grazing contentedly in fields divided by neat stone walls.

The track began to climb steadily before the pasture gave way again to moor and the track dwindled to a path. Pen-y-Ghent dominated the middle-distance; its sharp edge looking even more formidable at closer quarters.

The gradient increased, but Hannah's pace barely slackened. In fact, it was Paul who noted with relief that their route was not leading them to a head-on confrontation with the end of the ridge but was beginning to zigzag up its flank. Fortunately, the path had been laid in the form of a rough stone staircase, at first reminiscent of Jacob's Ladder near Edale. It soon became considerably steeper and rockier, however, and required considerable care.

"This is like mountain climbing now," Hannah said delightedly. Paul followed close behind her, full of admiration for her boundless energy.

They reached top of the ridge and saw that the path now led gently up to a small square tower, or cairn, about four feet tall. From this elevation, there seemed to be a profusion of ridges and hills stretching into the distance all around them.

Hannah took a deep breath and grabbed Paul's hand with a sudden surge of enthusiasm.

"This is fantastic!" she exclaimed. "We're very privileged to see it on a sunny day; it would be a desolate place in bad weather!"

"One thing surprises me," Paul said. "There's been a low stone wall close to the path all the way up here. Look, we even have to cross a style to carry on! Surely sheep don't graze up here?"

"It could mean that one side of the ridge is more dangerous for them than the other," Hannah suggested.

Eventually, they descended to farming land again and joined a stony track that ran between walls to protect the fields. The village of Horton-in-Ribblesdale nestled in the valley, and, some distance beyond, a rather ugly stone quarry. After another mile, they came out on to the road through the village.

"We need to turn left to get to our guesthouse, according to the sketch I made from Google Map," Paul said. "But I notice there's a café just up there in the other direction. Let's have some tea if they're still open."

Hannah looked at her watch. To her surprise it was just after five o'clock. Fortunately, the café was open and had several thirsty walkers like themselves. Unusually, the tea was provided in huge cups and the slice of cake was very generous.

Outside again, Hannah looked for any sign of shops. To her surprise, only one village store was in evidence. "It's nothing like Malham!" she said.

"We really are in the wilds of north Yorkshire now!" Paul replied as they went into the store to get some bananas and chocolate.

A fairly young man opened the door when Paul rang the bell. As they signed in, he said: "I'm Andy. My wife and I run this place. She told me your friend was here earlier with your luggage and paid your bill. Did he let you know?"

"Yes, he said he'd do it because we're helping him out at the moment. We tried to refuse, but he insisted!"

"You were lucky! We'd just had a cancellation for our en-suite twin room and he paid the extra for that as well," Andy said.

"That's a nice surprise!" Hannah said happily, looking forward to a shower after such an energetic day.

When she and Paul got to the room, she was even more pleased; although quite small, it was quiet and homely with a tranquil view of Pen-y-Ghent in the distance.

After they had both had a shower, Hannah washed some underwear and shyly offered to do some for Paul at the same time. He looked slightly embarrassed but she insisted that it was no trouble. She had even had the foresight to bring a plastic clothes line and some miniature pegs with her.

Soon after seven o'clock they walked the short distance back to a pub they had passed earlier. The Golden Lion was quite crowded and their meal took some time to arrive, but they were not in a hurry and just enjoyed relaxing over a long cool drink.

Needless to say they slept well after all the exercise and fresh air, but were down for breakfast at the earliest opportunity because the day's walk would be about thirty-two miles.

If anything, the breakfast was even better than at the guesthouse in Standedge. When they mentioned how good it was, Andy was delighted.

"I'll tell my wife," he said. "She cooks the breakfast as well as doing a lot of the other things. I have a part-time job in the village. It is hard work running a guesthouse and nice to be appreciated!"

"We're really set up for the day now!" Hannah declared in eager anticipation of the hours ahead. Paul smiled at her enthusiasm.

They had just thanked Andy for an excellent stop-over and were about to shoulder their rucksacks when the doorbell rang. He opened the door in some surprise at this early caller – it was just before eight o'clock.

"Good morning. I'm sorry to call so early," a man's voice said. "I believe you have a young lady of about twenty staying with you – quite short and slim with dark brown hair. She's walking north up the Pennine Way. There may be a young man with her."

Hannah looked at Paul in shock and he took her hand.

"There are several people in the breakfast room," Andy replied. "I'll go and look but must close the door for a moment."

He shut the door and turned to Paul and Hannah. "Is he looking for you?" he said, in a whisper. "He's quite smartly dressed and looks like a prosperous businessman!"

"We'd better see him. Otherwise he'll only wait until we leave," Paul said.

"I must get back to serving the breakfast; just give a shout if you need me. I'll leave you to open the door."

They tucked their rucksacks under the hall table and Paul opened the door. "Come in," he said. "You may be looking for us. You're only just in time; we were about to leave."

A man of middle age entered with a business card in his hand. Andy's description was a good one, except there was something disquieting about him. Not a man to be crossed was Paul's immediate reaction. He went back to stand beside Hannah as the man smiled and handed her the small card.

"There's nowhere else for us to go, I afraid," Paul said. "There are still people having breakfast."

"No problem. I won't take up much of your time," the man said. "First, I must apologize for the appalling behaviour of one of my employees; it was disgraceful of him to threaten you in the way he did and order his companion to chase after you. I only extracted the truth yesterday; the tale I was being spun earlier was that you picked up the little USB device when everything fell out of the attaché case, refused to give it back and ran away!"

"No, I accidentally crushed it with my hiking boot," Hannah said. "I called out an apology for the damage, but the small dark man looked and sounded so fierce and angry that I panicked and ran. It was only later that I realized I still had the thing in my hand."

"That's very understandable. I'm sorry you were treated so shamefully. If you can forgive me, however, I'd very much like the device back. Without it, my precious laptop and its contents are unusable. I've discovered that the small company making these security devices has gone out of business."

"His first lie," Paul thought, as the man paused to look at Hannah with a rather artificial smile.

"That's why the one you have is so important to me," the man continued. "I know you have kept it because it sends out a homing signal every so often. My two idiots have a detector; the only problem is that its range is very poor.

"Actually, I must give them credit for spotting you in Sheffield just before the signal moved into the Peak District. The first guess was Derby; you were wearing hiking boots and might have been heading for the southern edge of the National Park. They hired a car in Derby and drove up to Sheffield after failing to find you. Meanwhile, I was left biting my finger nails in London with each negative report. Then they almost succeeded several times on Tuesday!"

Paul looked at Hannah. "So that's how they've been tracing you! I thought you were dreaming when you said you thought you'd seen the blond man at Edale railway station on Tuesday morning and then again later in the day."

He looked back at their visitor. "I just didn't believe her, thinking her fright had made her imagine things!" he confessed.

The man looked at them and a faint flicker of suspicion crossed his face.

"What puzzles me," he said slowly, "is why my men picked up a strong signal late on Tuesday evening and then suddenly lost it again; they assure me that they looked all over the area but without success. The next day, they were reduced to zigzagging gradually up the path of the Pennine Way again until I insisted they came and picked me up at Leeds airport yesterday morning. Then, to our great relief, we picked the signal up again."

He stopped and waited.

Paul pretended to think back. "Last Tuesday night…?" he muttered slowly and then smiled as he recollected and spoke more loudly: "That was the night my brother picked us up from the pub in Standedge and took us to stay with him. He dropped us back on the Pennine Way a few miles further north."

He nodded to Hannah and turned back to the man. "It's high time we gave you what you want. We must get going."

Hannah produced the dongle, carefully folded in a paper handkerchief, and placed it in the man's extended hand. He opened the little parcel eagerly while Paul hoped that his explanation had passed muster and also that the damage to the dongle would be sufficiently convincing.

To his relief the man seemed satisfied.

"I'm really sorry you've been put to so much trouble and expense," Hannah said charmingly. "If only I'd had the sense to throw it down before fleeing!"

"Entirely the fault of my people," the man replied silkily, putting the dongle carefully in his pocket.

"I'm still extremely annoyed with them – the expense and delay have been most inconvenient. It serves them right that they're exhausted; I've left them stuffing their faces at the Golden Lion where I managed to get them beds in the bunkhouse for what was left of the night after we caught up with you. My own room there was noisy until well past midnight. You were wise to come somewhere nice and quiet like this. Anyway, I'm going to have my breakfast now and then we'll take the car back to Derby before returning to London by train."

He shook hands with them both as he bade farewell and Paul opened the front door. "Thank you for your help," he said and walked briskly back down the road in the direction of the Golden Lion.

Hannah gave a relieved smile. "I think we got away with it!" she exclaimed quietly and looked at the small business card in her hand. "Apparently he runs an antique business in Mitcham; that's a mile or two south of Tooting." She passed the card to Paul.

"I must 'phone Tony at once," he said. "Perhaps it would be better if I do it from our bedroom while you find Andy and thank him for his help. You could say that we hope to come again on the way back if we can get the timing right!"

Up in the peace of the bedroom, Paul was relieved to get through to Tony almost immediately.

"The item was successfully transferred two minutes ago to no less a person than the boss of the organisation!" he reported triumphantly. "A prosperous-looking man rang the doorbell here at 7:55, just as we were about to leave, and apologized profusely for his subordinates' threatening behaviour in London. He even gave us his business card – if it's genuine – and has gone back to have breakfast at the Golden Lion before he and his two minions return the hire car to Derby. He said they would then take the train back to London. I can't understand why he volunteered so much information!"

"Are you leaving now?" Tony asked, and, when Paul replied in the affirmative, carried on quickly. "Tim and I have been staying at the Crown Hotel on the northern edge of Horton. We'll leave in four minutes and drive down towards you. I'll get out at the café, while Tim goes and parks near the Golden Lion. Meet me at the rear of the café car park and give me the man's card and your GPS devices. You've done amazingly well. Thanks." He signed off abruptly.

Hannah was waiting for Paul in the small hallway, rucksack on her back.

"Tony is going to meet us outside the café where we had tea yesterday," he said as he shouldered his own pack.

Just north of the Golden Lion, Tim passed in his car with a cheerful wave. Tony was standing at the back of the café car park speaking into his mobile and gave them a smile and nod of greeting as they approached. It was clear that he was in contact with Tim but signed off within thirty seconds.

"Well done you two!" he said as Hannah handed him the business card and her GPS homing device. Paul was struggling to remove his from the back of his belt as Tony continued briskly.

"I spoke to my boss before we left the hotel. The appearance this more senior man is an unexpected development. As you said, it's rather surprising you were told so much: it may just be a sign of his relief at getting his hands on the dongle or trying too hard to play the innocent businessman plagued by incompetent staff!

"The mention of Derby is correct, at least, because we've traced the car to a hire company there, thanks to your accurate observation of the registration number, and Tim reports that the black car is at the Golden Lion. However, it would be too good to be true if they all travel down to London by train from Derby. I suspect the boss will get himself dropped back at Leeds airport. We're checking flight times to London now."

An unpleasant thought suddenly occurred to Paul. "Is it possible that he brought the laptop with him and is going to try out the dongle immediately?" he asked anxiously.

"No, he won't have the password or the expertise. He's definitely just the middleman being paid a tidy sum to steal and deliver the goods to a Mr X! But I must rush off and join Tim, because we need to keep fairly close when they leave the Golden Lion. I just hope they don't take the precaution of putting the dongle in a metal box! My boss is arranging a watch on that Derby garage as a precaution."

"I don't suppose they know anything about electromagnetic screening," Paul replied.

Tony shook them both by the hand. "Many thanks again. Have a good trek to Tan Hill – your booking at the pub has been confirmed and paid for. Stay out of sight here until I'm well on my way."

With a cheerful smile and wave, he returned to the road and disappeared.

Hannah had been completely silent, except for bidding Tony farewell. She was surprised when Paul turned to give her a quick hug.

"You played your part of the innocent superbly!" he said. "Now let's enjoy our freedom."

"Your play-acting was much better than mine," she replied. "It's a good job you'd already thought up that story about being collected from the pub by your brother: it made the loss of signal just about believable, especially in view of the fact that the man thinks his subordinates are morons! Come on, let's go!"

She took his hand enthusiastically and almost dragged him up the road.

CHAPTER 14

The Crown soon came into sight at the top of the road where it turned sharp left to cross the River Ribble.

"The Pennine Way starts again beside the hotel," Paul said.

The lane they entered soon became a gravel track running up between pastures carefully protected by neat stone walls. The rolling landscape, fringed by distant hills, was beautiful even under an overcast sky.

"There's Pen-y-Ghent over on the right!" Hannah exclaimed.

"Yes, the Pennine Way makes quite a long detour to come to Horton, presumably to give walkers somewhere to eat or stay overnight," Paul explained. "But, of course, we're seeing the opposite side of the ridge and it must be at least two miles away as the crow flies!"

Even though their pace was rapid, he could feel himself relaxing. It was obvious that the last twenty-four hours had been a period of greater tension than he had realized at the time, partly, he thought, because he felt some responsibility for Hannah. He looked at her; she seemed to be revelling in their new-found freedom and was obviously enjoying every minute as she stepped out energetically.

"Is it possible I'm beginning to fall in love?" Paul wondered to himself. "I couldn't have a better walking companion. Whereas my last girlfriend would have objected strongly to walking more than four miles or so, this girl takes everything in her stride with delight. I'm so glad we met on the train from London."

They were now on moorland covered in coarse grass and occasional rocky outcrops and tiny streams, but it was not long before the track descended slightly to run along the edge of a wooded ravine.

"This is Ling Gill," Paul said looking at the guidebook. "A large stream called Cam Beck runs through here."

A surprising amount of vegetation was being sustained by the water: not just bushes but quite substantial trees.

Beyond the ravine, the path crossed a neat stone bridge spanning the water and began to climb gradually. Without the guidebook and Hannah's sharp eyes to spot the small wooden signposts, it would have been easy to miss the correct route because there were several junctions where other paths and tracks disappeared in various directions. They could not afford to get lost. Although it was only about 14 miles from Horton to Hawes – home of the famous Wensleydale cheese – where Paul planned to stop for refreshments, they had 18 miles to cover in the afternoon and early evening if they were to reach Tan Hill in time for dinner.

Hannah noticed a long viaduct in the distance. "That's the Ribblehead viaduct," Paul informed her. "It carries the Carlisle to Leeds railway across the Ribble valley and was completed in 1874 according to the guidebook. The river and railway both pass through Horton."

"Together with the rest of the scenery, it reminds me of that advert for Yorkshire Tea on television a couple of years ago!" she said, striding along almost effortlessly, even with a fairly heavy rucksack.

Paul kept pace with her in silent admiration, walking beside her when the track was comfortably wide, but dropping back to follow when the path narrowed.

Several times they passed small piles of stones – some quite carefully constructed – presumably intended to mark the way in bad weather.

"These cairns must be very helpful to sheep farmers and shepherds when there's snow on the ground," Hannah observed.

After over three hours of hard walking they caught a distant glimpse of Hawes in the valley below them.

"We've gradually climbed over 300m this morning to about 570m at the highest point," Paul said. "That's lower than Pen-y-Ghent, but this afternoon we've got the Great Shunner Fell at no less than 713m! Look ahead." He pointed to a distant ridge well beyond the Wensleydale valley.

Hannah beamed at him; she seemed to be metaphorically rubbing her hands in anticipation.

"We need a good lunch break first," Paul continued. "The Wensleydale factory is just outside Hawes now, having outgrown the old central site. The latter is now a cheese-making exhibition centre with a good café. Several reviews mention the excellent cheese toasties!"

They entered a tarmacked lane for a short distance and then another stretch of path that took them into Gayle Lane on the outskirts of Hawes. "We must turn left here and the Centre should be about 200 yards on the right," Paul said. Sure enough, they soon reached a signboard that announced the Wensleydale Creamery.

Ten minutes later they were sitting at a table with cheese and tomato toasties, cold drinks, and a pot of tea. Hannah had insisted on paying for everything.

"This is delicious," Paul said. "Thank you, but the meal at Tan Hill is definitely on me."

Afterwards they made their way carefully through the rather crowded and confusing centre of Hawes and across the River Ure. The narrow road led them up a hill, where, to Paul's relief, the Pennine Way appeared again on their left by a clump of trees.

"Now the real walking begins!" Hannah exclaimed delightedly. "I feel ready for anything after that cheese toastie: the best I've ever tasted." Paul could only agree with her.

They marched quickly along the edge of a field beside a stone wall. At that moment some rays of sunlight broke through the cloudy sky, as if to welcome them, and lit up a ridge in the far distance.

"That ridge has a steeply-sloping edge rather like Pen-y-Ghent," Hannah said. "I hope we haven't gone round in a circle!"

Paul laughed. "That's far behind us! Perhaps rock formations in this area all formed in similar ways. By the way, this path is very short; within minutes we'll come out in the small village of Hardraw."

Once in the village street, they turned left to cross Hardraw Beck and went along the road as far as the village school before a wooden sign indicated a narrow track on the right that went up a gentle slope past a stone cottage and back into the attractive countryside.

"We've now got about four miles to the top of Great Shunner Fell," Paul said.

Before long, the gradual climb left the track and entered moorland. Occasional stretches of paved path protected the turf and peat. Near the top, stones were set in the form of a staircase. There was even a very welcome stone shelter at the summit.

"I bet people are glad of this in bad weather!" Hannah remarked, as they stopped for a drink and a few squares of chocolate.

The path very gradually descended in an arc that swung to the east and reverted to a narrow gravel track. A wide valley opened out in front of them.

"Swaledale," Paul announced, looking at his map.

The scenery, which had been quite bleak over the fells, was now much more attractive. They dropped down rapidly and came out on the narrow B6270, turned left and walked down the hill to the small village of Thwaite.

"Time for tea, I think," said Paul as they passed the window of a little tea shop that seemed to be part of the Kearton Country Hotel. "This is on me and I think we need more than just a slice of cake!"

About forty minutes later, much revived, they were on their way. The route of the Pennine Way commenced again just beyond the hotel and led them up fields surrounded by neat stone walls. They turned to look back at Thwaite; shafts of sunlight had broken through the clouds again and bathed the peaceful valley, even touching the slopes of Great Shunner Fell beyond.

The view to the rear became even more impressive as the narrow path twisted and turned up the side of Kisdon Hill. They passed a farm and continued along the eastern flank of the hill. The scenery was now quite delightful and Paul could sense that Hannah was enjoying herself.

The path became rough and stony before descending beside a wood that seemed to be clinging to the side of a ravine. They dropped down steeply to reveal the small village of Keld in the distance. Trees and bushes surrounded them and the River Swale appeared a short distance below. As the path began to drop even more steeply, they reached a signpost at a junction.

"The Pennine Way doesn't go down into Keld but takes this right turn to cross the river," Paul said.

A bridge took them across a surprisingly wide bed of stones partly covered with water and flanked by luxuriant trees and bushes obviously benefiting from the continuous supply of moisture.

"This is probably a foaming torrent in bad weather," Hannah remarked.

They started to climb again and Keld appeared again below them. Soon they were heading due north along a narrow stony path that continued to climb steadily and yield views to the rear of them that were worth stopping to gaze at every few minutes. The whole of Kisdon Hill appeared to rise from the floor of an enormous valley; even the route that the Pennine Way had taken from Thwaite was visible on its eastern flank.

After about forty-five minutes, the path reached open moorland and became almost completely level.

"We've got about three miles to go, so should be able to get to Tan Hill at about seven o'clock," Paul said.

Hannah gave him a broad grin and speeded up perceptibly. He took the challenge and matched her pace.

It must be confessed that the rest of the journey was rather dreary; not only because the cloud cover had intensified and the light was rather poor, but the route wound across almost featureless moorland. Eventually, the path began to drop slightly and an isolated building appeared in the distance.

"That's Tan Hill; it claims to be the highest pub in England at 536m," Paul announced. "We've covered about 32 miles today."

"I could have done more quite easily if we'd started earlier," Hannah replied. Inwardly, however, she was quite pleased to see the pub and the prospect of a shower and a good meal.

"If we decide to attempt to get as far as Dufton tomorrow, it's just over 38 miles! So an early start really is a good idea."

"I'm game if you are!" she said bravely.

Tan Hill turned out to be a fairly large building with a dozen or so cars parked outside. Their bedroom was in a wing at the rear; it was small but clean. Very soon Hannah was having her eagerly anticipated shower, but she was quick because she knew Paul was waiting. When she emerged, he was lying on his bed letting his feet air by allowing them to hang over the end.

"Sorry about the whiff!" he said. "I'll wash my socks. It's also my turn to wash yours."

Hannah smiled her thanks and rolled the socks into a ball before tossing them towards the open door of the shower room. She was impressed when Paul caught them on the move as he entered.

"I used to be good at cricket at school!" he chuckled over his shoulder.

After a good meal in the crowded restaurant, Hannah and Paul went outside for a final breath of air before having an early night.

"Thank you for a nice meal," Hannah murmured as she linked arms with him to stroll a short distance down the road.

They were too tired to go far, but, in any case, it was necessary to keep within the radius of the light shining from the pub to see where they were going. When they stopped beside the narrow road, she said something she had been meaning to say all day.

"I'm so pleased I decided to come with you; not only because you've been a fantastic help with the dongle affair but also because I'm thoroughly enjoying myself. I hope I haven't cramped your style. I'm also embarrassed by the amount of money you've spent on me."

Paul turned to face her and gripped her shoulders lightly.

"I'm glad you came and will always be thankful we met on the train. You've been an even better companion than John. Although he's a good friend, he would've found some of my plans overambitious. His wife feeds him too well and he needs to lose some weight! When I arranged the first four overnight stops, I forgot to allow for the extra time and effort needed to tackle the gradients. He would have been grumbling by the end of the day to say the least! But you've been amazing and taken everything in your stride."

"I've enjoyed rising to the challenge," Hannah replied, saying the words as if she really meant them.

He paused and looked at her, although her face was almost invisible.

"Another thing: I don't want you to mention money again. I was prepared to use some of my ill-gotten winnings to keep the cost down for John and am more than willing to do the same for you. Anyway, we've had two totally unexpected free nights!"

"I'm really thankful and promise not to raise the subject again," she replied quietly.

On impulse, Paul seized the opportunity offered to say something that had been on his mind for several hours. It helped that they were standing in almost complete darkness.

"Instead of referring to you as my walking companion, as I did when we were with my brother, would you be my girlfriend? I think

I'm falling in love with you; the rest of this trek could be regarded as a rather extended first date."

There was silence for what seemed like minutes to him but was really only a few seconds. Then Hannah replied so quietly that it was almost a whisper.

"Yes, I'd like that. I've been a loner all my life and you're the first man I've ever felt really comfortable with. But please be patient with me: I've allowed a protective shell to build up over the years and it needs time to dissolve!"

"I understand....completely," Paul responded equally quietly.

He removed his hands from her shoulders and slowly hugged her to him. With a little sigh, she rested her cheek against his chest and they remained completely still. Then he gently placed a single kiss on the crown of her head.

Again they were still, until she slowly raised her face to him and their lips met for one brief soft kiss. She gave another little sigh, but it was one of happiness, and he felt, more than saw, her smile at him.

She broke away to stand beside him, gripping his hand tightly. "We need sleep," was all she said as she drew him back towards the pub.

The atmosphere was now very close. "It feels as if a thunderstorm is coming," Paul said. "Hopefully we'll sleep through it, because we need to have breakfast at 6:45 to get an early start. A cooked breakfast has been ordered for us for seven o'clock – the earliest the kitchen can manage – but we're welcome to help ourselves to cereals etc. a little earlier."

As they approached the car park, two men emerged from the door of the bar talking loudly in the slurred speech of those who have drunk too much. They appeared to be aiming rather uncertainly for one of the cars.

"I hope they're not going to try to drive home!" Paul said as he moved quickly to the other side of Hannah to screen her from them.

She felt his protective arm surround her body, but, although the men looked rather blearily at them, they made no attempt to come closer.

"Thank you," a faint whisper sounded in Paul's ear.

Once in the bedroom, neither of them referred to what had happened outside; they simply got ready for bed.

When Paul turned the light out, however, he could not resist saying: "I'm getting quite good at interpreting the delightful little expressions that flit across your face!"

"I'm not aware of them and sorry it's such a plain face!" Hannah responded.

"Nonsense! You've got a sweet face and a lovely athletic figure, but, more important, I'm becoming increasingly attracted by what's inside! The mistake I made with my girlfriend at university was to fall for her looks and fail to get to know the real person."

"Was she beautiful?" Hannah asked, almost timidly.

"Very," he acknowledged truthfully. "But it's totally different with you – you're special!"

"Thank you for saying so. I'll allow those words to sink in: they'll be part of my healing process. Sweet dreams!"

Four hours later, they were both woken by a loud clap of thunder. Several seconds later there was a bright flash of lightning followed almost immediately by an even louder clap. Heavy rain began pounding against the window. The bedroom was so small that one side of Hannah's bed was very close to the curtains. As a lover of fresh air, she had unwisely left the lower half of the sash window open several inches.

"Paul! Are you awake?" she whispered.

"Yes! Are you OK?" he answered.

"Not really; the rain's coming in and I'm ashamed to say I'm frightened!"

He came over quickly and shut the window before sitting on the edge of the bed and taking her hand. There was another flash and he felt her hand tremble.

"I've never got over my childhood fear of thunder," she whispered.

He pulled her gently up to sit beside him and put an arm around her.

"Thank you." She laid her cheek against his shoulder; it was warm and comforting.

The storm passed over quickly and the rain died down to a steady patter.

It was not long before Hannah pulled away and lay down again. Paul opened the window a small fraction. Before he returned to bed, however, he quickly bent over and placed a kiss on her forehead.

"I'm sorry to be such a wimp," she murmured.

"Lots of people have a thing about thunder storms. I'm glad I was here to help!" he whispered.

It was only as he sank into a deep sleep again that he realized the short episode had revealed his true feeling for her – one of tender care and affection.

CHAPTER 15

They had left Tan Hill early on a dull Saturday morning and were well on the way across Sleightholme Moor by eight o'clock.

After a good breakfast, Paul felt well set up for a long day, despite the brief disturbance during the night. Hannah, however, had been very quiet since daybreak and he hoped he had done nothing to upset her. As they marched quickly over the rather barren and soggy moor, however, she began to unburden herself.

"I feel very ashamed of behaving like a frightened child," she confessed diffidently. "I try to be capable and self-reliant and then blot my copybook big-time! What must you think of me?"

Paul kept on walking but reached out to touch her encouragingly.

"Phobias about things like thunder storms are very common," he said. "In reality, you're the most capable girl I've ever met! Just to take two examples: you handle PE classes for children up to sixteen years old, some of whom must be bigger than you are, and you set out on holiday last Monday prepared to hike alone for long distances in the Peak District. If that's not evidence of self-reliance, then I don't know what is!"

He slowed down slightly and looked across at her. "I admire your independent spirit, but am also attracted by the fact that you sometimes need a shoulder to lean on. That's what boyfriends are for!"

Hannah beamed at him. "Thank you for such a vote of confidence." Then she chuckled. "I haven't told you how I got the older boys to respect me," she said.

Paul gave her an encouraging smile, "Do tell me."

"Well," she continued, "my first ever Year 11 class was extremely difficult; the larger lads thought they were much too tough to be told what exercises to do by a woman, and, even worse, someone my size! Then I had a brainwave, although it was risky and could have backfired! When they arrived the second time, I asked the boys to choose their two toughest ones and the girls to select four of their number to act as umpires.

"I'm challenging the boys to a press-up competition," I said. "If either of you can beat me, I'll let you off the exercises you don't like until the end of next week." Some of the boys smirked; they obviously thought their champions would have no trouble in beating me!

"I told them the press-ups must be full ones and that one of the girls would keep us in step by counting aloud at roughly one second intervals. The three other girls would act as umpires to make sure none of us cheated, keeping a count of the incomplete press-ups to be subtracted from our scores at the end. I demonstrated what I meant by a full press-up and a sensible timing.

"Then we got going in earnest! Fortunately, one of the boys didn't last very long, but the other lad hung on with surprising determination, egged on by his fellows. At last he gave up and I went on to do five more presses before I got thankfully to my feet. When our disqualified presses were subtracted – I'm ashamed to say I had two – I was eight ahead of my opponent and astonished to be given a round of applause by the rest of the class! After that I had no trouble with discipline!"

"Well done you!" Paul said admiringly. "My girl's not only a superb walker but has muscles of steel!"

After nearly three miles, the landscape became more interesting and they encountered several small rock-strewn streams and gullies. The path joined a narrow track for some distance before branching off to traverse an attractive meadow before crossing the rocky Sleightholme Beck via a wooden bridge. The path then threaded its way beside the beck for a short distance before turning due north to approach the A66 trunk road near Barnard Castle. Shortly a three-way signpost confronted them.

"The Pennine Way offers a choice of route at this point," Paul reported. "The longer one goes east to the village of Bowes and the shorter one directly north across the A66. We'll take the latter and cross a very unusual natural limestone bridge over the River Greta. It's called God's Bridge, perhaps not surprisingly!"

Soon they were gazing at the natural marvel; the water ran under a massive slab of limestone forming a completely flat bridge from one bank to the other.

"It almost looks like a manmade concrete structure until you get close enough to see that it's a huge chunk of stone!" Hannah exclaimed. "How was it formed? Was it by erosion?"

"The guidebook mentions a cave in the layer of limestone," Paul replied, looking puzzled. "So I guess the water broke through this cavity and scooped out a path for the river to flow under the upper layer of stone. While this was happening, the main stream must have been somewhere else."

As they moved on the noise of traffic gradually increased and it was not long before the path took them down under a wide dual carriageway.

"It's almost like a motorway!" Hannah said, raising her voice above the rumble of heavy vehicles.

"The A66 links Workington on the west coast, just south of the Solway Firth, to Darlington and Middlesbrough in the east. On the way it joins the A1 for a short distance at the famous Scotch Corner," Paul explained. "Our next objective is Middleton-in-Teesdale, about nine miles away, where we can stop for coffee."

This leg of the journey involved a mixed landscape of moors and fields, helped considerably by gradually improving weather. By the time they reached the western end of the Blackton Reservoir, the water was sparkling in the sunlight. A stone bridge took them across a channel connecting Blackton to a smaller reservoir further west and they began to climb steadily before passing a Nature Reserve, fragrant with wild flowers and grasses, on a carefully constructed path. A wide moor then led down to Grassholme Reservoir where the Pennine Way joined a narrow road that crossed the water on a long multi-arch bridge.

After about two more miles of pleasant undulating countryside, Middleton-in-Teesdale could be seen lying peacefully in a shallow valley ahead.

"The route has gone up and down so much this morning that it's surprising to discover from the guidebook that we'll actually have descended 300m from our starting point at Tan Hill by the time we arrive at a mere 230m in Middleton," Paul said with a chuckle. "However, this afternoon we have about twenty miles of superb hiking to Dufton, including reaching a height of 600m before dropping down again. Can you manage OK after that disturbed night?"

"Of course I can!" Hannah replied. "My glumness this morning was sheepishness, not tiredness. But you've cheered me up no end!"

It was almost midday by the time the Pennine Way deposited them on a narrow road just south of Middleton.

"Our onward path is a hundred yards further up the road on the left," Paul said, "but we need to go a little further and cross the River Tees to find a café or hotel in the village."

A few minutes later they spotted a small hotel and entered thankfully. Hannah persuaded a reluctant Paul to allow her to treat him to both coffee and a light lunch. While they were waiting for the food to arrive, he 'phoned a farmhouse advertising bed-and-breakfast on the Pennine Way just north of Dufton and booked the only room still available.

Just as he was saying goodbye, the young woman interrupted saying: "Just a moment, my mother's calling from the kitchen. She's asking if you would like an evening meal at seven-thirty. It'll be one of her special chicken casseroles. Apart from the family, there are three other guests who have booked a meal. It's a very friendly affair: we all sit at a large table. There'll be pudding and a hot drink to finish. At £7 it's less than you would pay at the hotel in Dufton and much nicer!"

Her voice had dropped to a whisper at this point; obviously she thought highly of her mother's cooking. Paul readily accepted, thinking that it would save them walking over half a mile back into Dufton.

Forty-five minutes later, armed with a packet of sandwiches, some extra water and a bar of chocolate, they made their way across the pleasant farmland beyond the village. The path climbed slowly and it was not long before it led them alongside the Tees for a short distance before diverging again. However, about a mile later, they rejoined a lovely stretch of the rapidly flowing river and began to follow it upstream with frequent views of cascading rapids.

Hannah looked across at Paul in delight. "I love the sound of water running over rocks!" she said.

The path climbed steeply and they were quite high above the river when they heard the sound of even more water.

"That's Low Force," Paul announced, "a series of two or three waterfalls in quick succession."

These impressed Hannah even more, but she was astonished a little later when a jumble of dry rocks appeared to surge out of the river bed with very little sign of water anywhere. "Where's the water gone," she said in great surprise.

"Presumably it trickles down between the rocks in rivulets at this time of year," Paul replied. "There may also be a narrow channel somewhere out of sight. However, it must be very impressive when the river is carrying more water!"

The path climbed even more steeply. After another mile or so, the roar of water became really loud.

"That's High Force Waterfall," Paul said. "It's not the highest one in England but probably the largest!"

When they first saw it, framed by overhanging trees, Hannah stopped in amazement. She gripped Paul's hand tightly. "Oh Paul, it's wonderful!"

He beamed at her. He was certainly impressed himself, but, somehow, her delight was an even greater pleasure to him. "I really am falling in love!" he thought.

The river above High Force was wider and shallower, with water cascading past large lumps of rock. They followed the river for well over a mile before the path led them away from the water and up over a rolling landscape with beautiful views of distant hills.

About a mile later they rejoined the Tees, only to cross to the opposite bank. Almost immediately the river curved towards the east in a wide meander and the path appeared to be guiding them beside a beck that had just entered the river from the north.

Paul began to worry that he had missed the route because the guidebook indicated that they had not finished following the Tees. Very soon, however, they were relieved to come to a small bridge over the beck where the Pennine Way took them west over a rather desolate landscape before returning to the north bank of the river.

"We seem to have been going west a lot recently," Hannah commented.

Paul laughed. "You're quite right," he said. "Dufton is about sixteen miles due west of Middleton-in-Teesdale as the crow flies. The Pennine Way is taking us across the spine of England. On this side, water flows from west to east – as the Tees is doing here, give or take the odd meander. After we cross the highest point of our walk in about an hour's time, the rivers and streams will be running in the opposite direction."

The river flowed rapidly towards them in a narrow valley between two ridges. The path, now very rough and rocky, began to hug the bank and great care was needed underfoot. Eventually the path left the water for a short distance as the river performed a sharp swing towards the north.

Rounding a bend to rejoin the river, they were confronted by a remarkable sight; water was cascading angrily towards them over a jumble of rocks.

Hannah stopped abruptly and looked at Paul.

He responded to her unspoken question: "That's called Cauldron Snout! The Tees runs into a reservoir to the north of us. The water is held by a dam – we may catch sight of it in a minute – and the run-off channel comes down this steep gorge."

The Pennine Way now led them rather precariously up an extremely rocky path beside the raging torrent.

"Although it's flowing very fast, there doesn't seem to be enough water to account for the amount that was flowing past us down in the valley," Hannah said, stepping nimbly from one lump of rock to the next.

"That's because Maize Beck flows into the Tees just below Cauldron Snout," Paul replied with some difficulty as he struggled to follow her lead.

The river was calmer beyond the gorge and they crossed a stout footbridge about 200 yards below the impressive dam.

The Way now carried them south-west slowly up over a rather bleak moor, occasionally brightened by shafts of sunlight breaking through the cloud. Parts of the path were very carefully constructed and there were frequent warnings not to stray because they were passing an army firing range.

Maize Beck had appeared from time to time a few hundred yards to their left and now they began to drop down towards it. Paul pointed to a ridge beyond.

"That's High Cup Nick," he said. "Our path reaches its highest point today just below it."

Hannah grinned at him, not in the least worried by the prospect of a climb.

They crossed the beck on a fairly new bridge and, about a mile later, the gradient increased. The path, once again on grass, was aiming towards a wide gap between two ridges, but they were not prepared for the sight that awaited them just beyond.

As Hannah and Paul crested the ridge that Paul had earlier described as "the spine of England", they were met by a view far more impressive even than Pen-y-Ghent near Horton-in-Ribblesdale.

"Behold High Cup Nick!" Paul said almost proudly, as if he had personally arranged the view to delight his companion.

She responded in kind and surprised him by reaching up to kiss his cheek before whispering, "You've certainly set my adrenaline flowing! Do we climb to the top?"

"No time! Perhaps on the way back. We've already reached 600m," was the reply as he took her hand and led her onward.

When they crossed a tiny stream flowing over the tip of a rock-crested valley, the scene got even better. High Cup Nick was just to their right and they were gazing down the steeply-sided valley and out across the broad plain of the River Eden.

"This amazing valley or gill is called High Cup Gill," Paul explained. "In the far distance, about fifteen miles away, you can just about distinguish the hills of the Lake District National Park. I wish it was a better day and we had some good binoculars!"

"Or even a high resolution digital camera," Hannah suggested. "Presumably it would then be possible to enlarge small areas of the picture. Is Dufton down there somewhere?"

"I think it's just out of sight beyond High Cup Nick," Paul said. "What about sharing that sandwich I got in Middleton?"

Hannah nodded eagerly; suddenly conscious she was very hungry.

They sat on a convenient rock and had half a sandwich each and some squares of chocolate, together with a drink of water. A small group of walkers passed them coming up in the opposite direction and could be heard exclaiming in appreciation as they stopped to gaze down the Gill.

"Surely they're not going all the way to Middleton at this time of day!" Hannah remarked.

"No, they've probably just come up from Dufton to see this famous landmark," Paul assured her. "They'll either go back the way they've come, or, there's probably a circular walk that goes down another way."

After a few minutes, Hannah and Paul hurried on because it was getting late and Dufton was still about three miles away. He warned her that the path might be difficult, winding as it did down the steeply shelving southern face of High Cup Nick.

In the event, the early part of rough winding path was negotiated with relative ease and it began to descend rapidly over smoother grassland. They eventually entered a rough track that pointed directly at Dufton nestling in the valley below them.

"What's that curious conical hill just north of Dufton?" Hannah asked. Paul consulted his guidebook. "Probably Dufton Pike," he said, "but we can ask at the farmhouse where we're going to stay."

It was not long before they reached the attractive village green in Dufton and Paul stopped to ask for directions to the farmhouse. It turned out to be half a mile north of the village and very close to the northbound route of the Pennine Way.

Soon the now weary travellers were receiving a warm welcome from the farmer's daughter who ran the guesthouse side of the business with her mother.

"You've made excellent time from Middleton since I spoke to you on the 'phone," the young woman commented, as she showed them to a nice room. Hannah was pleased to see that it had a shower.

"Yes, thanks to my amazingly fit companion!" Paul replied with pride, failing to mention that they had not left Middleton immediately after his call. "Hannah teaches PE at a secondary school and certainly keeps me on my toes!"

Hannah looked a bit embarrassed and shook her head. "You're just as fit as I am," she muttered.

"The evening meal will be ready in forty minutes," the young woman said. "We have it at a large table in our kitchen; it's at the end of the corridor as you come down the stairs."

"We'll be on time," Hannah promised. "It smells delicious!"

The woman smiled at the compliment. "My name's Heather, by the way," she said as she hurried away.

Hannah and Paul had removed their boots thankfully before coming upstairs. There was just time for them both to have quick showers in the small but adequate bathroom before going down again.

"All this exercise has made me really hungry!" Hannah remarked.

"I should have got two packs of sandwiches in Middleton, not expected you to share one for our late afternoon snack," Paul apologized.

Hannah shook her head. "I'm fine," she whispered as she took his hand and led the way down to the kitchen.

Three people were already standing by the large kitchen table and smiled towards the door as the young couple entered. A kindly-looking man of about fifty stepped forward with hand outstretched.

"Mary," he said, nodding towards the farmer's wife, who was busily dishing up together with Heather, "has asked me to introduce ourselves. We're regular visitors here and staying for ten days holiday. I'm Brian; this is my wife, Sue, and daughter, Rachel."

Everyone shook hands and Brian ushered them to seats at the table. In true professional style, he placed the sexes alternately, with couples together, except that Rachel was placed next to Hannah. The reason became clear when the farmer and his son hurried in with an apologetic nod to his wife and quickly introduced themselves.

The son, Ted, a burly lad with a bright smile, slipped into the seat next to Rachel. She smiled with pleasure; she had clearly lobbied her father earlier.

Dishes of steaming vegetables had already been placed on the table. Mary and Heather now served individual plates containing generous portions of the famous chicken casserole. The farmer stood up again as his wife and daughter took their places beside him. He looked towards Paul and Hannah.

"I hope you won't mind if I say grace," he said. "We're a Christian household and Brian over there is a Methodist minister, so he's used to it!"

He bowed his head and said a few short sentences of thanks. Paul, of course, was used to his family saying a rather formal grace at home, but to Hannah it was an eye-opener; the farmer seemed to be speaking to a much-loved friend in simple everyday language. She was also astonished when everybody said "Amen!" at the end.

People started chatting enthusiastically and passing the dishes of vegetables around. There was so much on offer that Hannah was pleased she had only had half a sandwich two hours earlier. Not only was it plentiful but the casserole was just a delicious as the aroma had promised. She turned to Mary.

"I've not had anything remotely as nice as this since my mother prepared a special dinner for me on my birthday visit home almost a year ago," she said. "My parents live on a small farm in Dorset. We grow vegetables."

Mary beamed with delight at her words. Mention of a farming background, however, caused a host of questions and it was at least five minutes before Hannah could lapse into silence and carry on with her meal, leaving Paul to explain his job briefly and that they were walking up the Pennine Way as far as Haltwhistle to visit his sister and her family.

He thought it best not to mention that he had only met Hannah the previous Monday; otherwise sharing a bedroom, even a twin-bedded one, might have seemed rather premature.

When Paul too managed to get on with his food, Brian took over most of the talking and became an excellent substitute host: the farmer was extremely friendly but not a conversationalist. Hannah sympathized; she knew how hard her father and mother worked on their modest farm and that they needed to relax at the evening meal. They did not have a stalwart son, only a part-time farmhand.

Meanwhile Rachel and Ted were having their own intimate conversation. Hannah overheard him asking how her recent A-level exams had gone. It transpired that she was hoping to go to agricultural college if she obtained the required grades.

The desert when it came was almost up to the standard of the main course – apple sponge pudding with homemade custard, followed by tea or coffee.

At the end, Hannah went up to Mary to say how much she and Paul had enjoyed the meal and to ask if she could help with the washing-up. The motherly Mary hugged her for the compliment and offer, but only allowed her to help Rachel with clearing the table and laying up the breakfast things.

"Even though it's Sunday, my husband and son have to get up early for the milking and so you can have breakfast almost anytime you like. I expect you want to get back on the Pennine Way as soon as possible." she said. Hannah suggested 7:15 and it was agreed.

While Hannah was helping in the kitchen, Paul stepped outside into the yard and 'phoned his sister. "We're staying in Dufton tonight in a lovely farmhouse," he informed Sue after they had exchanged greetings.

She was surprised that they had got so far so quickly and he chuckled. "Hannah's amazingly tough, even for a PE teacher!" he said, feeling a surge of affection for his new girlfriend, adding: "We've just done a trek of about 38 miles today!"

Sue was suitably impressed and said so; there was a note of hope in her voice, but she merely asked him what his plans were now and when they were hoping to arrive.

"Perhaps we should aim to get to you by lunchtime on Monday and then stay for two nights if we may?" Paul replied. "I'm not sure we should attempt to do the remaining 36 miles to Hadrian's Wall in one go, especially as the first 19 miles or so to Alston has some steep climbs."

Sue sounded slightly disappointed and asked him to wait while she spoke to her husband. A minute later, she was back on the 'phone.

"Ian has a suggestion," she said. "He was planning to drive the four miles west along the road from Haltwhistle to pick you up at the point where the Pennine Way crosses the A69 to Carlisle. Suppose instead he takes the minor road south to Knarsdale on the Pennine Way and picks you up there mid-afternoon tomorrow? It's only about seven miles from Alston. I have a slightly ulterior motive for suggesting this, but must keep it to myself for now!"

Paul laughed: he knew his sister. "Your motives are never ulterior, but always aimed at doing good! I guess you have a meeting at church tomorrow evening that you're hoping we'll agree to attend!"

"You know me too well!" Sue replied. "Actually, it's not a church service but a talk by someone with an amazing story to tell! No more details for now."

"I'll have to speak to Hannah about the evening but we'd love to be picked up at Knarsdale if Ian doesn't mind spoiling his Sunday afternoon. Shall we aim for four-thirty? I'll 'phone to report our progress about an hour before that. We'll have a proper lunch in Alston, however, because I know you have your main meal at half past one on Sundays."

He could tell that Sue was pleased when they bade each other farewell and sweet dreams. Turning back towards the farmhouse, he saw Hannah coming out to look for him. She took his arm and they strolled a short distance while he told her the plan.

"I'd love to come to the talk tomorrow," she whispered. "It sounds mysterious and intriguing! I must say I've enjoyed this evening more than I thought possible. Everyone has been so kind and friendly."

"I'm glad," Paul replied softly. "You've also done today's long trek in fine style!"

"And my feet are paying for it," she said, laughing ruefully, "even though my boots fit perfectly and were well worn in before I came north."

She turned to face him and looked up with a shy smile. He took her in his arms and kissed her; she responded for a short time before pulling away to take his hand.

"We need an early night," she said.

Paul gave her hand an understanding squeeze.

"I must be patient and not try to rush things," he thought.

CHAPTER 16

They left the farmhouse just after eight o'clock. Mary impulsively gave Hannah a motherly hug in her warm-hearted way and said she hoped they would come again.

Rejoining the nearby Pennine Way, they swiftly traversed the attractive fields and meadows north of the village until reaching hilly ground again. A conical hill appeared not far ahead.

"I hope that's not Dufton Pike again; otherwise we've not made any progress at all!" Hannah exclaimed.

"Don't worry!" Paul laughed. "That's Knock Pike; so named because the small village of Knock is just to the west of us. Dufton Pike is over there to the east; we passed to the south of it yesterday. The Pennine Way effectively takes a 90-degree turn in the village."

A little later, after climbing steadily, they turned to look at the view: the distant Eden valley was framed between the twin conical hills, Dufton on their left and Knock on the right. The picture was enhanced greatly by the fact that the sky over Eden was almost clear and the peaceful fields and woods were bathed in sunshine.

"I wish we had sun overhead," Hannah said wistfully, looking up at the clouds above them.

"Wait until we really start climbing," Paul responded. "We may be glad of the cloud cover. At least it's fairly high and should be well above the tops of the fells: we've got a chain of four of them to negotiate with three dips or cols in between."

"Well, we'd better get cracking if we want to have time for something to eat in Alston," she said, speeding up. He was impressed once again by her stamina but thought it better to keep silent.

They dropped down briefly to cross the dry rocky bed of a beck before climbing again. "I must remember that streams are called becks in this part of the country," Hannah reminded herself.

The winding path climbed even higher, sometimes over grass strewn with small rocks and occasionally over carefully laid paving.

"We'll pass close to the 794m summit of Knock Fell soon," Paul said. "There's a tall cairn on the summit called the Old Man of Knock according to the guidebook. Unfortunately, the clouds will obscure any views, but perhaps we'll have better luck on the next fell – Great Dun!"

The Old Man was more of a landmark than a thing of beauty, especially in the rather poor visibility, but they soon left it behind and dropped down the northern spur of the hill to join a narrow tarmac road for a short distance. The road snaked all the way up to the Great Dun, on the top of which a giant golf ball appeared to be perched rather precariously.

"A radar station for air-traffic control," Paul announced. "That's the reason for this road."

Clearly walkers were not encouraged to get too close, because a signpost directed them off the road to pass slightly to the east of the facility. Fortunately, both the path and the weather improved as they began to descend again. The tops of the next two hills – Little Dun and Cross Fells – were both visible as the broad stretch of high ground curved towards the north-west.

"Little Dun is a mere six metres lower than Great Dun!" Paul volunteered.

Hannah's attention, however, was drawn south-west because the Eden valley was again visible in the distance beyond the entrance to a long valley that ran out from the col on which they were standing. A breeze had sprung up and the jagged clouds above them were retreating slowly towards the east, allowing the approaching fingers of sunlight to touch the slopes of fells. She gave a sigh of pleasure and took Paul's hand as she shared her enjoyment.

The highest point of the trek was reached at 893m on the top of Cross Fell where they found a stone shelter and stopped for a drink of water and share the last banana and a little chocolate. By the time they left a few minutes later the sky immediately overhead was clear of cloud and a remarkable panorama lay before them; the wide plain of the Eden valley stretched out to touch the line of hills marking the edge of the Lake District. Hannah gazed in appreciation, but Paul was more down to earth.

"It's probably possible to make out the town of Penrith about ten miles away if we knew exactly where to look," he remarked, before encouraging her to move on. "It's downhill from now on. Very soon the Way will turn north-east towards the village of Garrigill before bending north-west again to follow the River South Tyne to Alston."

Marching onwards, Hannah asked: "Is the South Tyne the same river as the Tyne that runs through Newcastle-upon-Tyne?"

"It becomes the Tyne proper somewhere near Corbridge, twenty miles this side of Newcastle," he informed her.

The path was very rough in places but fairly direct. Hannah was moving forward so rapidly on the downward slope that they covered six miles in not much more than one and a half hours, but even she was pleased to see Garrigill in the valley below them.

They joined the road through the small village for a short distance before the Pennine Way led them over a mixture of meadows and woods. They managed to miss the path once, but their closeness to the river helped to keep them on course. Pleasant pastoral scenery surrounded them, especially nearer to Alston when the path led them up on to higher ground, giving them the chance to appreciate the beauty of the surrounding hills.

As they walked through Atston looking for a place to eat, they passed the Angel Inn. Paul suddenly remembered that he had seen it recommended in Google reviews. It was not long before he was ordering food and cold drinks at the bar while Hannah disappeared briefly after pressing £15 into his reluctant hand.

About thirty-five minutes later they set out on the last leg of the trek northward. "Only seven miles now," Paul said encouragingly, "but we'll have to step on it if we're going to make Knarsdale by four-thirty or soon after. Can you manage?"

"Of course I can!" Hannah replied, sounding almost cross. "The terrain will be far easier than we've had recently."

They crossed the South Tyne on the road bridge just south of Alston and almost immediately turned into the track that formed the first section of the Pennine Way. It was possible to glimpse the river to the right through the trees.

The Way soon reduced to a path again, and, less than a mile later, deposited them on a road. Hannah looked at Paul in surprise.

"I forgot to mention that the main road from Alston to Carlisle also keeps fairly close to the river, so we'll be seeing both more than once before we get to Knarsdale," he said. "I'm going to 'phone Sue to let her know that we should arrive by 16:40."

When he came off the 'phone, he said: "Sue asks us to wait on the north side of an old railway viaduct over the Carlisle road; we can stand at the entrance to a service road immediately on the left beyond the bridge. I've also told her that we'd like to come to the church meeting; it's at seven o'clock."

They continued walking at a good pace. Their route took them through a pleasing mixture fields, small woods, and sections of higher moorland. At one point the path squeezed through a tunnel under a high embankment.

"I believe we're passing below what used to be a narrow-gauge railway line between Alston and Haltwhistle," Paul announced. "Sue said something in a letter once about an enterprising group of enthusiasts who are restoring one of the tracks. My brother-in-law, Ian, goes to help occasionally."

More by luck than judgement, their timing was immaculate and they dropped down a gentle grassy slope to the Carlisle road beside a surprisingly well-preserved viaduct two minutes before the agreed time. A modest family hatchback was parked rather precariously at one side of the wide entrance of a private road.

A young man, a few years older than Paul, got out of the driving seat with a smile that conveyed both welcome and relief.

"My brother-in-law," Paul whispered.

"Hello, you two intrepid travellers!" Ian gave Paul a vigorous double handshake. "I'm so glad you're on time. Sue, bless her, hasn't chosen a very good place for me to stop!"

He turned to Hannah. "You must be Hannah; you're a really welcome replacement for Paul's unfortunate teacher friend, John."

They shook hands and he took her rucksack to stow with Paul's in the rear of the car. "There's a reasonable amount of legroom if you two want to sit together on the back seat," he said.

As they drove off, Ian continued to talk. "Sue and young Toby would have come with me but she thought she ought to get some sandwiches ready for tea and Toby bathed and prepared for bed before the baby-sitter arrives – she's coming at six-forty prompt. Although the church is only a five-minute walk away, we need to leave in good time; the building is quite small and the speaker should be quite a draw."

The road ran almost directly north for about three miles but then veered west towards Carlisle. "We have to turn right just here and go along a winding lane to get to Haltwhistle," Ian explained. "I'll stop talking and concentrate on the road!"

Hannah took Paul's hand and smiled at him. After almost eight hours of actual walking, it was good to relax in close proximity to the man she not only liked but was beginning to fall in love with. As the car twisted and turned on the narrow country lane through delightful fields and hamlets, she almost fell asleep against his shoulder.

Tony noticed in his rear view mirror and smiled to himself. "Paul needs a wife; perhaps she's the one," he thought.

The young couple were suddenly aware that the car had negotiated a sharp loop to go under a busy road.

"This is the A69 between Carlisle and Newcastle," Ian explained, speaking for the first time for fifteen minutes.

They crossed the South Tyne and then went under a railway line.

"Both the railway and the main road follow the river valley," Ian said. "We're now joining a road that runs parallel to the A69 and skirts the southern edge of the town centre. We'll turn right here and avoid the centre now. You can investigate it tomorrow. We live to the north-east of the centre just off a road called Shield Hill. It's very convenient because I only have a mile to walk to work."

"Ian's just been promoted to chief pharmacist," Paul whispered to Hannah.

Ian heard and laughed. "It's only a small place," he said modestly. "Don't make me sound too grand, otherwise Hannah will wonder why we live in one of the many terraced houses that are popular in this area."

The car climbed about 200 yards up a fairly steep hill and turned right into a cul-de-sac.

"It's in a similar situation to the one that Mark has in Skipton," Hannah observed.

"Yes, the width of the frontage is about the same, but, being at the end of the terrace, the previous owners added a two-storey side extension to the rear," Ian said. "Several windows now have a nice view of the valley." He pulled up in the sideway. "We also have off-street parking, which is very convenient."

As he extracted their luggage, he had another thought. "Before I forget; about two miles up the road, you can join the Pennine Way as it runs alongside the ruins of the old Roman wall. I'll draw you a sketch; you might like to do the walk together tomorrow."

"How lovely," Hannah exclaimed. "It will prevent us getting lazy on our day off!"

As she said this, the side door of the house opened and a smiling woman rushed out to greet them, followed, rather unsteadily, by a small toddler.

"I thought I heard the car! Oh, it's so good to see you!" Sue said as she hugged Paul and turned to greet Hannah, a really genuine smile of welcome on her face.

"You must be Hannah. Come in – you must be tired and hungry. Ian will take you both up to your rooms while I make the tea; the kettle's boiling. The house is bigger than it looks. We have a double and three singles, although Toby's is really a box room. There's a bathroom upstairs and even a shower room and WC downstairs, so you can both have a shower after tea if you think there's time. We need to leave in one and a half hours."

Sue's words suddenly stopped as they reached the foot of the stairs. Hannah was reminded fondly of Paul's mother who sometimes spoke in a similar flood of words.

"I can't thank you enough for allowing me to come with Paul," she managed to say, speaking for the first time.

"Any friend of Paul is a friend of ours!" Sue replied and would have hugged Hannah if she had not had a rather overwhelmed Toby in her arms.

After visiting the bathroom, Hannah stood at her little bedroom window looking out over the town and Tyne valley. A tear of gratitude ran down her cheek: she had obviously been given the best single room.

A few minutes later, they were all gathered around the kitchen table. Toby was in his high chair waving a small monkey that Paul had fished out of the bottom of his rucksack for his nephew. "I'm sorry it got a bit squashed," he said, "but it should recover!"

The wholemeal bread sandwiches, with egg mayonnaise and cheese and tomato fillings, were delicious and the tea more than welcome after such an energetic day.

When Hannah expressed her appreciation, Ian told her that his wife was famous at church for her egg mayonnaise made of fresh local eggs and homemade mayonnaise. Sue blushed modestly at all this praise.

With a shower over the bath upstairs and a separate shower room downstairs, Hannah and Paul were both able a have a shower before everyone gathered at the front door to leave the house. Sue issued final instructions to the baby-sitter, who turned out to be a sixteen-year-old girl from the church youth group.

Even at ten minutes to seven, the small church building was well over half full, but the four of them managed to find seats together in a row rather too close to the front for Hannah's comfort.

A remarkably young but skilful lad played quietly on an electronic keyboard while the room filled up and everyone waited expectantly.

Just after seven o'clock, three men entered from a side room at the front of the church. Two sat down – one Afro-Caribbean and the other Asian in appearance – close to a table bearing a white cloth and simple wooden Cross.

The third, a burly local man judging by his Geordie accent, stood at the simple lectern and introduced himself as the church pastor. He could see a good number of visitors, he said, and hoped they would feel welcome and able to relax. They had two special guests from Leeds and were about to hear a quite remarkable story. However, in view of its rather sensitive content, he would be grateful if any portable recording devices could be turned off.

After a brief pause, he went on. "I'll just say a prayer committing the evening to God and then Mark here will lead us in a very tuneful Christian song by Stuart Townsend, the words of which will be projected on the wall behind me. It's one of our congregational favourites and so everyone will soon find it easy to join in if they wish."

He then said a short prayer, at the conclusion of which the young man on the keyboard struck up with the opening chords of the song. The regular members of the congregation stood up and the visitors followed obediently, some rather uncertainly. The tune was so catchy, however, that it was not long before most people were joining in. Consequently, there were smiles of pleasure on many faces as people sat down and the pastor called the Afro-Caribbean visitor to the lectern.

"This is an old friend of mine, John, who leads a church in Leeds," he said. "Some of you may recognize him because he preached here about eight months ago. This time, however, he has brought a friend with him who recently joined his church."

The pastor sat down as John thanked him and said how pleased he was to be able to visit Haltwhistle again and bring friendly greetings from his church in Leeds. He then signalled to his friend to step forward.

"This is my good friend for whom I must use the pseudonym Peter: you'll discover the reason later. I had the privilege of baptizing Peter – using his real Christian name, of course – about five weeks ago, and he's now a dear friend and regular member of our congregation. He's not yet used to public speaking but has such an extraordinary story to tell that he feels the Lord wants him to share his experience when the opportunity arises. I won't say anything more but let Peter tell his story."

John smiled encouragingly and returned to his seat.

Peter stood rather unsteadily at the lectern, holding it firmly for support, as he looked out at the audience with a shy smile. He swallowed nervously and began to speak.

"Good evening. I'm most grateful for the opportunity to come here with Pastor John tonight and share my story with you," he said slowly with a slight Midlands accent; it was clear that he had spent most of his life in England.

It was what he said next, however, that caused Hannah to stiffen in shock and grip Paul's hand tightly.

CHAPTER 17

"Four months ago, I was a dedicated jihadist and had just joined Islamic State in Syria," Peter announced calmly.

A sharp intake of breath could be heard from many in the audience. Peter, however, continued as if nothing had happened.

"Then, within the space of two days, I changed from a man prepared to do almost anything to further the cause of Islam to being a Christian who believes that Jesus Christ is the Son of God and that the Cross is the only way by which we can approach a holy God. All that has happened to me is entirely due to the grace and mercy of Almighty God!"

Peter took a sip of water as murmurs of astonishment and delight arose from various quarters.

"Let me explain how it happened," he continued, warming to his theme. "My family have always attended the mosque in the city where I grew up. For their sake, I won't be more specific. Unfortunately, I began to mix with the wrong friends and became radicalized: not only believing Islam to be the only true religion but also that we are called to act in the same way that the Prophet Mohamed did fourteen centuries ago. I therefore responded eagerly when invited to join my spiritual brothers in fighting to establish a caliphate, now calling itself the Islamic State, in the Middle East. From now on, I will refer to them as Isil, a name commonly used in the West.

"I willingly bought flight tickets to Turin in northern Italy on the web, as instructed in a coded message, and a coach ticket from Turin to the coastal holiday destination of Savona. I was not going to use the latter: it was just part of my cover story. In Turin, I paid cash for a flight to Istanbul, where I was met by an agent who smuggled me across Turkey and over the border into Syria. I cannot give you any more details, but the British authorities were given the information during an uncomfortable two-week debriefing on my return to the UK. I still have to report to a police station in Leeds once a week.

"However, it is relevant to my story to say that, although my father believed I was going on holiday in Italy with a friend, I could not bear to leave my mother entirely in the dark and so I hinted that I might be joining an aid group preparing to help in a Turkish refugee camp near the Syrian border. She extracted a promise from me that I would buy open return tickets so that I could get back quickly if I was in danger and also to take great care of my passport.

"Anyway, I was sent to join the Isil group in a small town situated between the headquarters in Raqqa and Kobani close to the Turkish border. This made our location particularly important as a staging post for supplies going to our forces fighting the Kurds.

"Along with several other newcomers, I was put through an induction process. At one point, we were instructed to go to a table and hand over all our documentation and any remaining money. We stepped forward in turn and handed items, one at a time, to a man who sat putting them into piles. Fortunately, I had nearly two hundred pounds in £10 and £5 bank notes plus a little Turkish money. Having handed over my driving licence, I produced the bundle of bank notes. The man's eyes lit up and he began to count it, probably planning to keep some back for himself. Intent on the task, he absentmindedly nodded to me to move on to the next stage of the processing. Later, I managed to conceal my return tickets and passport in the second-hand military-style jacket I was issued."

Peter paused to take another sip of water. He was clearly coming to something that he found difficult to put into words.

"The Arabic speakers in Isil," he continued, "tend to look down on the others, especially the Europeans, because they think we may lack fervour and dedication to the cause. We are subjected to a particularly rigorous hardening-up process during our induction. By far the worst episode came one day when a group of us were ordered to witness an execution; three Iraqi Christians from Mosul were to be given one last chance of converting to Islam or being beheaded. It was planned to film the event for propaganda purposes.

"When we arrived, the handcuffed Iraqis were already kneeling down, each with a hooded brother – we had to refer to each other as brothers – standing behind holding a vicious-looking knife. A tall-hooded man, obviously in charge of the proceedings, was waiting beside the first Iraqi, who, it transpired, had been placed in that position because he could speak quite good English.

"To my surprise, at the last minute, a man considerably darker than the others was brought in and placed at the end of the short line of kneeling figures; he was obviously very frightened and seemed to have no idea why he was there.

"The leader nodded to the camera crew and filming commenced. The first Iraqi was asked if he would convert to Islam. He started to tremble, but then I saw something remarkable: the faces of all three men appeared to glow. I now know that I was being given the privilege of seeing the Holy Spirit surround them with his love and strength. The man straightened up and spoke loudly in a heavy accent: "I believe that Jesus Christ is the Son of God; I will not deny my Lord and Saviour!"

"The man in charge looked so angry that he failed to translate for those who didn't understand, but there must have been a sufficient number who got the gist of the brave man's words for there to be a moment of respectful silence. The leader, however, nodded to the knife-wielding jihadist and the Iraqi's head was jerked back and his throat sliced open. Worse followed that is too horrible to mention.

"I felt sick inside and it must have shown on my face because the man next to me whispered: "Be careful; we're probably being observed to note our reaction."

"This barbarity was repeated twice more. The challenge was now made in Arabic, but each replied with similar declarations of faith that were translated into English for the benefit of the film.

"When the questioner came to the terrified man at the end of the line, he spoke in English again: "You've seen the fate of the others. If you are a Muslim, declare it, or else this is your chance to convert and live!" As the shaking man looked at his interrogator, the same glow I had seen on the others also touched him.

"A moment later he gave a reply that not only stunned me but even surprised his interrogator: "The God of these three men is also my God!" he declared loudly. There was a howl of rage from the man behind him and he died in the same horrible way as the others.

"I am sure that four men, not three, entered Heaven together that morning and beheld the glory of their Lord!" Peter said with quiet conviction. He was becoming quite emotional and had to stop for a short time to recover, taking a sip of water.

Hannah had been feeling a sense of utter disgust that human beings could be so barbaric; now this revulsion was overlaid by a much stronger emotion. For the first time in her life she was face-to-face with real faith; not only the sort prepared to die in the heat of battle but one that would rather chose death than deny their God.

Paul must have had some appreciation of what she was experiencing because he took her hand again.

"After this traumatic experience," Peter continued, "I came away in turmoil but had to go through the pretence of giving the impression that I was glad four unbelievers had met their just fate. It was even worse during the following night and I hardly slept at all.

"Early the following afternoon, I was summoned to see one of the group commanders. I went with some trepidation expecting a reprimand: perhaps my reaction the previous day had been noticed. It turned out, however, that he wanted me to accompany a more senior brother who was acting as a courier and taking some sealed orders to an outpost about seven miles north of the town. We were to wait for a written reply and then come back as quickly as possible. Lack of suitable transport meant that we would have to walk and we were told to take some food and an extra bottle of water in addition to the water flasks we always carried strapped to our belts.

"While my colleague waited for the package to be prepared, I went to collect the water and a couple snacks from the canteen. We agreed to meet again in twenty minutes. As it happened, the canteen had run out of any small items of food that could be conveniently carried or survive the heat and so provided two emergency high-energy biscuit bars normally provided to our fighters in the field. I was not to know then that these would prove extremely useful.

"Soon after the agreed meeting time, my would-be companion appeared looking quite ill. "I feel very sick," he complained. "Something I've eaten probably. You'll have to go on your own. Here's the package, our permit to travel and a map of the local area." With that he rushed off in the direction of the latrines.

"It was surprising that he was prepared to let me go alone, but I assumed he was sufficiently senior to make that decision and so set out with some trepidation. The road, such as it was, deteriorated even further after about three miles. My map indicated that it curved around the base of a low hill just in front of me and so I decided to take a short cut over the top. Joining the road again – now no more than a rough track – I trudged on under the hot sun.

"I was pleasantly surprised by the friendly welcome at my destination; they had clearly been alerted to the delivery of the package and someone had been delegated to look out for us. When I was introduced to the commander, he did not seem too disconcerted to find I was on my own. I was even given hospitality while he examined the orders and wrote a reply for me to take back.

"It was on the return journey that the impact of what I had witnessed the previous day really hit me in earnest. I still believed Islam to be the only true faith that needed to be defended and spread with single-minded determination, but I had been shattered by the ruthless savagery of the beheadings. Seeing them for real had had far more impact on me than merely reading or hearing about such things in news reports. I had also been amazed at the complete faith and devotion of the Christians. Would I act like that in defence of my faith if faced with the prospect of such a horrible death?

"By the time I was halfway up the low hill, I was at my wits end. It was almost as if the atmospheric pressure had increased and was trying to crush me. The thought of having to return to the town and pretend that I was eager to become a dedicated and ruthless soldier of Islam was intolerable.

"There was a low slab of rock just in front of me, and, on sudden impulse, I threw myself down before it in the Muslim attitude of prayer, pressing my forehead to the ground so hard that I could feel the grit penetrating my skin. In despair, I cried out to Allah to help me and reveal his will. Was it right to spread our religion by fear and ruthless killing?

"There was no reply and no lessening of my agony. Then, totally unexpectedly, some childhood memories surfaced. In our religious education classes at school, we had been taught about the main world religions. I could now picture the teacher telling us about Christianity. My parents had warned me beforehand that Jesus is not, and could not be, the Son of God – in Islamic teaching he is merely a prophet and teacher – and so I obediently discounted this. Nevertheless, I took on board the fact that Jesus portrayed a God who embodies not only perfect holiness but also amazing love; a God who reaches out to the people he has created. Jesus himself was very much a man of peace and never took up the sword to fight those who opposed him. What had really astonished me, however, was that he encouraged his disciples to call God, "Father".

"As I recalled this last fact now, prostrate on the stiflingly hot hillside, I tried to imagine any Muslim having the audacity to address Allah as Father; it was unthinkable! The Quran and the Bible, especially the New Testament, were completely at odds in their depiction of the character of God. But what if Jesus was right? All my previous convictions would be turned upside down – the thought made me tremble with fear and apprehension. Even so, and totally unexpectedly, a tiny seed of hope seemed to have been planted in my heart.

"In that barren place, I cried out with the question burning inside me: "Almighty and all seeing God, which one of these Holy Books reveals the truth about you?" I waited forlornly, not really expecting an answer.

"Suddenly, I felt a cool fragrant breeze sweep the hillside. "The one that calls me Father," a gentle voice said quietly.

"I shook with shock. There was no possibility that the words had come out of my fevered imagination: the voice, although quiet, had spoken with total authority.

"I was trembling even more when I cried out: "Then I am totally evil and without hope! I came to Syria to fight to establish an Islamic Caliphate. Yesterday, I even stood by and said nothing while your servants were slaughtered. Why do you not destroy me in your wrath?"

"The voice came again, speaking slowly and emphatically. "Because I love you and my Son died for you. Look up!"

"Suddenly, I found myself no longer grovelling on the ground but on my hands and knees looking up at the low slab of rock a few feet away. A man clothed in a radiant white garment stood there – but a man like no other. His face shone with a glory so great that I could only just make out the faint outline of his features. My trembling increased. I knew I wasn't dreaming because my forehead was still painful from the contact with the rough ground; this person was far more real than the barren landscape around us.

"He raised his hands in a gesture of welcome and then lifted them slightly further to indicate that I should stand. As I rose to my feet a wave of peace flowed over me and my trembling ceased.

"Are you Jesus?" I croaked and sensed rather than saw his head bend slightly in acknowledgement. "So you are far more than a prophet and teacher?" Again his head inclined, but this time he smiled and it was as if a mantle of love and acceptance enfolded me. But such was the darkness in me that I could not accept it. I just felt more and more unclean the longer I stood there.

"After a few moments, I heard myself saying: "Lord, I don't think there is any hope for me. I feel so dirty. How can my past be forgiven and my heart changed?"

"For the first time, Jesus spoke. The sound of his voice was far too beautiful to even try to describe, but it penetrated right to the core of my being. "My blood was shed for you. Believe, ask and receive."

"I sank to my knees. "Lord Jesus, I believe you are the Son of God. Please forgive me and cleanse me!" the words poured out of me with a great sigh of relief.

"A wave of incredible power swept through me. Something I can only describe as a heavy weight was plucked from my chest and it felt as if a tide of filth was draining out into the ground.

"Stand up!" the quiet command came. I did so and saw Jesus smile again. Wave after wave of love and joy swept over me. This time it was different; the waves also seemed to flood through me. The feeling was so overwhelming that I began to weep.

"Lord, how can I thank you for your love and mercy?" I eventually managed to ask.

"Seek to know me and follow my plan for your life," he replied and then raised his arm to point. "Walk to the Turkish border. There you will be told what to do." Then, with a hint of humour, he added: "Take your gun and get rid of it where it will not be found; you will not need it again."

"I turned and saw that Jesus was pointing in the direction of a large rock some distance to the west of the road down which I had recently returned. I heard him say, "Remember, I will be with you always," but, when I turned back, he had gone.

"My shock only lasted a fleeting second before I was conscious of an all enveloping sense of freedom, lightness and peace.

Although I had already walked over ten hot miles, I now seemed to be full of energy.

"I had a small military-style compass in my pocket with a fold-out direction-sighting device. It had been a treasured possession since my early teens. Before leaving the point where we had been standing, I was therefore able to take a bearing on the distant rock. Descending the hill and arriving at my objective, I used the compass to locate another distinctive object before sitting down and leaning against the base of the rock to drink the small amount of water remaining in the bottle provided by the canteen.

"Now I only had my water flask left and it suddenly struck me that it would not go very far on a trek of sixty miles or more; neither would the two high-energy biscuit bars, each not much bigger than a small bar of chocolate. I also wondered about the terrain that would confront me. At the moment, I was surrounded by an arid landscape liberally scattered with small rocks and dotted with a few larger ones and stunted shrubs. However, the small map I had been given indicated that my route would approach within a few miles of the Euphrates as it wound south-east from its source in the mountains of Turkey to the Iraqi border and on down towards the Persian Gulf. The land should therefore become more fertile and there might be more chance of coming across a source of water.

"I was just about to get up and start moving again when I saw a hole in the ground near the base of the rock. Hoping it was not the burrow of some unfortunate animal, I managed to jam my gun, followed by the magazine, far enough down to be completely out of sight. I could now step out with nothing except a small satchel, water flask and what I had in my pockets.

"Guessing that a search party would be sent out to look for me and so anxious to get as far from the town as possible, I walked as fast as I could for about two hours until it began to get dark. The need to stop to take a fresh sighting every so often had delayed progress, but it was obviously wise to look for somewhere to rest before I tripped over in the rapidly gathering gloom and broke a limb. Eventually, I found a recess at the base of a rock big enough to offer a small amount of concealment and protection from the cold night air, helped by the fact that the rock had absorbed some heat from the hours of strong sunlight.

"I had a few sips of water from my flask and a quarter of one of the high-energy biscuits, before committing myself to God's protection with a thankful heart and lying down as comfortably as I could on the hard ground.

"I woke from a deep sleep three hours later both cold and stiff. It was not coldness that had roused me; it was bright moonlight. I found it was possible to see sufficiently clearly to travel in reasonable safely, although distinguishing distant landmarks was almost impossible unless they were very close. Perhaps, I reasoned, I could use a star, assuming I could read the compass in this level of light. I opened the lid and saw something long forgotten: the cardinal points on the dial, the needle and the hairline marker were all faintly luminous. With a sigh of relief, I managed to pick out a fairly bright star after a little trial and error.

"After another quarter of biscuit, I was really thirsty, but dare not take more than two small mouthfuls of precious water before setting out and travelling cautiously until my star faded in the eerie light of dawn. Sitting under a bush, I took a small mouthful of water to enable my parched mouth to manage the remainder of the biscuit. Still famished, I looked longingly at the remaining one, still sealed in its foil wrapping, but knew it must be kept for later. After another few sips of water, I struggled on, only settling down for a few hours of fitful sleep under a large bush during the hottest part of the day.

"Perhaps I should mention that I was still in territory under the control of Isil and so had to keep a sharp lookout for the familiar pickup trucks, although the ground was often too rough for them. Fortunately, there was no sign of any Isil fighters at first and only one or two distant sightings of their outposts and vehicles later as I neared the Turkish border. I did, however, try to avoid the occasional shepherd looking after a few sorry-looking animals grazing on the extremely sparse grass. None of them took any notice of me, even when looking in my direction. It was as if I was invisible!

"My flask appeared to be half empty by nightfall and I was now almost light-headed with dehydration. In desperation, I took several small mouthfuls and then felt very guilty. Suddenly, I remembered the parting words of Jesus about being with me always. If he wanted me to get to the Turkish border, then it would happen and I would not die of thirst. I even dared to drink a little more and began to feel better.

"I walked most of the night after managing to find my guiding star; it was much easier than the stop-start process during the day. At breakfast, I finished the remainder of my last biscuit and had a good drink of water without even thinking what I was doing. Suddenly worried, I shook the flask anxiously: to my astonishment it still felt and sounded half full! Of course, I was ignorant then of the Bible accounts of the prophet Elijah and the widow's jug of oil and jar of flour that lasted all through a long famine, or of Jesus feeding over 5,000 people with five small loaves and two fish.

"I set out on my now very sore feet. The going was getting harder because the further north I got, the hillier it became. After about an hour, cresting a ridge, I stopped to take one of my frequent sightings. To my amazement, a range of mountains had appeared in the far distance. "Those must surely be the mountains of Turkey!" I thought delightedly, travelling on with renewed energy after a celebration swig of water.

"About two hours later, bone weary and not paying sufficient attention to where I was going, I suddenly realized that two soldiers had appeared a short distance away. They were pointing their guns at me and shouting angrily. I put my hands up in despairing resignation, but then recognized their uniforms: I was in Turkey!"

Peter stopped and looked at his audience with some relief. It had not been easy to describe the remarkable change that had happened in his life and he wanted to make sure that everyone realized it had been God's grace alone that had brought it to pass.

"I'm almost finished," he said slowly. "I'm not allowed to go into details of what happened in Turkey and how I returned to the UK. Suffice to mention two remarkable things. The first is this; as the soldiers were escorting me to their frontier post, I indicated that I wanted to take a drink from my water flask. The senior man nodded and I took about three mouthfuls of water before it suddenly stopped flowing: the flask was completely empty!

"A little later, I was transferred to the area headquarters. There, after being given a meal and allowed a shower, I was interviewed by two army officers – a major and a captain, both of whom spoke fairly good English. One of their first questions was to ask why I wanted to return to England. Suspecting that they might not take kindly to the fact that I had become a Christian, I dodged the issue by merely saying that, after less than three weeks in Syria, I had realized the truth about the Islamic State and wanted to return to England to warn others not to go. The major looked at me intently for a moment and then ordered the captain to leave us.

"After the door had closed, he turned to me and said: "Now tell me what really happened; I'm a Christian, not a Muslim, and I'll be careful what I write in my report."

"With considerable astonishment and relief, I gave him a brief outline of my experience at the beheading, what had happened on the hill, and the miracle of the water flask. At the end, he gave me a smile and simply said, "Praise be to God! I'll do my best to write a report that helps to smooth your way through Turkey." With that, he shook hands and told an orderly to find me a bed where I could catch up on some sleep."

Peter smiled at the recollection before trying to sum up. "I'm not an evangelist who can give a carefully-reasoned exposition of the

Christian faith. As a four-month-old Christian, all I can offer is my personal experience of the love of God and of a Saviour who died on the Cross so that all who confess his Name can be forgiven and released from the power that sin has over our lives."

"Through my experience, I have learned the glorious truth that God patiently watches over each one of us. The moment he sees the merest hint of unease about the way we are conducting our lives, he does something to turn our eyes heavenward and is ready to respond if we make any sort of appeal for help. Only he can reveal the truth about Jesus to us and help us come to the foot of the Cross. If God is willing to respond to the cry of a sinner like me, he is more than ready to do the same for you! My prayer is that each person in this room, whatever their circumstances, will feel the touch of Jesus upon their lives tonight."

He stood for a moment with his head bowed and then seemed to make up his mind about something. "There are several people here for whom God has a message. I'll wait to one side of the platform at the end of the evening, ready to speak to anyone the Lord prompts to come forward. God bless you all!"

There was complete silence for a moment and then the whole room erupted in loud applause; there were even a few cheers. The church pastor came to the lectern and held up his hand for silence.

"We've been really privileged to hear a most amazing testimony to the saving grace of Almighty God," he said. "Some of you will have been greatly encouraged; others will need more time to allow the implications of Peter's story to sink in. John and I will be here at the end of the evening ready to spend time with anyone who would like prayer. However, there will be some in the audience who are being prompted by the Holy Spirit to respond to Peter's invitation; John tells me that he is being increasingly given what the New Testament calls "words of knowledge and prophecy" that have been a great help to folk in their church in Leeds."

"I'm now going to ask John to say a prayer to close the formal part of the evening. Then Mark will play quietly on the keyboard while those who need to leave can do so quietly and others can come forward. It only remains for me to thank you all for coming tonight and ask you to join me once again in showing our appreciation to Peter and John for blessing us in such a remarkable way!"

The pastor turned to his two guests with a beaming smile as everyone applauded for a second time. Hannah noticed that Peter was so moved that he was close to tears and had to turn away to recover. Strangely, it was this very human reaction that finally gave her the courage to go forward to speak to him.

"I'd like to go up and see Peter," she whispered. "Will you come with me?" Paul nodded, before turning to his sister to explain what they were about to do.

Sue smiled in delight. "Go forward while Ian and I hurry back to relieve the baby-sitter. I'm sure you can find your way home!"

Hannah and Paul joined the short queue waiting to see Peter. As Hannah watched him speaking to people, she was struck by his gentleness – a total contrast to what he must have been like a few months earlier. He invariably prayed briefly for each person or couple before they turned to leave.

When the man in front of Hannah departed, Paul gently pushed her forward in case she had something private she wanted to say, but she took his hand and they both went together.

Peter gave them a smile that lit up his face. "I'm glad you came together because Jesus has a message for you. When you met on the train to Sheffield last Monday, it was not a coincidence but part of his plan for your lives."

The young couple looked at him in complete shock: they had not told anybody that their acquaintance had been quite so recent or had started during the journey to Sheffield.

Peter seemed to know what they were thinking. "Don't worry," he assured them, "God only tells me things intended to help people, not embarrass them. I'm certain that your attendance here tonight is no accident. Jesus wants you to know that he loves you and longs for you to find new life in him. It may not be easy – as I'm finding to my cost – but nothing else could be more satisfying than having Jesus as a friend! Finally, and this is a word you may not understand now, Jesus is inviting you to "seek righteousness." Please hang on to that phrase; I believe it to be important."

Peter looked at them for a moment. They had never seen eyes so full of love and understanding before.

"May I pray for you?" he said quietly.

Hannah and Paul bowed their heads while Peter prayed in a way that seemed to surround them in glory. All the young couple could remember later was that they were being entrusted to the love, power, and mercy of God: that Jesus would become real to them and draw them to himself.

Hannah was shedding tears by the time the short prayer was finished. Peter asked permission to hug her and murmured, "God bless you and keep you!"

Then he shook hands with Paul and whispered: "Look after her – you have a remarkable future together – and remember the message "seek righteousness"!"

As Paul thanked him, he was extremely moved but still very perplexed. How was it possible to hear from God so directly? He took Hannah's hand and led her away. Outside in the cool air they walked arm in arm back towards Sue and Ian's house.

After Hannah had dabbed her eyes, she simply said: "I'm so glad we were able to come tonight. I need time for all this to sink in, but I believe it's a turning point in my life. I've not thought much about God, even when I've been with my parents to church on special occasions."

"It's the same for me," Paul replied, "even though I've probably been to church more than you have."

CHAPTER 18

Sue and Ian were wise enough not to quiz Paul and Hannah on their return to the house and simply sat with them at the kitchen table having a bedtime drink. Sue even had the insight to restore a sense of normality.

"When you come down for breakfast, please bring anything you'd like put in the washing machine," she said. "I'll also do any socks you have by hand."

"No, please, I'll do our smelly socks!" Hannah laughed. "You have more than enough to do."

"When is your lunch hour, Ian?" Paul asked out of the blue.

"I usually take the 12:15 slot, but must return an hour later to take over from my assistant," Ian replied. "Why do you ask?"

"Because I'd like to take you all out to lunch tomorrow as a small thank-you for having us to stay with you. Do you know of a restaurant that would be suitable for Toby?"

"That's a very kind of you, although the real treat for us is to see you again after so long and to meet Hannah for the first time," Sue said. "I've one of my special trifles in the 'fridge, ready to celebrate your visit, but we can have that in the evening."

After breakfast, Hannah washed the socks to the accompaniment of the washing machine's quiet rumbling as it dealt with their other clothes as part of the first Monday morning wash.

"Washing never ends with a toddler!" Sue remarked wryly as she prepared the next load. "I've a friend looking in for morning coffee shortly; she's got a little girl of three and Toby enjoys their visit. I expect you and Paul would prefer to have a look around the town? Toby and I could either meet you at the restaurant or you could come back here first."

The centre of Haltwhistle was so close that Paul and Hannah opted to return at 11:45 so that they could all go back together.

After spending half an hour happily exploring the centre of the town and beginning to think of coffee, they happened to pass a women's boutique. Paul noticed that Hannah's eyes were drawn to a mannequin wearing a white short-sleeved blouse printed with a variety of small flowers: a very summery and colourful display.

"That would look good on you!" Paul said. "If you like it, I'll get it for you as a holiday present."

"But you've spent too much on me already!" Hannah exclaimed, only for Paul to shake his head. "Rubbish! I can give my girlfriend a present if I want, and I do want!"

A short time later, they were sipping coffee in a nearby café with a carrier bag beside Hannah's chair. She was looking at her companion with a smile that set his pulse racing.

"You're the most generous man I know," she whispered.

"And there I was, foolishly believing you didn't know any others!" he teased her.

To his delight, she appeared wearing the blouse just as they were about to set out for lunch with Sue and Toby.

The happy group went down the hill towards the town centre with Toby dozing in his pushchair after an energetic playtime with his small friend. Hannah asked if she could take over the task and was soon pointing out things of interest to the boy as they passed. Sue, walking with her brother a short distance behind, noticed that Toby had perked up again, delighted to be the focus of attention.

"Hannah would make a good mother," Sue said quietly. "Are you in love with her?"

Paul looked at his sister fondly; Sue had always been blunt and to the point.

"Yes, but she's asked me to take things slowly. She's never had a boyfriend before," he whispered. Then, as Hannah seemed to be fully occupied with her new charge, he explained a little further.

"We only met last Monday morning. When I 'phoned mum from Sheffield station to say I was bringing a girl in place of John, I didn't tell her that we'd only just met on the train: she might have been rather shocked! As it turned out, they got on like a house on fire and she really took Hannah to her heart, as did dad. Normally, I'm not so rash, but there seemed to be something special about Hannah."

Sue nodded. "Yes, mum 'phoned to tell me that you might be bringing a really nice girl up the Pennine Way."

"Hannah only agreed to change her original plan of exploring in the Peak District and come with me at the last minute," Paul continued. "For the first few days we referred to ourselves as walking companions – incidentally, she's a much better walker than John – but on Friday evening at the pub in Tan Hill, I asked her to be my girlfriend and she agreed, provided we took things slowly."

Then he suddenly remembered the previous evening. "Telling you about our meeting on the train, reminds me that Peter astonished us last night by declaring something no other human being could possibly know – apart, that is, from somebody who had been in the same carriage. I quote his exact words: "Jesus has a message for you. When you met on the train to Sheffield last Monday, it was not a coincidence but part of his plan for your lives." He also said Jesus wanted us to know that he loves us and longs for us to find new life in him, adding that we must "seek righteousness", although we wouldn't understand this phrase immediately."

Sue pondered for a moment. "I think I can give you a clue. Although all Christians are expected to seek to live a righteous life, there's something even more crucial; one of the names for God in the Old Testament translates as "The Lord Our Righteousness" and the New Testament teaches that we must be clothed in the righteousness of Jesus because we have none of our own...."

She paused suddenly to call out a change of direction to Hannah and watched rather anxiously as Toby's pushchair was manœuvred across the road.

"The restaurant's 100 yards on the right!" she called. Hannah nodded and Toby poked his head out of the pushchair to wave at his mother. Sue laughed happily as she turned back to her brother to finish what she had been saying.

"Ian tells me that you plan to take a walk up to the Pennine Way and Hadrian's Wall this afternoon while Toby has his rest. He's left a sketch of the route beside telephone on the shelf by the front door. Tell Hannah what I've just told you and take one of our small Bibles with you in case God gives you any more clues. In fact, you can keep it for your return journey."

"Thanks Sue, you've been a real help," Paul whispered as he hurried forward to open the door of the restaurant for the pushchair. Thankfully they managed to find a table that could fit them all in.

A waitress brought up a high chair. Sue was about lift Toby into it when he shook his head.

"Anna do it," he said and held out his arms towards Hannah.

Sue grinned as she stood back. "He's really taken a shine to you!" she said. "Be careful, he's quite heavy."

However, she was surprised when Hannah lifted her young son with almost effortless ease and deposited him safely in the chair.

"You forget that I've got a really fit PE teacher for a girlfriend," boasted Paul, guiding Hannah a chair beside Toby, who chortled in delight.

"I'll deal with you later!" she whispered, but her happy smile took the edge off her words.

Sue, grinning at this exchange, took the seat on the other side of Toby and left a space for her husband between Paul and herself. She selected main courses from the small menu for herself, Toby and Ian, whilst Hannah and Paul did the same. The friendly waitress brought some cold drinks, and, while Hannah kept Toby happy by talking to him, Paul and his sister caught up on some family news.

Ian's arrival coincided with the delivery of food to the table. "Sorry to be late! There always seems to be an urgent and complicated prescription when it's time to go to lunch."

The lunch was a great success even though Ian could only be with them for barely an hour. Hannah felt increasingly relaxed in the company of such a friendly couple and their delightful two-year-old son. She was sorry when it was time to go.

When they were halfway home, Toby decided he wanted to walk and insisted that it must be Hannah who held his hand. One of his reasons became clear when they passed a toy shop and he made a beeline for the open door.

"It's a long time since I've been in a shop like this!" Hannah laughed as she guided him inside. Sue was about to follow when Paul stopped her. "I think Hannah's enjoying herself!" he whispered.

"Toby certainly is, but I'm worried he may start demanding something," Sue said, anxiously looking through the window as her son disappeared behind a display stand. It was not long, however, before they appeared again with Toby waving a small car.

"Look mum nice ka, vroom vroom!" he said triumphantly.

"CAR not ka, dear," Sue responded automatically. "That's very kind of Auntie Hannah. Have you said thank you?"

The little lad immediately stopped and put his arms around Hannah as far as they would reach. "Tank you, tank you!" came a small muffled voice.

She stooped down and lifted him up. "You're very welcome," she whispered as she kissed the top of his head.

That was the moment Paul definitely decided he was going to ask Hannah to marry him.

It was only when they reached the bottom of the hill not far from home that Hannah deposited her young charge back in his pushchair for Sue to push him back to the house. Paul followed with Hannah holding his arm.

"You were amazingly good with him and very generous too!" he said fondly.

"It was a pleasure to see his delight," Hannah retorted. "Anyway Sue and Ian have been so hospitable to me!"

Paul and Hannah set out from the house just after two o'clock. This time, however, they did not turn south into the centre of Haltwhistle but in the opposite direction up the steep hill that led to the fells north of the Tyne valley. Their plan was to join the Pennine Way as it ran for a short distance east-west along the line of Hadrian's Wall before turning north again towards the Scottish border. A note on Ian's sketch map suggested stopping at a distinctive crag just over two miles along the path and spending a little time exploring.

Sue had given Paul a small Bible to put in his map satchel before they left the house. "I've put a slip of paper in at Psalm 145," she said. "After you've found some quiet spot, I suggest you read aloud the passage I've noted down; it's very pertinent to last night and what we were speaking about a short time ago."

The steep road soon left the outskirts of Haltwhistle and cut through fields that lay peacefully under the afternoon sun. The air smelt delightfully fresh after the rain of the previous night and a couple of brief showers during the morning.

Hannah almost bounced along in happy anticipation of her first view of the two-thousand-year-old landmark. If she had known all that would happen that afternoon, she would have scarcely been able to contain her excitement.

"It's lovely to walk so freely without our rucksacks!" she exclaimed. Paul looked at her with pleasure: her face seemed to be shining with happiness.

Soon the fields petered out and moorland took over. About one and a half miles out of Haltwhistle, they came to a junction beside a rather lonely-looking pub and crossed over into a narrow lane leading to the intersection with the Pennine Way. They were now on the type of path that had become so familiar over the last few days.

The scenery became gradually more spectacular as they climbed the grassy path beside the ruins of the ancient wall, some sections original and others reconstructed using original blocks of stone where possible. Hannah was amazed as they crested the hill and saw the undulating ridge that the soldier-builders had followed so carefully. Almost at their feet was a square marked out by a low stone wall; clearly the site of one of the frequent lookout posts or small forts that would have been manned by Roman soldiers.

"This is extraordinary!" Hannah murmured. "Thank you so much for bringing me." She squeezed Paul's hand gently.

"Those legionnaires must have been extremely versatile," Paul exclaimed. "Just think! Those stones were last shaped by a Roman hand, using simple tools, over two thousand years ago!"

They followed the path that led along the south side of the wall; it was nearly three feet thick and varied in height – typically about four feet. Occasional small wooden gates had been inserted, presumably for the convenience of shepherds and their sheep.

"The amount of stone needed must have been enormous when the wall was at its original height!" Paul exclaimed. "I wonder if we'll see any complete sections."

Sometimes the slope was so steep that stone steps had been set into the turf. The young couple were increasingly glad that they had no luggage to carry. They were going generally uphill and the view was breathtaking, especially behind them to the west and south over the Tyne valley.

Eventually, at the top of a steep incline, they reached a square-tapered trig point. "We've reached about 350m," Paul announced.

The path now descended beside a more recently constructed wall of smaller stones. A lake was now visible in the distance.

"That water is Crag Lough according to Ian's map," Paul said. "He suggests we stop before going as far as that. Shortly after crossing a road not far below us the wall climbs a steep crag – marked with a red arrow – where there are plenty of places to perch for a rest and enjoy a view of the surroundings."

"I'd like to stop there," Hannah said. "It sounds a good place to consider what happened last night. We need to get off the path anyway so that we're not interrupted!"

Ten minutes later, they were scrambling up the extremely stony flank of the crag to find a flat rock wide enough for them both to sit on.

"It's a good job we wore boots and not trainers!" Hannah laughed, as they finally found a rock well away from the path.

She produced a bottle of water from her shoulder bag. They shared some of it while Paul opened the small Bible at Psalm 145 where his sister had inserted a slip of paper with "8 to 9, and 17 to 19" written on it.

"I presume that means we should read those verses," he said and proceeded to do so while Hannah listened.

The majestic words flowed over her: "The Lord is gracious and compassionate, slow to anger and rich in love…good to all…has compassion on all he has made……The Lord is righteous in all his ways…loving towards all he has made…near to all who call on him, to all who call on him in truth…fulfils the desires of those who fear him…he hears their cry and saves them."

Hannah turned to Paul. "That's exactly how it happened for Peter – when he called on God in truth," she said softly. "In fact, he was so moved at the end of sharing his experience that he shed a few tears. That was what really tipped the balance for me and I just had to go up and speak to him. God the Father and Jesus were so completely real to him. That man has been totally transformed!"

"I'm glad you did want to go up because it stopped me being frozen in my chair," Paul replied. "If we'd stayed put, Peter would not have told us something that no human being could possibly have known. That's what clinched it for me; I knew that I had to take God seriously and look at my own relationship with him, or lack of it!"

Hannah looked pensive for a moment. "You remember Peter said how he asked God a question – two, in fact? So far, your sister has helped us by giving us these verses from the Old Testament. Do you think we could ask God to give us something from the New Testament?"

"I suppose we could try," Paul said doubtfully, "but don't forget that Peter was desperate and needed a miracle. We've already had one, in a sense: the words Peter said to us about our first meeting being on a train."

"I'll try to pray," Hannah said. She shut her eyes.

"Lord God," she whispered rather nervously. "I've never prayed aloud before and Paul and I are almost completely ignorant of the Bible. Like Peter, we feel so very far away from you. We are also confused by Peter's last words about the importance of seeking righteousness. All we do know is that we could not possibly claim to be righteous. Would you please show us something about this from the New Testament? Thank you. Amen."

She opened her eyes and looked at Paul. He smiled at her uncertainly and took her hand, leaving the Bible rather precariously perched on his lap, optimistically open somewhere in the New Testament. They waited.

Suddenly, they felt a slight breeze on their cheeks. A few of the thin pages of the little book flipped over to St Paul's second letter to the Christians in the city of Corinth (2 Corinthians, Chapter 5). They looked at the two pages revealed. Was it their imagination or did some of the words in a short paragraph beginning at verse 16 appear to be brighter than the rest of the text?

Paul began to read them: "...if anyone is in Christ, he is a new creation....God was reconciling the world to himself in Christ, not counting men's sins against them....God made him who had no sin to be sin for us, so that in him we might become the righteousness of God."

Hannah looked as stunned as Paul felt. "God actually cares enough about us to answer us!" she said slowly. "I'm totally convinced. I want to become a Christian; not simply someone who goes to church on special occasions but one who is prepared to allow God to change them. Do you want to join me in asking Jesus to help us?"

"I certainly do!" Paul replied. "But how do we pray?"

"Do you remember what Jesus answered when Peter asked the same thing?" Hannah said, as she struggled to remember.

Then it suddenly came to her: "My blood was shed for you, just believe, ask and receive."

With one accord, they knelt down hand-in-hand on the hard ground beside the rock.

"Lord Jesus," Paul prayed. "Please forgive us for our neglect of you all these years. I, for one, should have known better because I've had the example of the strong faith of my parents and sister. We don't deserve your grace and mercy, but please forgive us and cleanse us from all unrighteousness. Please show us how to make you Lord and follow your will for our lives. Thank you. Amen."

"Amen, Amen!" Hannah echoed, and they waited in silence, not sure what to do next.

A gentle gust of wind came a second time. They immediately looked towards the Bible, now lying on the rock where they had been sitting, but it was still open at the same passage as before.

As they looked more carefully, however, eight short words seemed to stand out so clearly from the page that they almost glowed: "…the old has gone, the new has come!"

Their hearts were filled with joy. God had received their prayer and responded. They would never be the same again. They both tried to verbalize their thanks at the same time, but everything came out in a jumble; it did not matter because they seemed to know instinctively that the Lord looks, not at the words, but at the heart.

CHAPTER 19

It was quite painful kneeling on the rough ground, especially for Hannah who was wearing shorts, and so Paul helped her up to sit on the rock again. Sitting beside her, he looked at her knees; they had grit on them and some sharp bits seemed to have penetrated the skin. Taking out his handkerchief, he gently brushed the debris away, only to find that some tiny wounds remained and looked quite sore. He reached over to the bottle of water on the rock behind her and sprinkled a little on a clean portion of the cloth.

"I hope you don't mind me bathing the sore skin. It will hopefully feel better!" he said.

Hannah remained silent but thanked him with a smile and a nod of the head. Her eyes were still full of tears. He had never seen her looking so young and vulnerable and yet so peaceful and full of joy.

He came to a decision. Although they were both in an emotional state and this was probably not the ideal time, he was not only determined to ask her to marry him but to do so now.

He stood up and tenderly pulled her up with him. Turning to face her, he looked deep into her eyes.

"Hannah, will you marry me?" he whispered.

Hannah looked up at him, but with no hint of surprise. The most wonderful smile he had ever seen gradually spread outwards from her lips until her whole face had lit up.

"Yes, Oh yes," she breathed. "I've been hoping you would ask all day!"

Paul, overflowing with emotion, took her in his arms and they gently came together for their first real kiss. Hannah then laid her cheek on his chest as tears of emotion streamed down her face. Paul continued to hold her close; the love he felt was like a liquid flowing into as well as over her, just as real as the moisture on his chest from her tears.

They had no idea how long they remained clasped together, but eventually he led her down on to the path and back the way they had come. They were conscious that they were passing through scenery that had delighted them earlier, but they were too full of happiness to pay much attention now.

Back on the road and heading down towards Haltwhistle, Paul looked at his watch for the first time since they had first sat on the rock and opened the Bible. It was now five minutes to six and they had been out for almost four hours. Hopefully, Sue would not be worried, although they knew she was planning a light meal at seven o'clock when Toby had been tucked up in bed.

Fifteen minutes later, Sue opened her front door to find two beaming young people on the doorstep.

"It doesn't look as if I need to ask you how the walk was!" she exclaimed.

"We've both become Christians!" Hannah blurted out.

"And Hannah has agreed to marry me!" Paul added excitedly.

Sue hugged them both with tears in her eyes. "I've been praying since last night that the Holy Spirit would bring you to the foot of the Cross," she said. "Your engagement is the icing on the cake! Come and tell us all the news."

They went indoors and Toby rushed out of the kitchen in his pyjamas to greet them waving his new car. He held it up for Hannah to admire; she scooped him up in her arms and carried him into the kitchen where Ian was just finishing a cup of tea.

There was general rejoicing as Paul and Hannah shared their experience in a little more detail, leaving some things untold because, somehow, they were too special and personal to talk about.

As Sue finished preparing the meal, Ian took Hannah upstairs, still holding Toby, to help put the little lad to bed.

Meanwhile, Sue made a generous suggestion. "It would be good for Hannah to wear an engagement ring as soon as possible. It's going to be quite difficult to find one in a hurry. After Haltwhistle, your next opportunity will probably be Skipton, if you're going to call in on Mark again."

"When Ian asked me to marry him," she continued, "he had very little money and so we chose the simplest ring we could find: a nine-carat gold one with four tiny channel-set synthetic cubic zircons. I can't wear it any more because my finger has thickened slightly as I've got older and the band is too thin to enlarge. More recently, Ian replaced it with a diamond ring and so I would be very happy for Hannah to use it temporarily, or even to keep it if she likes. Anyway, I'll give it to you to see what you think."

"That's very kind of you Sue. Thank you. It'll save getting something in a rush," Paul said gratefully. "By the way, after supper, I must 'phone mum and dad with the good news."

"Then use our landline; we have free evening calls," Sue offered. "You might also like to book that nice farmhouse in Dufton for tomorrow night. I'm not trying to get rid of you, but you did say you only wanted to be here for two nights. In fact, if it helps, I could drop you both in Alston by about ten o'clock, say. It would give me a change of scenery and Toby would love the ride."

The evening passed so very happily for them all. Sarah and Jack were absolutely delighted with both lots of good news and Simon even 'phoned his younger brother to let him know about the engagement.

"I knew it was in the offing!" Mark said knowingly. "I'm so happy for you. Come and see me on your way back. In fact, stay for two nights and I'll drive you to Harrogate next Saturday; Hannah would love to see it."

Then he paused in dismay. "Oh dear, I've suddenly remembered I'll be away from Skipton from mid-morning Saturday until Sunday evening. If you can get here by Thursday night, however, I could take Friday off work. I'll be happy to pick you up in Gargrave late afternoon. You can update me on the dongle affair over another Italian dinner!"

"That sounds a good plan," Paul replied. "We can make it if we save a day by using the Carlisle to Leeds train. There's a station near Dufton – Appleby, I think – and we could go south about 35 miles to Horton-in-Ribblesdale."

"Fine! I look forward to seeing you on Thursday. I left Hannah's bed made up in the hope you would come again! Let me know about the pick-up; I can manage any time after five-thirty. I'll book a table at the Italian restaurant for eight o'clock."

As soon as Paul came off the 'phone he reported Mark's invitation before calling the Dufton farmhouse to book a twin room for the following night. He was able to speak to the farmer's wife, Mary, who said how much she looked forward to welcoming them a second time so soon after their first visit.

"They really are a splendid family!" Hannah exclaimed.

Paul nodded in agreement as he made a final call to the guesthouse in Horton, where they had stayed on the way north, and was pleased to find that their old room was free for Wednesday night.

While all this was going on, Ian used his laptop to find out that trains from Appleby to Horton run roughly every two hours and take about fifty minutes. Looking at his road map, he reckoned that Appleby was not much more than four miles from Dufton.

"Just a mere stroll!" Hannah murmured.

They all sat comfortably in the small parlour with a bedtime drink. Sue began to give some advice about finding good churches to attend when Hannah and Paul got back to their respective homes.

"It needs to be friendly and welcoming, but, most important, have biblically-based teaching," she said.

This subject brought them neatly on to the subject of the wedding and Hannah described the little Anglican church in her home village a short distance south of Sherborne.

"My parents go there fairly regularly and will want us to get married there," she said. "Our farmhouse is quite large and probably big enough for some sort of reception afterwards. Also we have three spare bedrooms, two of them double, and so you, Sarah and Jack, and Mark can all stay there. Hopefully, you can cope with Toby in your bedroom! I can sleep on the settee downstairs for one night and I'm sure my uncle will put Paul up; he lives on the outskirts of Sherborne."

"Hannah and I haven't had much time to discuss all this!" Paul added. "But we reckon the earliest we could get married is during the Christmas school vacation because one of us will need to give a term's notice. Christmas Day is on a Thursday this year and most schools will break up the previous Friday. So we could get married on the Sunday afternoon, if that's possible, and have a very short honeymoon somewhere for three nights before the holiday rush and then come back to the farm for Christmas."

"The other problem is the weather at that time of year!" he added, now slightly worried.

"We'll get there somehow!" Ian promised.

Hannah looked thoughtful. "I'd just like a simple wedding with the immediate families," she said. "No palaver!"

Then she looked at Paul. "I'm the one who should change schools; Paul is too valuable where he is and he's only been there for two terms. Anyway, Basingstoke is much closer to the countryside and decent walks than Tooting!"

"In a year or two's time, you might even move north somewhere closer to us," Sue said hopefully. "We'd both be delighted; everybody seems rather far away at the moment!" she added wistfully.

"We need to seek God's will before making too many plans!" Ian said with a broad smile. "Shall we have a short time of prayer before we go to bed?"

CHAPTER 20

Sue drove Hannah and Paul the fifteen miles or so to Alston the following morning. Toby, carefully strapped into his child's seat, was delighted to have Hannah all to himself in the back of the car. He talked almost non-stop, although she could not make out all he was saying and his mother had to interpret occasionally. Hannah felt sad to be leaving such a happy and friendly family and wished that she could be there to see Toby growing up. At least they would soon be part of her family!

Just before ten o'clock, they were sitting in a café in Alston having a last cup of coffee together. After returning to the car to collecting their rucksacks, they thanked Sue once again for all her kindness and hospitality before kissing her and Toby goodbye.

His little faced crumpled as he began to realize that they were leaving and Hannah slipped a small bouncy ball into his hand in the hope it would deflect his attention. She had bought it in the toyshop at the same time as Toby's car.

The young couple walked slowly down the road leading to the point at which the Pennine Way re-commenced its southbound route, turning every so often to wave at the two increasingly small figures in the distance.

Three hours later, Paul and Hannah reached the top of Cross Fell, at 893m the higher of the four peaks to be encountered on the way to Dufton. Although there had been rain recently, it was now beautifully sunny and the view across the valley to the distant Lake District in the east was superb. They found a good place and sat on Paul's waterproof to soak up the scenery and eat the sandwiches Sue had thoughtfully provided.

When they had finished eating, Paul took Sue's old engagement ring from his pocket and knelt beside Hannah.

"Sue and I were worried that we might not have a chance to choose an engagement ring that you like before we get back to Sheffield or even London," he said, "and so she has given me a ring for you to use temporarily. It was the first, fairly cheap, engagement ring she had until it became too small for her finger and Ian bought her one with a real solitaire diamond; this only has small manufactured cubic zircons, I'm afraid!"

He took her hand and kissed it gently before slipping the ring on her finger: fortunately it fitted. "This comes with more love than I can possibly express. Regard it as a sort of IOU from me to get you a ring you really like eventually!"

Hannah looked down at her hand for a moment. When she turned back to him her eyes were shining.

"It's lovely! Just what I would have chosen anyway and so sensible for an active person like me who handles a lot of gym equipment; anything with more prominent stones would get damaged and I don't want to keep having to remove it!"

"I'll get you something similar with small real diamonds then, although it would be sensible to stick to nine-carat gold because it's tougher than the higher-carat alloys," Paul said as he stood up and drew her with him. "I love you so much that I want you to have something really nice!"

They came together in a kiss that lingered as they stood blissfully in the warm sunshine. Then Hannah laid her cheek against his chest and remained there for several minutes gazing out over the broad valley that lay before them.

"I'm so happy!" she murmured, whereupon he kissed her again so lovingly that she shed several tears, giving him the opportunity to kiss them from her cheeks.

Reluctantly, they packed up, shouldered their packs and moved on. They still walked at Hannah's normal fast pace, but the giving of the ring seemed to have cemented their sense of togetherness even more than before.

They kept glancing at each other with little expressions of pleasure and Paul was suddenly filled with an almost overwhelming tenderness for his fiancée. It had first occurred, but with much less intensity, during the meal in the pub at Standedge on the first night of their trek up the Pennine Way. Outwardly, Hannah was strong and competent, but inside there was a vulnerability that pulled at his heart strings. He was determined to protect her to the utmost of his ability.

Such was their fitness after so much exercise over the last few days that they followed the path almost effortlessly from one peak to another until commencing the downward descent from Knock Fell to Dufton.

The view over the Eden Valley was superb and prompted Hannah to exclaim, "We're so fortunate to see it like this! So much better than when we were coming north on this leg of the journey."

It really seemed to be no time at all since having lunch that they found themselves ringing the farmhouse doorbell. Heather, the farmer's friendly daughter, opened the door with a flourish.

"Welcome!" she cried. "When you left last Sunday morning, we had no idea you'd be back by Wednesday evening, because you told us that you planned to spend two nights in Haltwhistle. Mother couldn't believe you would be able to walk so far so quickly!"

While these words were tumbling out she hugged Hannah and shook Paul's hand enthusiastically.

"We cheated; my brother-in-law saved us a few miles on Sunday and my sister gave us a lift all the way to Alston this morning!" Paul confessed.

Mary emerged from the kitchen at the sound of their voices and more hugs followed. Then she noticed Hannah's ring.

"You're engaged!" she exclaimed. "I'm so glad. Many congratulations to you both. I knew it wouldn't be long before you had good news: it was something about the way you looked at each other three nights ago! Do tell us all about it over the meal. We're having beef tonight. Our old friends, Brian, Sue and Rachel are still with us. Heather will take you up to your room; it's the same as last time."

The meal was almost as good as it had been the first time, although very little could reach the standard of Mary's chicken casserole in Hannah's opinion. As before, Brian was the life and soul of the party, supported by his charming wife.

Their daughter Rachel chatted happily to Ted, the stalwart son of Fred and his wife. As last time, the farmer had lapsed into a benevolent silence after saying a heartfelt grace at the beginning of the meal; he was clearly trying to let go of the pressure of a busy day's work.

Poor Mary and Heather had to keep getting up and attending to everyone's needs and it was not until the cold desert and cups of tea and coffee had been provided that Mary was able to turn to Hannah and Paul.

"Now tell us all your news. I sense there is more than the splendid fact that you've just become engaged!"

"You're right, although I've no idea how you know!" Paul replied. "My proposal to Hannah – at no less a place than Hadrian's Wall – came a few minutes after we'd prayed together and asked Jesus to be our Saviour."

There was such general rejoicing at this news that Hannah realized she and Paul were not only in the company of delightful people but ones who really cared about the welfare of two relative strangers. Her heart warmed at the knowledge and it took a second or two before she became aware that Paul was inviting her to recount the events of the previous Sunday evening.

"It all started," she said slowly, "when Paul's sister and her husband took us to their church in Haltwhistle to hear the testimony of an ex-jihadist recruit to Islamic State in Syria. His pseudonym was

Peter to protect his identity but his experience of the grace of God was amazing to say the least ...."

To say that Hannah's listeners were glued to her words is an understatement. All the women in the room were in tears by the time she recounted what Peter had said to them at the end.

"So you see," Paul took over, "it took us some time to let all this sink in, but, on Monday afternoon, we walked up to Hadrian's Wall intending to spend time looking at the small Bible my sister had given me. She had put a bookmark in Psalm 145 and I read part of it aloud as we sat halfway up the stony flank of one of the crags overlooking the fascinating sight. The whole passage seemed to be so relevant to Peter's experience that we dared to ask God to reveal himself to us.

"We could scarcely believe it when there was a puff of wind and some pages of the Bible flipped over to 2 Corinthians, Chapter 5 and we read, "...if anyone is in Christ, he is a new creation....God was reconciling the world to himself in Christ, not counting men's sins against them....God made him who had no sin to be sin for us, so that in him we might become the righteousness of God." After all, Peter's last two words to us had been "seek righteousness"!

"This prompted us to kneel down and respond in the best way we could, before waiting quietly wondering if we had prayed correctly. When we looked at the passage again, a few words literally seemed to shine out of the page, "...the old has gone, the new has come!", and we knew the Lord had heard us and responded."

"Thank you for sharing something so personal," Brian said. "I never cease to be amazed how God calls people in all sorts of ways; there's no set pattern. Not surprisingly, very few people have awesome testimonies like Peter, but it led you two to a remarkable one of your own!"

He thought for a moment and then turned to Mary. "Mary," he said, "before we help you clear the table could we all pray for this dear young couple? Also I think it would good to pray for Peter's protection; he's likely to incur a lot of enmity from his erstwhile colleagues if he's discovered, even more so for daring to speak about Jesus as Saviour. Fred, would you like to start?"

The farmer had been almost silent since saying a prayer at the beginning, but he now readily obliged and prayed beautifully for Paul and Hannah. His wife followed with some very sensitive and perceptive words and even Rachel joined in. Hannah was dabbing her eyes before they had finished.

It was left to Brian to pray for Peter, asking for God's protection to surround him and give him the ability to share his story in such a way that many people would be moved to respond.

Everyone helped with the clearing up and it was not long before they all sat down again with another hot drink.

Mary asked Paul and Hannah what they were planning to do the next day. Paul explained that they were aiming to catch a train from Appleby to Ribblehead at 12:36, the station just south of the Ribblehead viaduct. They would then walk back to look at the famous structure from below and carry on towards the 730m top of the Whernside ridge before walking back past Ribblehead and down Horton where they had booked accommodation. Earlier tomorrow morning, however, he wondered if it would be nice to walk to the top of Dufton Pike.

To his surprise, Rachel answered.

"A very good idea!" she said. "There's a good five-mile circular route that goes north up the Pennine Way, then climbs the northern flank of Dufton Pike, comes down the south-eastern side and back into the village. You'll love it," she ended rather wistfully.

Suddenly, Hannah found herself saying: "Would you like to come with us if your parents haven't planned a more exciting trip somewhere?" She smiled invitingly at the girl.

Ted whispered, "Go on, you'd enjoy it!"

Sue nodded encouragingly. "It would also be a nice change from walking with us old folk!" she said.

Rachel looked delighted. "I'd love to come. If we go at about eight-thirty there'll be plenty of time."

She paused for a moment. "Does the train actually go over the Ribblehead viaduct? That must be wonderful!"

Paul nodded and smiled at her. "As a thank-you for acting as our guide to Dufton Pike, I'd be happy to buy you a day-return ticket to Ribblehead, provided of course that there's a train coming north again at a reasonable time. The journey takes about fifty minutes."

"That's very kind of you, but I do have some money," Rachel said, looking rather embarrassed that her hint had been so obvious.

"Not if you've only just finished A-levels," Hannah cut in quickly. "We'd be happy to treat you."

"That's settled then," Paul said, "subject to checking the train times." Then he saw that Sue was already tapping the screen of a small tablet she had produced from her bag.

It only took her a minute to find an answer: "The 12:36 gets in at 13:17, and there are trains coming back at 14:05 and 16:01."

She turned to her husband. "It looks as if we're going to have a nice afternoon in Appleby," she said. "If we leave here at midday, we can drop the young people off at the station and then have lunch somewhere and look around the town. When do you want to come back, Rachel?"

"If you're happy to do the whole walk with us, it'll have to be the 16:01. Otherwise, you could come as far as the viaduct and then return to the station to get the earlier train," Paul said.

"I'd love to do the whole walk," Rachel said hopefully, "if it's not making you spend too long in Appleby, mum?"

"Not to be outdone by all these kind deeds," Mary announced, "Heather and I will make you some cheese and tomato sandwiches to have on the train."

After a good sleep and an excellent breakfast, Rachel, Hannah and Paul set out for Dufton Pike. Joining the Pennine Way, they walked about two miles back the way they had come the previous evening before Rachel guided them on to the path that zigzagged up the northern flank of the fascinating 480m conical hill. Over halfway up, she told them to look behind them to the north-west where Knock Pike rose proudly in the middle distance, its top bathed in bright sunlight. This, however, was only the prelude to even more impressive views from the smooth grassy top of its larger twin.

At first, their eyes were drawn to the south-west where the broad expense of the Eden valley lay peacefully under wispy clouds that were moving at a sedate pace across the pale blue sky.

Then they turned towards the north-east and the wide sweep of the North Pennine ridge. Their delight propelled them forward a few steps. Paul heard Hannah gasp in astonishment; it may have been an optical illusion but the Pike seemed to be amazingly close to the massive bulk of another hill and only separated from it by a deep ravine.

"That's Brownber Hill," Rachel informed them.

"It almost feels as if one could topple down into the valley!" Hannah exclaimed.

Reluctantly, they moved on after a drink of water. Rachel was now much more talkative as she walked ahead with Hannah: no doubt Hannah's friendly enthusiasm had broken the ice.

Back at the farmhouse, Mary bustled out of the kitchen and insisted that they come in for a farewell cup of tea or coffee. Brian and Sue were already sitting at the kitchen table having their refreshments; a bag of sandwiches and three bananas sat beside them for the train journey and Rachel added them to her small rucksack together with the refilled bottles of water.

"There's no need to ask if you had a good time," Brian remarked with a big smile, "I can see that you did!"

"It was brilliant," Hannah replied, "and Rachel is an excellent guide – not even one wrong turn!"

Half an hour later, Hannah and Paul said their sad farewells to Mary and Heather, the latter having just completed her chambermaid duties. Both were quite overcome by the compliments they received and especially by Paul's promise to keep in touch and hopefully bring Hannah back one day for a short holiday in such a delightful place.

Brian and Sue dropped the travellers at Appleby station. While Paul went in to get the tickets, Rachel hugged her parents a temporary goodbye and Hannah promised to make sure they finished their walk up Whernside in plenty of time for her to catch the four o'clock train at Ribblehead.

The southbound train was only two minutes late leaving Appleby. Paul insisted that the two girls took the window seats and he sat beside Hannah next to the aisle. Rachel beamed at him and thanked him for his kindness in buying her ticket while she began to distribute the sandwiches. Thoughtfully, Mary had even included three small plastic plates with strict instructions to the girl to make sure she returned with them.

As they travelled south, Paul remarked on the fact that the train had begun its journey in Carlisle and would finish in Leeds, only thirty miles north of Sheffield.

"A real cross-country route that stops over a dozen times on the 120 mile journey, including Skipton where my younger brother lives," he said. "In fact, if he didn't have a car he could use this train to visit our parents in Sheffield."

"Paul's brother Mark has a good job in a computer software company in Skipton," Hannah informed Rachel. "He lives on his own in a small terraced house overlooking the town and we stayed a night with him on our trek up the Pennine Way. He's invited us to spend two nights on the way back so that he can take us to Harrogate for a day trip."

"In fact, we'll be in Skipton tomorrow evening after walking from Horton," Paul added. "By the way, there are three stops before we get to Ribblehead. After the third one, we must watch out for a long tunnel that comes shortly before the viaduct."

Rachel nodded excitedly; this cross-country journey by train was a novel experience for her. She began to talk animatedly about the passing scenery and the various places she had visited over the last few days with her parents.

Paul watched with pleasure as Hannah responded warmly to her youthful enthusiasm: it was as if they had been friends for years.

It was not long before Rachel mentioned an outing that had been a highlight for her.

"Last Sunday afternoon," she said shyly, "Ted took me for a climb up to High Cup Nick and back, although we kept to the Pennine Way and didn't try to scramble to the top!"

She blushed slightly and fell silent, looking out of the carriage window.

Shortly after stopping just outside the market town of Kirby Stephen, the train entered the more rugged landscape of the Yorkshire Moors.

"We're passing about five miles to the west of Great Shunner Fell," Paul said, quite out of the blue.

Hannah hurried to explain. "Great Shunner was one of the really high peaks we tackled several days ago. I seem to remember that it was a rather murky day!"

"Mainly because the clouds were almost touching the tops of the fells," Paul added.

The train continued to wind through the attractive landscape, until, after the third stop, Paul warned them to anticipate the mile-long Blea Moor tunnel and, shortly after, the 400m Ribblehead viaduct.

Even so, when the train slowly entered the Victorian feat of engineering, they were not prepared for the experience of travelling so high above the floor of the valley on a narrow bridge of stone. The two girls almost had their noses pressed to the window, as did many of the other passengers.

All too soon, the train pulled into Ribblehead station and they disembarked with quite a lot of other tourists. To their surprise, the station was quite busy.

The reason became apparent when it transpired that it was run by the Settle and Carlisle Railway Trust. There was even a visitor centre with an exhibition illustrating the building of the Ribblehead viaduct and Blea Moor tunnel.

"I suggest we walk first and look around when we come back for the four o'clock train," Paul said.

Hannah agreed, although Rachel looked a little embarrassed that they thought she needed to be accompanied back to the station. Hannah noticed and linked arms with her.

"The problem is that the next train is over three hours later!" she said. "If you miss it you would have to come to Horton with us for a meal and travel back from there."

For a moment, Rachel looked as if this possibility appealed to her until she realized it would mean a second journey to Appleby for one of her parents.

Two minutes later, they emerged from the narrow service road linking the station to the road running north-east to Hawes. The Railway Inn stood immediately opposite and displayed a prominent notice advertising fresh ground coffee.

Paul guided them up a gravel track beside the pub car park. They had barely gone a hundred yards when Rachel spied the long expanse of the Ribblehead viaduct less than a quarter of a mile away.

"There it is!" she exclaimed as she hurried towards the famous railway landmark. All twenty-four semicircular arches were clearly visible now, supported by graceful tapered-stone columns.

When the path neared the viaduct and veered left to go under one of the huge arches, the spectacle became really stunning. The columns were well over a metre wide at the base. Every sixth column was double the width of the others and truly massive.

As Rachel gazed up completely fascinated, Paul took her elbow in a brotherly gesture.

"Are you sure you shouldn't be aiming for civil or structural engineering rather than agriculture?" he whispered.

"I would have needed A-level physics and the college didn't offer it owing to the shortage of teachers!" Rachel said rather sadly.

"I'm sure Ted would prefer you to study agriculture," Paul said with a chuckle.

Rachel blushed. "Ted and I get on very well," she admitted, "but I think I'm too young for him!"

Hannah smiled kindly at her. "There can't be more than three years difference; that's nothing, particularly not after you've done a two-year agricultural course."

"He might not be prepared to wait that long," Rachel responded.

"He will if it's in God's plan for you to marry!" Hannah's words came out almost automatically. She was quite surprised at herself but then realized that her thoughts were beginning to be influenced by her new relationship with God.

"You're right, of course," Rachel agreed as she linked arms with her new friend and they walked on through the tall arch and saw before them a long ridge that ran in a roughly northerly direction and sloped gradually up to a peak.

"That's Whernside," Paul announced. "On the train, we were too intent on watching out for the viaduct to take much notice. We'll only have time to go up to a height of about 600m at the southern end of the ridge, quite a long way short of the 736m summit, but it will mean a climb of over 300m if you're ready?"

"You bet," Rachel muttered. "You two take walking seriously!"

Hannah laughed and took her by the hand as they marched enthusiastically onwards.

Paul guided them in a clockwise direction around the first section a circular tour of Whernside that he had quickly noted down from a map displayed at Ribblehead station. Their passage was helped considerably by small direction signs.

Eventually, the climb began in earnest; in the space of half a mile, they scaled 260m. Rachel took it in her stride. So much so, that not much more than an hour after leaving Ribblehead station, they reached the point at which Paul called a halt and reluctantly said they would have to turn back.

"Well," Hannah remarked, "Whernside itself is not an object of beauty but the views make up for it! What's that large ridge to the south of us?"

"I think it must be Ingleborough Hill," Paul said "Together with Whernside and Pen-y-Ghent, it forms the group of three major peaks in this region."

They descended the slope carefully but were then able to speed up considerably and it was not long before they reached the Railway Inn for coffee. Hannah had seen Rachel searching for her purse to treat them all as they entered the pub but got to the bar counter ahead of her.

"We're earning: you're not. You get yourself a drink at the station to take with you on the train," she whispered. "It's been a real pleasure having you with us!"

Rachel was really moved by her kindness. While they were standing waiting for the coffee to be prepared, she whispered: "May we exchange e-mail addresses?"

"I was going to suggest it," Hannah responded. "I'd love to keep in contact. You must come and stay with us when we have something bigger than a one-bedroom flat."

Paul had heard her words as Rachel put the tray of coffee on the table. "We're aiming for a two-bedroom place at least, once we decide where to look," he added.

Unfortunately, they could not linger over coffee and had to return to the station. There was just time for Rachel and Hannah to have a quick look around the visitor centre while Paul checked on the train timetable and consulted the local map again to make sure he knew how to get to Horton.

The northbound train was signalled and Rachel 'phoned her mother to let her know that she was just about to leave Ribblehead. The two girls hugged and promised to keep in touch. Rachel shyly thanked Paul for treating her to the rail journey.

Hannah and Paul remained on the platform waving to their new friend as the train pulled away.

A few minutes later, they were on the attractive lane that ran south to Horton. It was now late afternoon and the fields lay peacefully under the mellow sunshine, although well to the south of them there was a substantial amount of cloud.

"It looks as if we could have some rain later!" Paul remarked, but Hannah was too happy to care. Something had suddenly dawned on her.

"Do you know," she said, with a note of awe in her voice. "For someone who used to be a complete loner, I found it surprisingly easy to warm to Rachel and be really interested in her welfare and future. She actually asked if we could be friends and keep in touch!"

Paul took his fiancée by the hand, although this was a rather risky procedure on such a narrow road.

"Two things are changing you and helping you to come out of your shell," he said gently. "First, God is now in control of your life. Secondly, you have a fiancé who loves you and promises to encourage and support you."

Hannah gave a little cry, threw her arms around his neck and kissed him. "Thank you for those wonderful words!" she whispered.

Almost embarrassed by her outburst of emotion, she led the way down the narrow road at a brisk pace. The gradient was gently downwards, because they were now very close to the Ribble; in fact it was about half a mile east of the railway line that appeared from time to time on their left.

They passed through the attractive hamlet of Selside. The road veered slightly to the east and in the distance Hannah spotted a familiar landmark.

"Pen-y-Ghent!" she exclaimed in delight. "Can we please climb up there on our way back tomorrow?"

"Of course we can!" Paul laughed. "If we leave at eight-fifteen or so, there'll be plenty of time. We don't need to get to Skipton until five o'clock or soon after."

In Horton, they crossed the Ribble and went down the long road to the southern fringe of the village. Paul rang the doorbell of the guesthouse well before six o'clock. Andy, the young man who ran the small establishment with his wife, answered the door with a smile of welcome.

"I'm so glad to see you again!" he said. "My wife and I were worried that the businessman who called just before you left early last Thursday was up to no good, especially when he sent his chauffeur round about thirty minutes later to ask for your names and contact details! Of course, I said that they were confidential and could not be divulged."

Andy grinned as he recalled what happened next. "The man was just starting to get stroppy when one of the guests came into the hallway wanting to pay his bill and leave. So the chauffeur simply asked one more question: did I know where the young man's brother lived? I replied that I had no idea but was aware you'd stayed with him very recently. To my surprise, this shut him up completely. He thanked me politely and left!"

When Hannah had recovered somewhat from her surprise, she said: "Was this chauffeur tall and blond with long hair tied back in a ponytail by any chance?"

It was now Andy's turn to look surprised. "Yes, but how did you know?"

Paul chuckled, "We've come across him several times – at a distance, fortunately – but it's a long story. However, it was very helpful you told him that we'd stayed with my brother. It has almost certainly allayed his boss' suspicions about us. Thank you!"

"You're welcome! I'm glad to have been of help," Andy said. "Now let me take you up to your room; it's the same one as before."

He took Hannah's rucksack from her and led the way up the stairs. "By the way, if you like curry, the Golden Lion have an excellent curry night on Wednesdays – both hot and mild ones," he called over his shoulder.

Hannah was particularly pleased to see the familiar room again; it seemed no time at all since they were last there, even though so much had happened since. She looked out of the window happily and only vaguely heard Paul telling Andy that they'd like breakfast at seven-thirty.

Being hungry, the thought of a curry and all the trimmings speeded up their showers and they set out for the Golden Lion an hour later. Before finding a small table on one side of the crowded bar, Hannah insisted on slipping £20 into Paul's reluctant hand towards the meal and drinks. He ordered two mild chicken curries at the counter and returned with some very welcome cold drinks.

It was only while sipping coffee at the end of the meal that Hannah happened to look through a gap between the tables to the far end of the room.

Her coffee cup froze halfway to her mouth; it was as if a familiar film was being re-run. A tall blond man, glass of beer in hand, was sitting on a stool fifteen yards away staring at her in amazement.

CHAPTER 21

Hannah put her cup down with a shaking hand, causing Paul to look at her in surprise.

"Our blond nemesis is over on the other side of the room!" she managed to whisper, feeling quite sick.

Paul turned. The man was unmistakable and was even now threading his way towards them.

Paul's shock was instantly wiped out by a surge of adrenalin. He gave Hannah's hand a reassuring squeeze before standing to his feet.

"I'll flatten him if he tries to lay one finger on her!" was his first thought. Then he realized the man would be extremely unlikely to try anything violent in such a public place.

"May I join you?" the man said diffidently. "Although I try to maintain a tough-guy image, I'm quite harmless really!"

Paul nodded reluctantly and the man sat down opposite them, putting his glass carefully on the table.

"This is my first alcoholic drink today," he said. "But I would like to talk to you for a few minutes and explain some things."

He looked at them almost pleadingly.

Surprisingly, it was Hannah who recovered first. "Fire away then," she said.

It occurred to Paul that Hannah had employed a rather unfortunate phrase. But at least it lessened the tension, especially when, to their surprise, the blond man put his elbows on the table and his head in his hands.

"I'm at my wits end," he said. "My boss – the man who visited you five days ago – and Jake, my very unpleasant dark-haired companion, were arrested early last Monday morning. One of the people working in my boss' antiques shop 'phoned me with the news. I live in a tiny flat above the showroom, employed as the security guard and porter."

He paused momentarily as if he still found it hard to believe what had happened.

"My boss was arrested in a dawn raid at his home and my dark colleague when he arrived at the shop at 8:30; he was just bundled into a van! Several policemen remained on the premises searching for fake or stolen antiques and the two shop assistants were grilled for well over an hour. They gave the police my name and said I would be back from holiday tomorrow. So I can expect a grilling too, if not arrest! I'll have to go back because all my belongings are in the flat, together with some cash saved up from my wages over the last six months."

Paul thought it wise to register surprise at the news and then asked: "Why didn't you return to London with the others?"

"Partly because I'm in the doghouse, even though I managed to convince the boss in the end that all this trouble was caused by Jake's vile temper. No wonder the young lady was frightened; he frightens me most of the time, even though I could knock his daylights out with one punch! The boss handles him with kid gloves because he's a valuable asset. I've suspected for some time that some of his hush-hush missions have involved theft; I'm certain now after the attaché-case saga. The boss ordered me to meet him very early in the morning and escort him back to the shop as quietly as possible without using the company van or public transport."

"Anyway," the man continued, "when you gave me the slip at St Pancras, I 'phoned the boss in his office at the shop. Jake had already arrived to report what had happened. The boss was angry that we'd been careless with the latches of the attaché case and blew a gasket when I reported my failure. I was ordered to stay put and buy two single tickets to Derby – a guess based on the fact that you were wearing hiking boots. Over an hour later, Jake arrived with a small bag of his own and another he'd packed with things from my flat. As you now know, he also had a rather pathetic detector for tracing the signal from that memory stick or whatever it was.

"There was no sign of you anywhere in central Derby and so we rented a car to travel out towards the southern part of the Peak District. Then we tried Sheffield; it was like trying to find a needle in a haystack and getting very late by now. After having a meal, we got a few hours fitful sleep in the car before touring slowly around more of the suburbs in the early hours of the morning.

"To our delight, we eventually picked up a signal near the railway line from Sheffield to Manchester, but it faded so quickly that we deduced you were on a train heading into the Peak District. We did our best to follow by road, picking up the signal several times before getting a clear one in Edale.

"After missing you there, we saw that you were walking up the Pennine Way and nearly intercepted you several times, especially when we got a strong signal at that pub near Marsden. We were appalled when it suddenly disappeared! After that, we seemed to have no luck at all. Our boss was so cross that he insisted on joining us. We were extremely relieved, to say the least, when we got a good signal in Horton that stayed put!"

The man looked at them and smiled for the first time.

"My boss is ultra-cautious and always suspicious," he went on. "Even after I managed to find out from your guesthouse that you'd stayed a night with a relative living near the Pennine Way, he was still slightly doubtful. He decided to kill two birds with one stone by ordering me to stay here for a week. He thought it would be a punishment for me and confuse anybody who might be trying to keep an eye on us. He paid for my dinner, bunk bed and breakfast in advance and told me to return to London by train in six days time – that's tomorrow – after giving me a week's wages and some cash to buy a ticket home and a couple more shirts."

The man gave a rather hollow laugh. "In fact, my boss would be annoyed to know that I wasn't as bored as both he and I expected! In fact, I've had a surprisingly pleasant time walking around the countryside: until last Monday afternoon that is! I've been worried silly about what might happen to me since then."

The man lapsed into silence for a minute after what was, for him, a considerable linguistic effort. Then he looked directly at them.

"I've been in prison, you see, and I was grateful that the boss was prepared to hire me six months ago. I don't see how I can convince the police that I've been trying to go straight since coming out. The attaché case is the first stolen thing I've knowingly handled and that only when all the fuss started."

Hannah and Paul had been growing gradually sorry for the man's predicament and wondering what comfort, if any, they could offer him.

"Let me get us all a soft drink or something hot," Paul suggested. "Regard it as a peace offering!" he added quickly, when the man looked doubtful.

"Perhaps a tomato juice with plenty of sauce," the man said. "I used to crave that when I was inside."

"I'll have the same, please," Hannah echoed, "but no sauce."

Paul soon returned with three tomato juices. The ice cubes tingled as he placed the glasses on the table.

"I'm Paul and this is Hannah," he said.

"I'm Mike," the man replied, giving a faint smile of acknowledgement. "But why are you being so kind? After all, we probably managed to spoil the beginning of your holiday."

The young couple were at a loss to know how to reply until Paul suddenly had a thought.

"Because God loves you and wants to help you," he said.

Mike was completely speechless. Many things had been said to him over the years, usually critical or negative, but this statement was a first. He felt a strange sort of turmoil inside; various emotions were being stirred up, included those all too familiar to him – anger and fear. What emerged, however, was a glimmer of hope that there might be a way out for him after all.

Paul tried to explain. "Hannah and I knew nothing about God's love a few days ago. Then something happened in Haltwhistle that completely changed us."

He proceeded to give a brief summary of Peter's story and their eventual response. "We're now certain that God cares about each one of us and that Jesus died to make it possible for us to be forgiven and have a relationship with God," he concluded.

Hannah was so moved that she gently touched Mike's hand as it lay on the table. "We'll pray for you if you like," she said, "perhaps at one of the quieter tables outside."

Mike gave a strange sort of gulp and nodded. They moved into the garden, now fairly dark except in the vicinity of the occasional light. Finding a table in a gloomy corner, they sat down.

"I've never prayed before," Mike managed to whisper hoarsely.

"We've only been doing it ourselves for three days," Paul answered, "but have found that God hears even the most down-to-earth and simple prayers. When we stayed in a Christian farmhouse last night, the family prayed for us at the table after the evening meal; it was just as if they were speaking to a much loved and respected friend. Hannah and I have been trying to do the same on our own. May we try with you?"

"OK," came the faint reply; Mike sounded quite nervous.

Paul had the same feeling as he started to pray, hoping that Hannah would come to his rescue if he dried up.

"Heavenly Father," he said quietly. "Hannah and I believe that you love Mike and understand the predicament he's in. Please reveal Jesus to him and help him understand something of what was done for him on the Cross. May he come to that point of asking you to change him, first inside and then in his circumstances. Give him favour in the eyes of the police in London; may they accept that he did not want to get involved with anything wrong and that he really is trying to go straight. We ask these things in the Name of Jesus. Amen."

Hannah had just echoed, "Amen," when she noticed that Mike had his head in his hands again and his shoulders were shaking with emotion. Even though Paul's short prayer lacked the eloquence and emotion to move anyone to tears, she realized that God must already be at work in Mike's heart. She and Paul prayed in silence.

Then Mike spoke, "All this is so new to me and hard to take in. I think you said the man Peter knew something about you that he couldn't have guessed. Could you ask God to tell you something about me that you couldn't possibly know otherwise?"

Hannah felt that she and Paul had been given a tall order. She gazed out into the now dark night for a few moments. To her amazement, a picture formed in her mind. She turned back to the others with her eyes now closed.

"A really vivid picture has come to me," she said in a hushed whisper. "I'm in a street of dilapidated terraced houses. A small boy is standing at the open door of one of them crying bitterly. There's an old woman standing behind him with her hands on his shoulders. They're looking up the street at the retreating back of a woman – young, judging by her long blond hair – wearing a dark-brown coat and carrying a suitcase. She's walking rapidly away."

Hannah opened her eyes. "I've never had that happen before," she exclaimed, "except, of course, in a dream..." She was interrupted by Mike's exclamation of shock and emotion.

"That young woman is my mother leaving home very suddenly when I was six," he said. "I never saw her again, but learnt when I was older that she had gone to live with another man. My dad was shattered when he returned from work. I cried all night and most of the next day. The woman behind me in the doorway is my grandmother; she had come to live with us when my grandfather died."

He sat trembling as the painful memories flooded back. "Please God, help me!" he groaned. Then he turned to his companions.

"I want to become a Christian," he said very quietly. "If there's a special prayer, will you pray it for me?"

"The precise words don't matter," Paul replied. "God looks at the heart. I'll say one sentence at a time and pause for you to repeat it quietly. OK?"

Mike nodded. Paul collected his thoughts and began slowly, speaking in the first person so that Mike could copy easily.

"Lord Jesus, I am sorry I have been going my own way all my life and done so many wrong things...Please forgive me...Thank you for dying to take away my sin...Please come into my life and make me the person you want me to be...Thank you for loving me. Amen."

Mike's repetition had started very faintly but quickly became stronger. He gave a huge sigh at the end of the short prayer. There was wonder in his voice when he exclaimed: "Something's happening inside me. It's as if a huge burden is melting!"

Hannah felt the urge to add a prayer of her own. "Thank you, Father, for hearing our prayers and drawing Mike to the foot of the Cross. Thank you also for revealing something from his childhood to help him believe that you love him. Now, as you change him inside, please also heal these hurtful memories. May they never trouble him again."

"I don't know how to thank you," Mike said quietly.

"It's been both a surprise and a pleasure," Paul replied. "There's no need for thanks, although perhaps you would accept a small Bible – if Hannah has it in her bag – and promise to read it."

Hannah nodded and extracted the small book. "The print is very small, I'm afraid. I suggest you start with St Mark's Gospel, the second one in the New Testament section."

Mike took it with a smile that was only just visible in the light from the nearest lamp. "Thank you both. If only my old colleagues could see me now!"

Just then one or two drops of rain fell on the table. They all stood up hurriedly.

"I must get some sleep," Mike said. "I have to get the first train to Leeds in the morning."

They shook hands rather hurriedly as more drops fell. Paul put a small slip of paper in the tall man's hand. "My email address so that you can let us know how you get on. God bless you."

"We'll pray for you on the top of Pen-y-Ghent tomorrow morning," Hannah said as she quickly found the small folding umbrella she always carried when rain was likely.

"Thank you," Mike called over his shoulder as he moved quickly in the direction of the inn's bunkhouse. He turned at the door to give a final wave.

Paul held the small umbrella as Hannah squeezed as close to him as possible to keep dry. Fortunately, their guesthouse was only a short distance away.

"You were brilliant!" he whispered. "First, to get that vision; it really convinced Mike that God is real and cares for him. Secondly, to think of saying thank you for what God was doing in Mike's life and asking that those painful memories be healed."

"God did it all," Hannah replied softly. "Everything came so easily to me!"

CHAPTER 22

At 8:20 on Thursday morning, Paul and Hannah walked a short distance up the lane above the guesthouse to take a path that joined the Pennine Way on the southern side of Pen-y-Ghent. As a result, it was not long before they were scrambling up the same very steep slope they had tackled a few days earlier.

"When I suggested using this shorter route to the summit, I'd forgotten how steep and stony it was compared with the northern side," Paul laughed, "and, thanks to Tony, we didn't have our rucksacks the first time."

"We can cope!" Hannah called back with a rather breathless chuckle. "Anyway, we're fitter now after all the walking of the last nine days."

The ground was still quite wet after the hours of rain during the night. The sky, however, was almost clear and the splendid views made up for all the hard work. Paul spread out his waterproof so that they could sit down facing north-west over the vast expanse of the Ribble valley.

After a drink of water, Hannah suddenly remembered that they had promised to pray for Mike on the top of Pen-y-Ghent and so they took turns to pray quietly that God would be very close to Mike on his long journey back to London and his uncertain future there.

Just after one o'clock, following a bar meal in Malham, they set out for Gargrave, the village where Mark had dropped them off the previous Thursday morning. Hannah stepped out so determinedly that, by three o'clock, they were sitting in the Dalesman café having a pot of tea and a slice of cake.

"It doesn't seem possible that only just over a week ago Tony and Tim were setting us up in this very place to act as decoys with the fake dongle!" Hannah said wonderingly.

From Gargrave, it was about five miles along the A65 main road to Skipton. As they set out, Paul looked at his watch and reckoned they would be able to reach Mark's house by the time he arrived home from work. He therefore sent Mark a text message to say they were now fairly close and would not need a lift.

Their timing was so good that they were just walking up the short stretch of hill below Mark's cul-de-sac when the little blue Ford Ka drove past with a brief hoot.

Three minutes later, Mark was standing on his doorstep to welcome the two travellers.

"It's good to see you again so soon," he said. "I've been dying to hear how the dongle saga is getting on; the only thing you told me on the 'phone was that the decoy was successful. Tell me at dinner – I've 'phoned to move the booking forward to seven-thirty."

Paul put his rucksack beside the sofa in the living room and took Hannah and her rucksack upstairs to the little back bedroom while Mark made a pot of tea.

"This view is brilliant," she said happily, looking out of the small window, "so very similar to the view I enjoyed of Haltwhistle and the Tyne valley."

When she went down to the kitchen for tea, the two boys were sitting at the table. Paul was just finished telling Mark the family news from Haltwhistle. "I expect Sue has told you that Ian has been promoted to senior pharmacist," he was reporting.

Mark, however, leapt to his feet to take both Hannah's hands and kiss her check.

"I completely forgot to congratulate you on your engagement!" he said. "I've already shaken big brother's hand until it almost came off; perhaps I'm allowed to hug you instead!"

He did just that before adding: "He's a lucky fellow. Now come and have your tea before it gets cold and let me tell you why I'm going away from mid-morning on Saturday."

It transpired that Mark had recently met an attractive girl, Fiona, who worked in a hairdressing salon in her home town of Halifax, about twenty miles south of Skipton. She was working on Saturday morning but had invited him to spend from Saturday lunchtime to Sunday evening in Halifax. She had a spare bed in her flat and her parents had invited them both to lunch on Sunday.

"I've only taken her out to dinner once," Mark said. "Although it went very well indeed, I'm not sure about meeting her parents so soon!"

He somehow managed to look pleased and uncertain at the same time.

"Either she really likes you," Hannah said, "or her parents want to check you out as suitable husband material."

"Thanks a lot!" Mark said, giving a wry smile. "The first possibility is a pleasant thought; the second terrifies me."

"Rubbish!" Hannah replied cheekily. "You're a very eligible bachelor with a house and good job."

"And a small shabby car and very little money," Mark muttered. "Perhaps it won't be far to walk to her parents' home!"

"By the way, mentioning my car has reminded me that I could make a small detour on the way to Halifax and drop you at Hebden Bridge; it's only a mile from where the Pennine Way crosses the A646 and would save you about twenty miles. If we leave here about nine o'clock you can get a good distance further south by early evening."

"That would be a great help," Paul said gratefully. "We can then stop somewhere like Crowden, either in the little café-cum-guesthouse where we had tea on the way north, or there's a youth hostel in Crowden according to the map."

He looked at Hannah. "Is that OK with you? We'll miss out on that nice little place in Standedge, I'm afraid, but it will mean that we can get well south of Edale by next Sunday evening."

"I promised Hannah a couple of nights in the Peak District," he explained, turning to his brother.

Hannah gave her fiancé a warm smile. "That's fine by me. I'm happy to go anywhere with you," she added rather dreamily.

Mark gave a quiet chuckle but then became unusually quiet and thoughtful. Paul understood his brother quite well; it occurred to him that Mark might be hoping Fiona would say the same sort of thing to him one day.

At dinner in the nearby Italian restaurant, the two travellers told Mark what had happened to the dongle after they left Skipton and even shared some of the information gleaned from their surprise meeting with Mike.

"If ever the police contact you again, please don't tell them you know all this," Hannah said. "We're hoping that either Tony or Tim will let us know unofficially in due course, but there's always the chance that their boss – the detective inspector or whatever he was – will forbid any contact at all."

"The other news we've not yet told you is that we both became Christians in Haltwhistle," Paul announced unexpectedly.

"Yes," Hannah whispered. "Sue and Ian took us to hear an astonishing testimony given by an ex-Islamic jihadist. We'll tell you about it over coffee back at the house if you like; it's rather too public here."

Mark looked surprised. "Now that's something I didn't expect. I know mum and Sue have been working on Paul and me for years. Now I'll be the sole target; I'd better be on my guard! However, I'd like to hear the story – it sounds an unusual yarn."

Later, when they were back at the kitchen table again drinking Mark's coffee, they told him Peter's story in some detail. He sat listening carefully, not interrupting even once.

When they finished, he said: "That's an impressive story even when told second hand; it must have been quite riveting coming from the man himself! No wonder you were impressed. I'm still "sitting on the fence" but it has given me food for thought."

The following day, Mark drove them to Harrogate, about twenty miles east of Skipton. Paul had been to the famous spa town about six years ago on a family outing, but it was a new experience for Hannah. She relaxed in the back of the car just enjoying the drive and listening to the two brothers chatting happily.

"I'm following the A59 from Skipton that takes us just north of Harrogate town centre and then down the eastern side," Mark said. "I aim to park close to an excellent carvery called The Empress where I'll treat you to a late lunch after we've seen some of the town and visited a café that serves the best coffee for miles around!"

After leaving the car, they walked beside a large park, known as The Stray, and along a series of pleasant streets until Mark led them down a busy pedestrian precinct to a modest-looking shop bearing the unusual name of Baltzersens. There was a large notice on the window announcing, "47 Seats for Coffee Lovers Inside".

"This place may look plain and functional but they take coffee seriously," he said. "You're in for a real treat!"

It was only 11:45 and the busy lunch period had not yet commenced. It was therefore fairly easy for Paul to find a table and leave Hannah sitting there while he joined Mark at the counter. "Let me pay," he said. "You're kindly taking us to lunch later."

Hannah smiled as she watched them argue. Paul appeared to win, as she knew he would, and she started to look around her.

The white ceramic tiles on the walls were certainly functional but the colourful posters and other decorations gave the place a sense of friendliness. The Italian coffee machine on the counter certainly looked the part and the stout wooden table tops were spotless.

She sighed happily. "This is my sort of place," she thought, "I feel at home here."

The two boys joined her carrying large cups of deliciously aromatic coffee and three small jugs of cold milk. They all sipped appreciatively.

"This is excellent, Mark, as you promised it would be," Hannah exclaimed. "Thank you."

"Thank your fiancé," Mark replied with a grin, "he paid for it!"

"But you brought us here!" Paul interrupted. "If we'd been on our own, we'd never have found a café like this."

Later, Mark guided them past some of the landmarks of the town. First, they came to Bettys, renown for its afternoon teas. "Been here since Victorian times and extremely expensive!" he commented before taking them to view the outside of the Royal Pump Room, built in Georgian times to house a well producing water with the highest concentration of sulphur in Europe.

"It became really popular to "take the waters" in the Victorian era," Mark explained with a flourish of the hand, rather like a tour guide.

"Rich folk hoped the water's properties would heal them. Even Tsar Nicholas II of Russia and Charles Dickens came here. The water is now considered harmful if drunk in quantity and only a small taste is allowed – I'm told it's horrible – and the place is now a small museum."

They walked through the Valley Gardens, a long triangular area of carefully tended paths, flower beds, trees and small pavilions, some serving trinkets and refreshments. The gardens were surrounded by expensive-looking blocks of flats, terraced houses and small hotels.

Hannah bought them all an ice-cream. "I hope this doesn't spoil our lunch!" she said as she handed the cones out.

"Not a chance!" Mark laughed, "We've well over two miles to walk back, especially if I take you past the very old Majestic hotel and the enormous Holiday Inn near the Harrogate International Centre: a total contrast of old and new!"

The Holiday Inn was not only large but also extremely modern, appearing to consist mainly of glass.

"They must have spent a fortune on curtains!" Hannah exclaimed and the boys laughed.

Mark referred to the small town map he had been carrying and led them south across the busy A61 that cut its way through the town centre and directly into the relative quiet of Beulah Street.

"Another pedestrian precinct," he said, "with some expensive shops if Hannah wants to do some window shopping!"

"No, I'm just enjoying the walk," she said, giving a happy little chuckle and linking arms with her fiancé.

Beulah Street ended near the Victoria Shopping Centre. Mark guided them through and then out across the A61 again before turning left to go over the railway.

"We now follow North Park Road all the way back to The Stray and a late lunch," he said.

After an excellent carvery meal, Mark drove them back towards Skipton.

"The advantage of leaving just before four o'clock is that we avoid the Harrogate rush hour," he said. "Anyway, I hope you're going to fill me in with your wedding plans when we get back. I've also promised mum that we'd 'phone her at about eight o'clock tonight on my landline; my calls are free in the evening."

Hannah was surprised how quickly the journey passed. It seemed no time at all before Mark was parking the car beside his front door.

Over a cup of tea, Paul and Hannah repeated what they had told Sue and Ian about their plans for the wedding so far. Hannah finished by mentioning the accommodation.

"We have two spare double bedrooms at my parents' farm and my old single room, and so all Paul's family – including you, Mark – can stay there. I can sleep on the settee downstairs and I'm sure my uncle in Sherborne will be happy to put Paul up for the Saturday night. My only other close relative is my grandmother and she's in a rest-home; Uncle Tim or a friend will collect her for the wedding and breakfast afterwards – whatever form that takes!"

While Mark cleared up the tea cups and Hannah folded the clothes that had been washed the previous evening and left drying during the day, Paul used Mark's computer and broadband connection to plan the next part of their walk. He had booked a room at the guesthouse in Crowden earlier that day and was now looking at a possible route through the Peak District to give Hannah a glimpse of the area that she had originally travelled north to see. It would be nice, he thought, to go south from Edale and join the scenic Monsal Trail that ran roughly south-east from the outskirts of Buxton – famous for its spring water – down to Bakewell on the A6 between Buxton and Matlock.

      The Google map revealed the locations of a large number of guesthouses all over the area. Being the height of the summer season, however, it took several attempts on Mark's very convenient landline to book a twin room in two suitable locations, the first about four miles walk south of Edale for Sunday night and the second just outside Bakewell for Monday. After that, Paul thought it would be nice to go another eight miles or so down to Matlock before doubling back to Chatsworth House – a treat he had mentioned to Hannah several days before.

      Mark made the promised 'phone call to Sheffield just after eight o'clock. He greeted his mother cheerfully and passed the receiver to Paul, who had, of course, told her all the good news earlier. But, as usual, she was delighted to hear from him again and all about their happy day in Harrogate.

"I've been talking things over with dad," she said eventually. "I know you're leaving for London about midday next Friday and plan to spend Wednesday and Thursday nights with us. However, we wonder if you'd like to come here for Tuesday night as well. It would give us more chance to get to know Hannah. Dad says he would be happy to take next Wednesday off and take all four of us to see Chatsworth House. It would make a lovely day out!"

Paul could hear the longing in his mother's voice. "We'd love to do that, mum; it's an excellent idea. Please give dad our love and thank him but say that the entrance fee is my treat. Now Hannah wants to speak to you. As I pass the 'phone to her, I'll just tell her about your kind offer."

He did so and left Hannah to talk to her prospective mother-in-law. As he joined Mark in the kitchen, who was just beginning to prepare the supper, he heard Hannah's happy voice saying: "Hello Sarah, we'd love to spend some quality time with you both. An extra night and the Chatsworth trip is such a kind offer – Paul tells me that the house and gardens are really special…"

Mark was a surprisingly good cook, judging by the cheese omelettes he produced with only a little help from Hannah who prepared the cucumber and tomato salad.

They all had a very pleasant evening together before retiring early.

CHAPTER 23

Well before nine o'clock the following morning, Saturday, Mark drove Paul and Hannah the twenty miles or so south to Hebden Bridge. On the way, he commented that centre of the small town was well worth seeing, even if only briefly.

"I'm going to park in a place I know," he said, "and take you to an excellent café where you can treat me to a cup of coffee before I show you the route to take west along the A646 to the point where the Pennine Way crosses the main road – it's just over a mile."

"It's very kind of you to make this detour, Mark," Hannah said gratefully.

"Fiona doesn't get off work until 12:30 and I only have to go eight miles south-east to get to Halifax," Mark replied. "I'd prefer to spend some of the time with you rather than in Halifax, although I must allow time to find a nice café for lunch before meeting her."

"You've done us proud, Mark!" Paul said gratefully. "One day you must stay with us when we have somewhere bigger: Fiona too if she turns out to be the girl of your dreams!"

"I'm really attracted to her at the moment," Mark confessed. "Over coffee, you two must give me some tips."

The journey did not take long. After leaving the car, they walked a short distance down an attractive pedestrian precinct to the café Mark had in mind. Over cups of excellent coffee, Hannah and Paul did their best to give Mark a few pointers to developing a relationship, but it was difficult.

"I don't think we've been much help," Paul summed up in the end. "The trouble is that we were effectively given a head start by meeting precisely when Hannah needed advice and support in the face of a rather frightening and mysterious situation. I was attracted to her straight away but it's difficult to say how much was due to her as a person and how much the intriguing mystery she brought with her! Love only developed slowly."

"I wouldn't call a week slow!" Mark exclaimed.

Hannah gave a chuckle and he looked at her in surprise.

"After what happened in Haltwhistle, Paul and I can only conclude that God was the matchmaker," she said quietly.

Paul nodded. "That's the crux of the matter," he said as they all got up to leave.

Mark guided them back to the main road and turned right to walk with them for a short distance in a westerly direction. The road almost immediately crossed a small river and he paused in the middle of the bridge.

"This is the end of Hebden Beck," he informed the others. "It merges with the River Calder just beyond those trees." He pointed south to some small dense trees that obscured the view. "Now, if we carry on a little further, I'll show you something remarkable."

They walked down the main road past a row of small shops and turned left into a narrow road beside a car park.

"We'll be crossing two bridges in quick succession," Mark said. "Look down at the water and see if you notice any difference."

On the second bridge, he paused and looked at them expectantly, almost like a conjuror waiting for his audience's reaction after some clever slight of hand.

"There was a fast flowing river below the first bridge, but now we're looking down at what appears to be a canal!" Hannah exclaimed.

"And the water level is higher than in the river!" Paul added. He sounded intrigued.

Mark smiled. "You've got it in one! The river is the Calder; this is the Rochdale Canal. In the centre of the town, the canal actually crosses the river! I didn't have time to show you, but it'll be an interesting sight to show Fiona when I bring her here for an outing on some future date – if there is one!"

It was time for the hikers to depart. They returned to the main road where Paul and Hannah exchanged hugs with their kind host.

"Thanks for looking after us so well," Paul said. "Let us know how things develop with Fiona."

"Yes, thank you," Hannah added. "We'll pray for you both."

Mark looked quite moved at her words and simply nodded his thanks. He stood on the corner waving until they were out of sight.

Fifteen minutes later, they rejoined the Pennine Way by crossing the bridge over the Rochdale Canal in Charlestown.

"We're now on familiar ground," Hannah said as she marched on enthusiastically. It became even more familiar when they climbed up past Stoodley Pike, Hannah having commented on its ugliness on their way north.

About six miles later, they reached the A58 Rochdale to Halifax road and the White House pub.

"We had coffee here before if you remember," Paul said. "Would you like another drink now? It's just after one o'clock, so we could have a proper main course here and keep the sandwiches you made for this evening. Crowden is about seventeen miles further and I'm not sure what food will be available at that time of day."

"Safer to have something nourishing here then," Hannah replied, "but not too filling. I seem to remember that there's Black Hill to climb!"

A board displaying today's specials included lamb's liver with bacon, chips and fresh vegetables.

"It reminds me of home. My mother used to serve liver and bacon about once a week," Hannah said nostalgically. "May I have that and a nice long drink?"

"Of course," Paul replied and he ordered it for them both.
Feeling satisfied but not too full, they commenced the longer haul of the day. Two miles of undulating terrain led to the pedestrian flyover on the M62 motorway and then it did not need long at Hannah's impressive pace before they were dropping down towards the familiar Standedge Cutting.

As they were about to cross the busy road, Paul paused and looked rather anxiously at some thick clouds to the east of them.

"I would have suggested a short detour up the road to the pub where we had our first evening meal but it's getting a little late in the afternoon and I'm also worried about those ominous clouds. Are you OK with a short stop for some water?"

"Of course I am," Hannah said.

They perched on a bank in the small car park beside the road for a quick drink before carrying on steadily. When the rising mass of Black Hill was directly ahead, however, the first spot or two of rain could be felt.

"We need our waterproofs," Paul said abruptly. "Tops and bottoms this time, I think!"

They sat on the remains of a low stone wall to extract capes and leggings from their rucksacks. It was the first time since setting out on holiday that the sky had looked sufficiently ominous to warrant the use of waterproof trousers.

Unfortunately, it was necessary to remove their boots to get the leggings on, and so, by the time they had shouldered their rucksacks again and helped each other sort out the voluminous canopy capes, it was raining steadily.

"These capes look ridiculous!" Hannah said with a grin. "But at least they keep everything dry, including our rucksacks."

Paul laughed. "We'd be completely dry if I'd had the sense to suggest stopping earlier." As an afterthought, he added: "I'm always surprised how little room these modern materials take up when properly folded. Much less room than the first cape I had in my youth!"

They marched on up the gradual slope towards Black Hill, now really living up to its name in the rain-swept gloom. By the time they had climbed another mile on steeper gradient, the rain had become a downpour. Pools of water were forming rapidly and they were thankful for the stepping stones that marked the route.

They were now on the broad top of the hill. Just visible not far ahead was the white-painted trig point, "Soldier's Lump", marking the highest point. There was virtually no shelter provided by the tall pile of stones. Nevertheless, Paul took Hannah's hand and they crouched beside it with their heads down so that the rain cascaded off their hoods on to the ground and not down their faces.

They were completely alone on the plateau, made almost menacing by the dark cloud, rain and wind.

"Any walkers coming up from Crowden, about four miles away, must have been sensible enough to turn back!" Paul had to almost shout for Hannah to hear him above the noise.

The rain showed no sign of abating and they moved on, helped by the fact that the path was now completely paved. Hannah led the way for a time before stopping suddenly. She looked troubled.

"What's wrong?" Paul shouted anxiously, but she shook her head, smiled and moved on.

They had just carefully negotiated the path along the edge of Laddow Rocks and were on the steep descent when they noticed that the rain had lessened considerably. Looking ahead, the cloud cover over Crowden, now not far to the south, was pale grey in complete contrast to the darkness they were leaving behind. By the time they approached the A628 crossing, the rain had stopped completely, although the ground was still very wet.

Paul moved alongside Hannah and took her hand, almost in celebration. She smiled at him. He thought that she looked very relieved about something, but he did not press the point.

"The terrible weather has probably got her down," he thought.

The tea shop they had visited on the way north was closed by the time Paul rang the bell of the adjoining guesthouse. The woman who opened the door beamed at them in welcome.

"You look as if you've just been through the worst of this afternoon's weather!" she exclaimed.

"Yes, on the top of Black Hill!" Paul said.

"Well, come round the back. We've got a nice dry outhouse where I can hang your waterproofs. Your boots can go by the side of the kitchen range when you've cleaned the mud off them after a nice hot cup of tea."

Paul and Hannah removed their boots and outer clothing. Their kind hostess then showed them to a small but comfortable bedroom. Hannah was disappointed to see that it only had a hand-basin. However, the bathroom and a second WC were only a short distance along the corridor.

"We use the café for breakfast and also provide an evening drink in there at nine-thirty for people staying here. Your pot of tea and a couple of rock-buns I've just made for the café tomorrow will be ready in about fifteen minutes," the woman said. "I'm afraid we don't serve evening meals and the nearest pub is about two miles away in Tintwhistle."

"That's all right; we've got some sandwiches," Hannah told her, "but a cup of tea and cake sounds lovely. Thank you."

"You're welcome," the woman called as she hurried away.

Paul had noticed Hannah's disappointment. "I'm sorry, I should have warned you that this place doesn't have any en-suites," he said apologetically.

"I can't possibly grumble," she replied. "You've thoroughly spoiled me so far. After all, if I'd been on my own in the Peak District, I'd be using youth hostels!"

It was almost seven o'clock by the time they were seated in the little café. The tea was most welcome after their long wet walk.

"This rock-bun is delicious and not too sweet," Hannah said when the woman came in with some more hot water. She was so pleased at the compliment that she insisted on fetching two more from the kitchen.

"By the way," she said, "I'm expecting a party of four people at about eight-thirty tonight. If you want a bath or shower it would be wise to have one before they arrive."

The young couple took her advice and Hannah had a shower while Paul got the mud off their boots so that they could be left to dry in the kitchen. When it was his turn to have a shower, Hannah washed their damp socks in the hand basin and hung them out to dry in the bedroom.

While they were eating the sandwiches Hannah had made earlier that day, the sound of voices and doors banging could be heard in the corridor. Clearly the other guests had arrived.

"I hope they don't crash about late at night!" Paul remarked.

"I'm so tired I could sleep through anything!" Hannah said. Then she became serious. "Did you notice anything strange on the top of Black Hill?"

"Not apart from the atrocious weather!" was the reply. "Although I did see you looking worried at one point when we were on the way down."

"That hill certainly lived up to its name today," she said slowly. "I've experienced plenty of bad weather in the great outdoors before, but this time I actually felt that there was something menacing in the atmosphere; almost as if the place hated us for being there. It sounds crazy I know."

"Actually no," Paul said gently. "I'll tell you why. In Harrogate I slipped into a bookshop to buy a Bible to replace the one we gave Mike. The only small one I could find turned out to be the old King James' Version. This morning, as I was searching for Psalm 145 to see how much it differed from the more modern translation in Sue's copy, I chanced on Psalm 23. I'll find it again and read it to you."

He turned the pages of the small volume and began to read: "The Lord is my shepherd: I shall not want. He maketh me to lie down in green pastures: he leadeth me beside still waters. He restoreth my soul: he leadeth me in the paths of righteousness for his name's sake. Yea, though I walk through the valley of the shadow of death, I will fear no evil: for thou art with me; thy rod and thy staff they comfort me...."

"I think we were being given a lesson in trusting God," Paul concluded. "You sensed a feeling of menace on the hill. You may well be right, although the rain and wind were absolutely atrocious. But God wants us to know that we're under his protection."

Hannah looked at him and smiled gratefully. "Thank you for not thinking I'm a complete idiot! To find that passage from the Bible makes the whole experience well worth it. I still find it amazing that God actually cares about us."

As the truth of Hannah's comment sank in, they were surprised to find that they were experiencing a deep desire to give thanks to God for his love and for the provision of the Cross. As they tried to verbalize their thanks and praise, the next thirty minutes slipped past in no time at all.

They were interrupted by the noise of footsteps moving down the corridor and suddenly realized it was nine-thirty and a drink was now available. The thought of something hot was attractive and they left the bedroom to investigate.

The only people in the café turned out to be a friendly-looking couple who had driven up from London that day with two young teenagers, now in bed exhausted after the journey.

"The M1 was busy today and we stopped for an evening meal about ten miles south of here, which is lucky because I gather the nearest restaurant is some distance," the man said. "We've arranged to leave our car here and trek up the Pennine Way in short stages to Malham, where we've booked a place to stay. Then we'll come back here for one night before returning home."

"It's the first time we've tried bringing our two boys on a substantial walk," his wife added. "I hope they like it; they're only twelve and thirteen years old."

"When the weather's good, the route is splendid," Hannah assured her. "We've been lucky so far; the only really bad weather was this afternoon for the last few miles coming south."

"When you're in Malham you must make sure you take a short trip to see Malham Cove," Paul said.

"And climb up to the plateau above it," Hannah added quickly. "The rock formation up there is fascinating!"

"When your boys are a year or two older, one of the harder but more scenic parts of the Pennine Way is from Horton-in-Ribblesdale to Dufton, a distance of about seventy miles," Paul continued.

The couple were obviously interested in their experiences and so Hannah and Paul spent the next few minutes describing the highlights of their journey up to Haltwhistle.

"Are you Christians by any chance?" the woman suddenly asked quite out of the blue.

It took Paul a second or two to recover. "Yes, we both became Christians about a week ago. But how do you know?"

"I can tell," was the rather mysterious reply. "I've been a Christian for several years – my name's Martha – but George here is not, although I'm working on it!"

"Yes, she is," George said rather ruefully.

"Do you mind telling us how it happened?" Martha asked.

"Well, my sister and her husband took us to hear an ex-Muslim speaking at their church. The man – using the pseudonym Peter – had only recently arrived in Syria to join Islamic State when a traumatic experience – and I really mean traumatic – made him wonder if he was doing the right thing. The next day God spoke to him audibly and he met Jesus face-to-face!"

Hannah took over. "We were shell-shocked, as you can imagine," she said. "However, what clinched it was when we spoke to Peter afterwards; he told us not only that God had a plan for our lives together but described when and where Paul and I had first met – something we'd not revealed to anyone!"

"Please tell us more," Martha whispered almost pleadingly.

Paul managed to condense Peter's story into about ten minutes without missing out any salient features.

At the end, Martha had tears in her eyes and George sat staring down at the table looking completely stunned.

"After an experience like that I'm not surprised the man became a Christian," he said, almost to himself. "He must have been frightened to death!"

"Not frightened but in awe," Hannah said. "The love that flowed from Jesus was far too strong for Peter to feel afraid. Remember, Jesus gave him a choice when he said, "Believe, ask and receive"; there was no compulsion. As a result, Peter was totally transformed. In the space of four months, he has changed from a dedicated jihadist to a most humble, gentle and loving man."

"Your testimony to the love and grace of God has made me want to get closer to him," Martha declared. "I'm also sure it will have a beneficial influence on George."

The latter smiled slightly but did not say anything to contradict his wife's confident prediction.

It was nearly ten-thirty and so, extremely tired by now, Paul and Hannah got up to leave. Saying a warm goodnight to George and Martha, they said they hoped to see them and their two youngsters at breakfast.

As it happened, however, the family only appeared just as they were leaving the small café after finishing an excellent breakfast. The two lads were now full of energy and hungrily anticipating breakfast, but George and Martha looked as if they might have stayed up too long the previous evening discussing the testimony they had heard.

Nevertheless, when Martha asked Hannah if she would mind exchanging e-mail addresses so that they could keep in touch occasionally, the latter was happy to oblige.

CHAPTER 24

The early morning was bright and sunny when Paul and Hannah set out from Crowden; the only remnants of the appalling weather the previous afternoon being the damp ground and frequent puddles.

Hannah moved with her customary energy and enthusiasm even as the gradient increased sharply: climbing 200 metres within half a mile. About eighty minutes after leaving the guesthouse, they had covered four miles and reached the highest point of the Bleaklow Plateau at well over 600m.

Hannah took a deep breath of the clean-smelling air as Paul extracted bottles of water from the top of his rucksack. The sky was a cloudless blue and a thin heat haze lay over the distant panorama.

They continued steadily, first down slightly to Snake Pass Road and then generally up again on the winding route over Kinder Low.

By twelve-thirty they were standing at the top of Jacob's Ladder admiring the view south down the valley – a view etched in Hannah's memory by the impact it had made at the beginning of this remarkable trip on the Pennine Way. Even the diminutive figures she could see moving slowly up and down the lower path seemed strangely familiar.

She took Paul's hand affectionately. Looking down in surprise, he immediately discerned what she was thinking and his expression changed. As she led the way down the rough-hewn steps, her heart was singing for joy at the sight of the love in his eyes.

Over an hour later, they were sitting at a small table in the Old Nag's Head in the centre of Edale having a cold drink.

"Would you like something to eat here?" Paul asked, fingering the menu.

Hannah shook her head. "It's very crowded. I'd much prefer something simple in the café near the railway station. I'll always have a soft spot for that place: it's where our adventure together really took off!"

"You can say that again!" Paul chuckled, and, a few minutes later, they were walking south down the narrow road towards the main car park. Tourists seemed to be everywhere after the relative quiet of the Pennine Way. It was quite a relief to turn off down the little service road to the station. Being the weekend, however, even the small café was busy.

"I suppose we shouldn't be surprised," Paul said sadly. "It's Sunday in the height of the holiday season and the weather's good. Let me just get a take-away coffee and a packet of biscuits or something to keep us going. There's a delightful café I know that caters for real walkers just over three miles away. Is that OK?"

"Of course it is! We've only done sixteen miles so far. We can have the coffee on a bench outside the station," she replied.

It was quite strange to be sitting beside the station entrance, where, only twelve days ago a large black car had suddenly appeared and given her the shock of her life. A momentary quiver came over her. She turned to her companion and smiled: his presence was so comforting.

They walked west along the main road, parallel to the railway. After less than a mile, the road bent sharply south to cross the River Noe.

"That narrow lane coming out at the corner we've just passed goes up to the farm where the Pennine Way turns east towards Edale," Paul said. "We could have taken a short cut if I'd realized then how crowded Edale would be."

"But we needed something to drink – not to mention a visit to the loo!" Hannah said with a chuckle.

Very soon they came to a gate on the right-hand side.

"This is where we turn southwest and take a path known as Chapel Gate," Paul said. "We have a steep climb ahead and some brilliant views."

"Excellent," Hannah muttered as she stepped out briskly.

When the path levelled off temporarily and turned eastward, they paused to look back. The Edale valley looked so tranquil under the bright sunshine now that the bustle of the village was far behind. The massive bulk of the Kinder plateau lay beyond.

The path began to climb steadily again. Over the next half mile they climbed nearly 200 metres before reaching the crest of a ridge where the views in several directions were spectacular.

Just then the path arrived at a T-junction.

"Turning left here would take us up the peak of this ridge," Paul informed her. "It's called Lord's Seat – don't ask me why – and then goes on to another hill known as Mam Tor. I'll take you that way after we've been to the café. For that, we must turn right."

The path dropped quickly down to merge with a road going west. Paul took Hannah's hand and led her a few yards along the latter before turning left into a rough single-track lane with a sign at the entrance advertising holiday cottages and bed and breakfast.

"Almost there," he said encouragingly, "the café's not as far as the B and B."

Some trees came into view at last and beside them a stone building displaying a large sign: "The No Car Café welcomes walkers, riders and cyclists".

They entered thankfully and Hannah had a pleasant surprise. The room was cool and welcoming with spotless wooden tables and chairs and bright pictures on the white walls.

Paul greeted the people at the two occupied tables with a smile and nod – it seemed to be the sort of place where walkers felt amongst like-minded friends. He pulled out a chair for Hannah and helped her off with her rucksack.

A cheerful man bustled in with a tray for an adjacent table. Having put everything in place, he came over and looked approvingly at the rucksacks.

"Good afternoon. What can I get you?" he asked.

"I wonder if all customers have to show proof of using leg-power," Hannah thought.

"We'd love a large pot of tea and a slice of one of those nice-looking cakes," Paul said, nodding towards a small side table where two large cakes sat under transparent domes. "However, we missed out on eating anything in Edale because it was far too crowded, and so something more substantial would also be very welcome."

"We can make you up some sandwiches with white or wholemeal bread: cheese and tomato, beef and pickle, or salmon mayonnaise. Unfortunately, we've run out of ham. Alternatively, for something hot, we can do cheese toasties or scrambled egg on toast."

Paul looked at Hannah enquiringly. "A cheese toastie with a tomato halved would be lovely," she said.

He ordered the same for both of them, together with tea and two slices of fruit cake.

It was good to relax for a time in quiet companionship. The toasties, when they came, were excellent.

"Almost as good as the ones we had at the Wensleydale cheese museum in Hawes," Hannah whispered.

By four o'clock, well satisfied, they were making their way back to the road.

"No more than six miles to go to Castleton and our guesthouse," Paul said, "but two steep climbs; the first up to Lord's Seat and the second to Mam Tor. The views from both should be really special on a day like this."

"That's my sort of walk!" Hannah exclaimed with relish, as he made sure that she led the way at her preferred pace. This meant that within forty minutes they were standing beside a pile of rough stones marking Lord's Seat and admiring the stunning view of the Edale valley to the north. Directly east of them, the ridge began to drop away before rising again to the summit of Mam Tor.

"Mam Tor's 517m high according to the map," Paul said. "It's slightly lower than we are now."

He turned to look south and Hannah followed his gaze. "Tomorrow we'll make our way in that direction to Miller's Dale and join the major portion of the famous Monsal Trail down to Bakewell."

A couple of minutes later, after a drink from their water bottles, they moved on along the ridge and dropped down for just over half a mile to join a road for a few yards before reaching a gate on the far side that gave access to an extremely steep path up to the trig point on the summit of Mam Tor.

Even Hannah, for all her amazing fitness, was glad to stop at the top for a breather.

"You made short work of that!" Paul said admiringly. "Of course, the weather is good today. Walkers are warned that the path can be dangerous on windy days, especially after rain. The preferred route is to come from the other direction – the one we'll use shortly to go down. It's not so steep and less exposed to the elements."

Once again the views were superb, a particularly good one this time being to the northeast where several smaller hills stretched out into the near distance.

"We're going in that direction but will swing south-east before that first hill to go down towards Castleton," Paul said.

So far they had been lucky because the vantage points on the top of both hills had been empty, but now, suddenly, a group of three people appeared behind them, breathless from the steep climb. Hannah also pointed to the other gentler path; a large party of young people was approaching excitedly, cameras at the ready.

"I think it's time to go," she said.

They took their time on the two and a half mile decent because the views were well worth it, lying now under the gentle sunshine of early evening. Hannah felt herself absorbing the peaceful atmosphere like a healing balm.

This continued as they joined a narrow road half a mile north of Castleton and walked down between pleasant fields where sheep and cows grazed contentedly. Although they passed a couple of farms and several small dwellings, the edge of the village seemed to be defined by a bridge over a narrow stream. A moment or two later, Paul turned into a small close and stopped outside one of the cottages.

"We're here," he said as he led her up to the front door.

It was a long time since Hannah had seen such a charming place; it even had a climbing rose beside the door and the fragrance of the delicate pink flowers filled the evening air as they waited. An elderly woman opened the door and beamed at them.

She seemed to know exactly who they were because she stood back to let them enter as she greeted them in a Derbyshire accent stronger than Hannah had heard so far.

"There you are, in splendid time just as you promised. I always get a little worried when folk are late because I like to go to bed early. My dear husband, when he was alive, used to say, "Early to bed and early to rise makes a man healthy, wealthy and wise", although we seemed to miss out on the wealthy bit, I'm sorry to say! Do come on through."

She led them across a small hall. It clearly doubled as a breakfast room because there was a table against one wall already laid up with two breakfast settings, the cups carefully inverted on the saucers to keep them clean. Two mugs had been placed next to an electric kettle, together with what looked like a jar of instant coffee and a small jar containing tea bags.

Going down a short corridor, the old woman opened a door and ushered them into what must have once been the main bedroom of the cottage. It contained two single beds under tasteful counterpanes, a small child's bed under a protective cover – presumably for luggage when not in use – and a small dressing table and chair. The only place to hang clothes was on a short rail attached to the wall.

The reason there was no wardrobe became clear when the old woman opened a sliding door with a flourish and showed them the en-suite shower room.

"When my husband died five years ago, the thought of having to leave a home where we had been so happy was awful," she said. "One of my neighbours suggested using the larger of our two bedrooms for paying guests and advised that it would be worth giving up some of the floor area to put in a shower and so on. It was not too expensive because the original bathroom is just beyond."

The old woman sounded so pleased she was still able to remain in the home she loved that Hannah's heart went out to her. "The room is lovely," she said appreciatively as she moved over to the window, "and I see you have a charming garden."

Paul saw that the small garden was indeed beautiful: a little overgrown perhaps, but with a profusion of flowers.

The woman was delighted by Hannah's praise. "I try to keep the garden as best I can," she said. "By the way, I've made sure there is plenty of hot water for you to have a shower. The front door key is on the bedside table, but, if you want to lock this room when you go out for a meal tonight, you need to take the key from this side of the lock and use it on the other. I'll put a small jug of milk on the table in the hall at nine o'clock; so please make yourselves a hot drink when you come in. Lastly, when would you like breakfast? I'm up before six-thirty and so any time after seven o'clock will be fine if you need to get an early start."

They settled on breakfast at seven-thirty and the woman bade them goodnight.

"What a dear lady," Hannah said as she began to unpack a few things. "If you want to use the bathroom first, I'll look out something to wear tonight. Unfortunately, my smarter pair of jeans is at the bottom of the rucksack!"

When Paul emerged after a quick shower, she had sorted herself out and carried her clothes for the evening into the tiny room.

"It's a good job I'm small," she joked.

Paul was pleased to see that she was going to wear the blouse he had bought her in Haltwhistle; probably inspired by the profusion of flowers in the garden.

A few minutes after seven, they ventured down into the village centre. It was a balmy evening and even the grey stone buildings seemed to glow in the soft light. Hannah felt a surge of happiness as she linked arms with her fiancé and tried to express her thanks that he had found such an attractive place for their overnight stop.

Paul felt a gentle kiss on his cheek. He looked down at her happy upturned face and it was as much as he could do to resist giving her a huge hug in the middle of the street. It was a little too public: a number of holidaymakers were enjoying an evening stroll or looking for somewhere to eat. In the end, he had to settle for whispered, "I love you."

After they had consulted three menus outside what looked like quite crowded pubs, they found a fourth establishment that looked promising. It turned out to be a good choice; or, at least, the homemade steak and kidney pie with locally-grown vegetables was very satisfying after an active day. They even rounded off the meal with an ice-cream before exploring a little more; eventually walking a short distance up a narrow road going south-east out of the village, from which there was a splendid view of the valley bathed in a rosy glow by the sun setting behind a nearby hill.

"We must remember how to get to this lane – it's called Pindale Road – because we go this way tomorrow," Paul said.

They had neared the bottom of the hill again when he turned to Hannah and put his arms around her. "I wanted to tell you in the pub how wonderful you look, but felt too shy! You're totally adorable and I love you." With that he kissed her.

Hannah responded warmly before laying her cheek against his chest. "I'm so happy," she murmured.

Back in the little cottage, they made themselves a weak cup of coffee at the hall table before retiring to bed.

Shortly before nine o'clock the following morning, Hannah and Paul, after bidding a grateful farewell to their elderly hostess, were climbing up Pindale Road again. The weather was still fine, although not quite as clear as on the previous day.

"It was kind of you to add £10 to the bill when you paid it," Hannah said. "The dear old woman was a little embarrassed but clearly delighted."

"Well, it was quiet and comfortable and also the cheapest place we've been in. Our guesthouse in Bakewell will be the most expensive, with the exception of Tan Hill that Tony paid for us."

"Anyway, I'd like to share the gift and give you £5 when we next stop," she insisted.

By this time they had reached a wooded area and a fork in the road. A narrow lane descended through some trees directly ahead and the road they were following veered slightly right and began to climb through an attractive wood until it reached open pasture land.

Hannah wondered if the coarse grass would only sustain sheep, but, as the road meandered between the rough fields, they passed a small herd of cows grazing with apparent contentment. Pleasant vistas of distant hills came into view with every bend and they marched in contented silence until beginning the descent into the village of Tideswell.

"I expect you'd like some coffee soon," Paul said. "We've already walked over six miles."

Fifteen minutes later, after passing through the outskirts of the village and along the short High Street, they entered the surprisingly broad Queen Street and were intrigued by the name, Vanilla Kitchen, on the signboard above a small café.

"This looks far too unusual to miss!" Hannah exclaimed. "Please may we go in here?"

"Of course," Paul said fondly as he took her arm. "I'm sure they must do acceptable coffee."

Not only was the coffee good but they were tempted into sharing one of the delicious-looking homemade scones and so it was midday before they moved on down Queen Street.

"They probably have market stalls along here once a week," Hannah commented.

Paul nodded rather absentmindedly as he consulted the notes he had carefully made in Skipton when consulting Google Map on Mark's computer.

"There should be a lane called Sunny Bank going off on our right. It leads into Sherwood Road that runs south towards Miller's Dale," he said.

"There it is!" Hannah pointed.

"Well done!" Paul said with relief. "Thanks to your sharp eyes we've been saved some extra walking."

"But you did all the careful research in the first place," she replied as she took his arm to negotiate what turned out to be hardly more than a passage. "You've planned a lovely two-day tour of the Peak District for me. Thank you."

Sherwood Road took them past small terraced and semi-detached houses of grey stone, followed by a few newer bungalows and houses, to the edge of the village. Here the road abruptly reduced in width.

Paul was just about to continue along it until he glanced at his sketch map again. "A car would go straight on, but Google indicates that walkers can take a slightly shorter route down this lane going off to our left," he said. The entrance carried a notice announcing that the lane was "Unsuitable for motor vehicles".

"This looks interesting," Hannah said, "and the countryside looks really lovely. Come on!" She took Paul's hand eagerly.

It was not long before they passed a farm entrance and the lane got narrower; it even had patches of grass growing in the centre.

"Now we know why the sign was there!" Paul chuckled.

A little later, they passed a second farm and the patches of grass disappeared. "I think this means we will soon be coming back on to the road from Tideswell to Miller's Dale," he said. He was right; after less than two hundred yards they rejoined the road.

"We've less than a mile from Miller's Dale and the Monsal Trail," he continued. "Once we're on the Trail it may be quite difficult to find somewhere for a lunchtime snack and so we'd better stop at the Angler's Rest in Miller's Dale. We can have a proper meal in Bakewell tonight; I've already made a note of two places with good references on Google."

The narrow road curved gently to the right as they dropped down through a wood into the valley of the River Wye and then ran into the B6049 running west towards Buxton – famous for its bottled water. Almost immediately, Paul led Hannah sharp right down a small road running beside the river and they came to an attractive ivy-clad pub. "The Angler's Rest," he announced.

After modest refreshments in a pleasant environment, they returned to the B-road and almost immediately passed under what was obviously an old railway viaduct.

"We're going under the Monsal Trail," Paul announced. "To get on it we'll have to go a little further and then double back up a steep side road. The Trail actually starts a mile further west on the outskirts of Buxton."

The smaller side road climbed steeply up until they came to a car-park on their left. Paul guided Hannah across it.

"This is the old Miller's Dale station yard and here's the station building." He pointed to a grey-stone building, beyond which lay the original platform. A group of people were standing there chatting, their bicycles propped up against the wall.

"A party of cyclists must be having a pit-stop," he said as they entered the broad gravel track of the Trail and began to walk east.

It immediately became clear that Miller's Dale must have once been a junction because there was another viaduct running almost alongside them at a slight angle.

Hannah gave a little laugh of understanding. "Now I realize why we've gone under three rail bridges in the last quarter mile."

Having crossed the River Wye, the route of the old railway line remained fairly close to the water and followed the south side of the attractively wooded valley, occasionally cutting through outcrops of rock. In fact, about two and a half miles from Miller's Dale, the Trail entered a long tunnel through the hillside.

"The river must have done a large meander for so long a tunnel to be necessary to keep the rail line fairly straight," Paul said as they walked quickly and carefully through the relative darkness. Fluorescent lights were provided at intervals but it was still necessary to keep a look out for cyclists, some of whom had no lights.

They emerged from the tunnel with some relief. After another mile, the track crossed the river on a spectacular viaduct. Amazing views now appeared. Hills and ridges rose to over 300m behind and on each side, the river swept round in a large arc below and a flatter landscape appeared directly ahead.

Hannah squeezed Paul's hand in a gesture of appreciation as they moved on between pleasant fields, past small copses, over or under several roads and past the remains of small stations.

The last one of these had been turned into a thriving café; people were seated at tables on what was once the platform.

"This is Hassop Station Café," Paul said, "we'll come back as far as this tomorrow before continuing north. The Trail passes just to the east of Bakewell less than a mile from here. It would probably be a good idea to go to the guesthouse to drop our luggage and change our boots for trainers before having tea in the town centre."

The Trail bent gradually to the south and soon buildings began to appear through the trees on their right. "Here we are," Paul said. "We must watch out for a gate that leads into Station Road."

Once through the remains of the station forecourt, now flanked by commercial buildings, they followed Station Road for a short distance and then Paul took Hannah down a small side road.

He seemed so sure of the route that she was moved to say, admiringly: "You must have done an amazing amount of research on Google while we were with Mark!"

"Well, it was safer to find a good guesthouse and book in advance at this time of year because I was determined to get a twin with a shower at the very least, if not a full bathroom."

"You really are spoiling me!" Hannah whispered. "One day I'm going to make it up to you."

She took his arm affectionately, although it was quite awkward because they were both wearing rucksacks. Paul felt inwardly warmed by her gratitude and the rather ambiguous second statement.

Within a couple of minutes, he was leading her up a path to the front door of quite a sizeable building. Their welcome was warm even though the friendly woman seemed rather surprised that they had arrived at three o'clock in the afternoon.

"When I planned today's journey, I misjudged the distance from Castleton," Paul explained.

As in Castleton, their room contained three beds but was more spacious and had a larger en-suite. The window looked out over several adjacent bungalows to open countryside beyond.

"This is lovely!" Hannah exclaimed and gave Paul a kiss that he was not slow to return.

After unpacking and changing their footwear, he suggested it was time to find some a drink. "The two places I found on Google are less than half a mile away," he said. "Afterwards we could walk the short distance south to the start of the Monsal trail and follow it back up to Station Road before having a shower and going out for dinner."

"Sounds good to me," Hannah said eagerly.

It only took a few minutes to reach the bridge over the River Wye into the town centre. Almost immediately they came to the Castle Inn, an attractive-looking building standing in a prominent position overlooking a busy junction.

"That's the pub I thought might be a good place for a meal later, but, for a drink now, this café is highly recommended."

Paul pointed towards an establishment on the opposite corner with several black awnings jutting out over the pavement and bearing a rather unusual name, Lime Lounge Coffee House.

It was quite crowded with visitors enjoying late afternoon refreshments, but the tea and a shared toasted teacake were well worth the wait.

Emerging from the café, they passed a tourist map on a wall and were able to plan a circular tour of just over two miles that included some of the attractive town and the final section of the Monsal Trail. They took the walk slowly, arm in arm, enjoying the scenery, the pleasant weather and just being together. The short section of the Trail up to the Station Road exit was only a mile and Hannah was disappointed to find it so short.

"Never mind, we'll see it again tomorrow when we go up as far as the old Hassop Station before continuing north-east towards Sheffield," Paul assured her.

After leisurely showers, Paul gave a smile of approval when he noticed that Hannah had selected the rather faded but comfortable military-style shirt she had worn on the train two weeks earlier. She, however, misinterpreted his expression.

"I would have preferred to wear your floral blouse," she said hastily, "but wanted to keep it for the trip to Chatsworth House. I've already worn it several times and it really needs washing."

He shook his head. "I like that shirt and have done so since we first met. It represents some of the things I love about you; namely that you're neat, well-organized and like simple practical clothes. You look great to me and it's a pleasure to escort you out this evening."

He held out his arm invitingly and she took it with a happy little laugh and a quick peck on the cheek.

As they had expected, the Castle Inn was busy even at six-thirty. But there was no hurry and Hannah relaxed and simply enjoyed looking around the attractive room with its beamed ceiling and woodwork. Every so often, she exchanged a small smile of pleasure with Paul as she sipped the cold drink he had brought her from the bar.

"I never dreamt that I would ever meet a man I'm so happy and comfortable to be with," she thought as a feeling of joy filled her heart. A perfect evening was helped by the fact that the meal, when it arrived, was very good.

When they had finished eating, Paul suggested crossing the road to sample a cup of coffee in the Lime Coffee House.

"We only had tea earlier. Hopefully coffee won't keep us awake after a fair amount of exercise today," he said.

"I'll sleep like a log!" Hannah replied. "We must see if your Google reviews are accurate!"

They were not disappointed, although they did restrict themselves to small cups, and afterwards they strolled happily through more of the town before returning to their pleasant accommodation for a good night's sleep.

They remembered just in time, however, to make a brief 'phone call to Paul's parents reporting their progress and aim to arrive in Sheffield by about four o'clock the following afternoon.

CHAPTER 25

It may have been the coffee, but Paul woke suddenly in the early hours of the morning. Only later did he come to realize that it was not by accident that he being offered a time of peace and quiet to take stock of all that had happened over the last fifteen days.

As he lay there in the stillness, he became aware of the deep debt of gratitude he owed his parents and sister for their years of faithful prayer: something he and his younger brother had always shrugged off as rather quaint. He now knew that this expression of love and concern was the means by which God had chosen to work in his life. Outwardly, everything appeared to have started on the train from St Pancras to Sheffield, but the deeper reality was that things had already been happening in the heavenly realm.

Like a lot of men, Paul had always been attracted by beautiful women; indeed he had completely lost his head to a beautiful student in his second year at university. She had surprised him by returning his favour and being very willing to enter into an amorous relationship until their rather traumatic break-up three months later.

Hannah did not possess the beauty that normally appealed to him, but something about her had attracted him on that fateful train journey. So much so that, realizing she was a serious walker, he had caused embarrassment by suggesting she might like to accompany him on his trek up the Pennine Way. It was only his help with other things – the dongle, in particular – that had saved the day.

Things had progressed rapidly from there. They were soon walking together in such a friendly and relaxed way that she had been prepared to share the twin-bedded room in Standedge that he had booked when planning the trek with John. He was fairly certain that the shock caused by the crooks' sudden appearance in Edale had only partly influenced her decision.

His parents and other older Christians might have been shocked if they had known about the room sharing, but, even after

Hannah and he had become Christians, their consciences were clear: they had always behaved impeccably and given each other as much privacy as possible.

By the time they reached Tan Hill, Hannah had cautiously accepted the change of status from walking companion to girlfriend. No doubt, the dongle saga had brought them closer together, but the change had happened remarkably quickly, only four days after first meeting.

Then, of course, everything occurred with even greater rapidity: their arrived in Haltwhistle in time to go to the Sunday evening meeting in Sue's church; Peter's astonishing testimony to the love and mercy of God, followed by his almost equally surprising words to them privately afterwards; their time in God's presence sitting on a rock overlooking Hadrian's Wall, ending with their kneeling together at the foot of the Cross.

Finally, there was Hannah's willing acceptance of his proposal to get married, followed by the confirmation of God's outworking in their lives when they met Mike – their erstwhile blond pursuer – in Horton and witnessed the power of God changing his life and giving him peace.

As Paul gave silent thanks to God for the abundant blessings that had been bestowed upon him, the atmosphere in the room seemed to change and he was inwardly aware of a holy presence in the room.

"Lord Jesus, from the bottom of my heart I thank you for Calvary," he whispered quietly. "May I offer myself, my life and my marriage to you? Please surround Hannah, even now while she sleeps, with your Holy Spirit; indeed may your presence become greater in us and the things of this world less."

The room was still almost completely dark but the atmosphere seemed to shimmer with anticipation – could it be that he was sensing Jesus' response? The faintest possible breeze swept across the room and he was filled with inexpressible joy. Time seemed to stand still, although the extraordinary experience probably only lasted a few minutes before the room returned to normal.

Slowly he slipped into three hours of the deepest sleep he had ever known.

He woke with Hannah shaking his shoulder gently. "Wake up sleepy head. The alarm's just gone off: it's ten past seven!"

By nine-fifteen they were back on the Monsal Trail going north. "I don't understand it," Hannah was saying. "I know I slept well and the breakfast was good, but we've had good nights for most of the holiday, so it can't be that. However, I don't think I've ever felt so well or full of energy. I feel like running all the way to Sheffield!"

Paul took her hand and drew her to the side of the track. "Let me tell you what happened in the middle of the night," he said.

A few minutes later, they continued on their journey rejoicing. Paul, to his surprise, found a well-know hymn of praise echoing in his head. Being in such an exuberant mood, he surprised Hannah by bursting into song. Although she was unfamiliar with most of the verses, she managed to join him with the chorus, somewhat to the amusement of several passing hikers.

They left the Trail at Hassop Station Café and made their way on to the B6001 road leading to the village of the same name, rather surprisingly well over a mile north of the old station. The narrow road made its way through a pleasant flat landscape of green fields.

"I hope it doesn't rain soon," Paul said, looking up at the increasing clouds overhead.

In Hassop, the road took them past an attractive pub called the "Eyre Arms" that made them think of coffee. Although it was not yet half past ten, they decided to stop and were soon enjoying a very pleasant coffee break. In fact, this turned out to be a good decision because it began to rain just as they were preparing to leave.

"At least we can put our waterproof capes on in the dry," Hannah remarked thankfully.

The rain was still quite light and so they decided against waterproof leggings.

"This is the last day we'll need to use our walking jeans," she said. "They can't get much worse after wearing them almost every day for the last two weeks, except when we had shorts."

The B6001 continued north for two miles towards the village of Calver through what would have been an extremely attractive wooded valley if the weather had been better. Passing quickly through the surprisingly large village, they had to cross the A623.

"This is the main road east to Chesterfield," Paul commented, "our last stop on the train to Sheffield. So we're less than twelve miles from home now."

The road began to follow the valley of the Derwent for two miles towards the small village of Grindleford. The scenery gradually got even better as the route got closer to the western bank of the river. When the gaps between the trees allowed, there were splendid views across the wet valley to the ridge opposite.

The road now merged with the B6521 as they approached the outskirts of the village. After another half mile, Paul guided Hannah into a small road running up a hill on their left and signposted for Hathersage.

"There used to be a nice hotel just up here where you can get something to eat," he said.

Just past the village school, they came to an attractive stone building bearing a hanging sign announcing "The Sir William Hotel" and surmounted by a portrait of a be-wigged gentleman in a red coat.

Once inside, Hannah whispered: "Aren't we a little too damp and scruffy for a pleasant place like this?"

Paul shook his head. "It also acts as the village pub."

Indeed, the friendly young woman behind the reception desk did not seem at all surprised to see two wet hikers and gave them a warm smile of welcome.

"If you'd like to hang up those wet capes, there are plenty of hooks in the corridor by the cloakrooms," she said. "Don't worry about your boots; they'll be fine in the bar."

Paul thanked her and they headed in the direction indicated. "I'll meet you in the bar in a few minutes," he said. "As soon as I get there I'll find a table and collect drinks from the bar and a menu."

A few minutes later, they were studying the lunchtime menu at a table in the popular bar. Hannah tried to slip two £10 notes into Paul's hand but he would only accept one. The prices were surprisingly reasonable and it was good to relax in such a warm, dry and welcoming place. In the end, they both chose baked potatoes and side salad, but with different fillings.

While they were waiting for the food, Paul began to explain his plan for the early afternoon.

"I'm hoping the weather will allow me to take you up a lovely path through a narrow wooded valley beside Burbage Brook: a tributary of the Derwent. It's about two miles long and called the Padley Gorge Trail. It comes out on the Edale road about seven miles from the centre of Sheffield. From there we can get a bus for about four miles and then walk the short distance home."

"Alternatively, if the rain gets worse, we can catch the train from Grindleford to the next stop, Dore and Totley, where we started out just over two weeks ago. We've got to walk up to Grindleford station anyway because that's where the Trail starts. Just in case, I'll see if the hotel has a list of train times."

He stopped to ponder for a moment before glancing over at Hannah to see if she agreed with his suggestions, only to find that she was looking at him with one of her slightly amused smiles.

"I love the way Paul plans everything so carefully," she was thinking. "I suppose it's because I like being well-organized myself, although I've been happy just to relax on this holiday and let him take care of everything. I love him so much!"

She was just about to say this when he spoke again.

"It only seems two days, not two weeks, since leaving Sheffield; I've enjoyed the time so much, not least because I've met the most wonderful girl in the world!"

Hannah's eyes became moist, but her rather quirky humour took over. "I'm so pleased for you. I look forward to meeting her."

"Well," Paul said, now pretending to be speaking into a 'phone, "if you can get here within the next forty-five minutes you can do so today. She's sitting opposite me right now looking rather bedraggled but totally adorable!"

He was prevented from saying any more by the appearance of their baked potatoes, but Hannah, not even caring about the lock of rather damp hair that had dropped over her forehead, gave him one of her special smiles that made his heart miss a beat.

By the time they were ready to leave, the sky looked considerably brighter. They left the hotel through a rear entrance into the garden and car park. From this vantage point, the view over the valley was really lovely even through the fine drizzle that was still falling.

"Come on, we can easily manage that walk through the gorge!" Hannah said as she took Paul's hand in a warm grip and almost pulled him back to the lane and down towards the main road. Turning left, they followed the road down as it approached the river before going over a stone bridge.

"This village has what looks like a cricket pitch," Paul said in surprise. "I've not noticed it on earlier visits."

"Probably because it's a popular commuter village for Sheffield," Hannah said sensibly.

As they passed a rather imposing hotel and some larger houses, Paul observed: "There's a hotel that would not be pleased if we went in with wet muddy boots and I guess these houses are for wealthy city folk who prefer not to walk far to the station."

"But surely they're two car families!" Hannah said.

Paul laughed as he guided her left up a narrow road to the station. "Wait until you see the parking facilities!" he said. "It's first come, first served. It must be difficult if you have to drive a long way and arrive late. But perhaps they don't have parking wardens here."

He was right. Even in the middle of the holiday season, all the spaces were taken and several cars were parked against the verge.

"Where's the station?" Hannah asked, suddenly realizing that they were level with the top of the railway bridge just ahead of them: there was no sign of a building, except for a small café.

Paul pointed to pedestrian path that dropped down out of sight through the trees. "Just down there; we'll see it from the bridge when we cross. Would you like a coffee? I completely forgot to offer you one after lunch. That little café is said to be good. Walkers are looked after even if car owners are not!"

"Probably also helpful for commuters who have to find a place to park back in the village and miss the train!" Hannah said. "But yes please for the coffee."

The entrance to Padley Gorge Trail was immediately in front of them beyond the railway bridge. The rain had now stopped completely. They climbed up the winding path past huge moss-covered rocks and under ancient oaks. Drops of water fell from the wet leaves and the pleasing sound of Burbage Brook could be heard splashing merrily as it hurried down to join the Derwent. Hannah was so intrigued that she drew Paul off the path more than once and scrambled to the bank just for the pleasure of seeing the water tumbling over rocks and cascading down small waterfalls.

A short distance further, the path turned to climb up and over a wooden footbridge cleverly set into enormous rocks that edged the brook.

Paul put his arm around Hannah's shoulders as they stood admiring the scene. Upstream, the sides of the gorge tumbled down to the water's edge in a profusion of rocks and foliage. Trees were clinging desperately to the steep slopes and a few had even given up the struggle and were leaning precariously inwards. On the bed of the brook many rocks of differing size caused the water to babble and swirl delightfully.

Eventually they moved on, the route now following the western side of the brook. They were still climbing and the trees became fewer as they left the ancient woodland behind. The rapidly improving weather seemed to have encouraged the birds into greater activity, flitting excitedly from one tree or bush to another.

An attractive open landscape was now evident on their left, but it was to the right that Hannah's eyes kept being drawn; Burbage Brook was still churning its way past rocks and over small waterfalls. They even passed a small weir.

"I expect the water flow has to be controlled in very wet weather," Paul said, "or there might be flooding further down. By the way, a lot of this landscape has been created by quarrying that took place a hundred years ago to provide stone for building."

As if to prove his point, they passed a huge pile of moss-covered stones on the open ground to their left.

The Trail took them back over the brook. Fifty yards further on, Paul stopped and pointed to a path that led off to their right.

"The Trail finishes just ahead on the main road from Hathersage to Sheffield," he explained. "This other path runs parallel to the road and comes out on the B6521 from Grindleford just before it joins the main road near a pub and bus stop."

The Fox House turned out to be a large building situated on a bend on the A6187. Just beyond was a bus stop where two people were standing and looking expectant. When questioned, they said that a Sheffield bus was already overdue by several minutes.

It turned out to be quite a pleasant place to wait now that the sky was almost clear of clouds and the sun was lighting up the surrounding slopes. By the time the bus came there were not many seats available and Paul had to stand beside a seated Hannah after he had left their rucksacks in the luggage bay.

After a four-mile bus journey and a walk of about fifteen minute, Paul rang the doorbell of his parents' modest house.

Sarah opened the door with a cry of pleasure. "How lovely, you're a few minutes early!" she cried. "Come in, come in. Take off your rucksacks and let me give you both a big hug – my prospective daughter-in-law first!"

She greeted the couple with such delight that Hannah had tears in her eyes as she returned the greeting. In fact, both women had to wipe their eyes before Sarah managed to continue at the rapid rate that Hannah remembered from her first visit.

"I'll put the kettle on. You must be dying for a cup of tea. Take your things upstairs and come down when you're ready. Start bringing down any clothes you want put in the washing machine; I'll do one load tonight and another first thing tomorrow morning – perhaps the heavier things like jeans and trousers. Dad's promised to be back in time for a meal at six-thirty. You can share the most important part of the news then."

She stopped abruptly, beamed at them and disappeared into the kitchen.

Hannah spent fifteen minutes upstairs unpacking, changing her clothes and sorting out some things needing washing. Going downstairs with a bundle of dirty things, she saw that Paul had already arrived with his own bundle.

"The teapot has stood for long enough. Please pour some tea, dear," Sarah said, "while I start putting your clothes in the machine."

Over tea, the young couple described some of the highlights of their long walk. To her surprise, Hannah found that Sarah had never seen any of the Pennine Way, except for its beginning in Edale.

"You must both be extremely fit," Sarah declared. "I never thought you'd walk that far in such a short time. I hope Paul didn't push you too hard!"

"On the contrary, I had a job keeping up with her," Paul said with a chuckle and a loving look across the table at his fiancée.

"I don't believe that," Hannah exclaimed, "you were always very considerate, adjusting your pace to make sure I was comfortable."

"Anyway, I could not have asked for a better walking companion," Paul said with complete seriousness.

Sarah smiled gently when she saw that Hannah was quite moved by the compliment, even more so when Paul added in a soft voice, "…or companion full-stop."

When Jack arrived there were more hugs and expressions of delight. A happy family meal followed, during which Paul and Hannah gave an edited version of all that had happened on their first evening in Haltwhistle and on the Hadrian's Wall the following day.

To say Jack was astonished would be an understatement and Sarah was even reduced to tears. Paul moved over and put his arm around his mother's shoulders. "God is so gracious," was all she could whisper through her tears.

Later, they were able to discuss the arrangements for the trip to Chatsworth. With a careful eye on the weather forecast, Jack had decided to book four tickets on-line for the following day, Wednesday, rather than wait until their last day in Sheffield.

"The tickets are expensive and I want to contribute towards the cost," Paul said as he handed his father a cheque for £50.

Jack did not want to take it but the young couple insisted. "We also want to take you both out for a meal either tomorrow or Thursday," Hannah added.

CHAPTER 26

The next day was warm and fine. It was a happy party who set off at nine-thirty on the fifteen mile journey to Chatsworth House, seat of the Dukes of Devonshire for over three hundred years. Paul and Hannah held hands in comfort on the back seat of Jack's taxi.

"This is one of the advantages of being an owner-driver," Jack said as they drove. "You don't need to get the boss' permission to use a taxi and pay a mileage charge."

They drove past the small Dore and Totley station, where their walking adventure had started a mere fifteen days ago, and south down the A612 for twelve miles or so until joining the A619 going south-west. Almost immediately, they passed the private entrance to the Chatsworth estate on their left, but Jack knew that the public entrance to the House and grounds was two miles further.

"Strangely enough, we're four miles north-east of Bakewell where we stayed on the last night of our walk," Paul commented.

Chatsworth House stood close to the east bank of the River Derwent. As Jack turned the car into the entrance of the enormous grounds and drove towards the river bridge, Hannah gasped in amazement. "It's magnificent!" she exclaimed.

The western face of the palatial baroque house stood at the foot of a wooded ridge, a small part of its formal gardens visible to one side. The honey-grey stone of the building seemed to glow even though the sun's rays had not yet reached the façade.

"Welcome to the work of the famous landscape gardener, Capability Brown," Paul said as he waved his hand towards the picturesque scene. "The gardens and park were all designed by him; he was lucky to have a nice river going through the grounds."

Jack drove over the river and a cattle grid to enter the inner part of the estate and soon found the large car park.

"If we go into the house first, it would probably be a good idea to leave our lunch in the car to be collected later," he said.

The inside of the great house was so impressive that all four of them were almost lost for words; Paul and his family had visited the gardens before but not the house. Sarah immediately thought of the amount of work the domestic staff would have had to do in the days when the house functioned solely as the family home of the duke and duchess and their extensive family.

"Managing the cleaning of a large hotel was a mere nothing in comparison," she exclaimed, "and we had all the advantages of modern appliances!"

"I thought you said your mother was a chambermaid," Hannah whispered to Paul.

"She started as a chambermaid in Sheffield when she was seventeen and eventually worked in the Leopold Hotel in the city centre for about ten years before retiring towards the end of my final year at university," he replied quietly. "However, during her last eight years she was promoted, first to head chambermaid and then housekeeper, where she was in charge of all the cleaning staff."

"In fact," he continued, "the manager was so pleased with her that he persuaded her to stay on for an extra year. It's a hotel of the old style, not like the modern type where all the rooms are identical. Perhaps we'll see it tomorrow."

Then he realized they had just entered the large music room. His parents were standing with a group of people peering through an open door. He knew what was attracting all the attention because he had read about a remarkable feature in this room.

He took Hannah's arm and held her back until there were fewer people in that part of the room. Then he took her over.

"Come and look at what's on the other side of the door," he whispered. His parents looked on with some amusement.

Hannah looked and saw a violin with its bow hanging on a hook on a second door on the other side of the thick panelled casement.

"That violin looks very old and valuable!" she said in surprise. "Why isn't it locked up in a glass showcase?"

Paul laughed. "Because it's a painting!" he said, "done over three hundred years ago by Jan Vander Vaardt. There's a French name for this particular technique, meaning to "fool the eye". What amazes me is how it has been kept in such good condition."

Although they continued on through a succession of magnificent rooms containing elaborate antique furniture and expensive-looking paintings, it was the violin hanging on the back of a door that was to remain etched in Hannah's memory.

Nearly two hours after arriving in the car park, they left the great house and went to find a cup of coffee. Having finished his drink, Paul left the others while he returned to the car to collect the picnic lunch.

When he returned, they began to tour the formal gardens. It was a good job that Jack had a visitors' map of the layout because there was so much to see: the tall "Emperor" fountain at one end of a long rectangular pond; the even more spectacular cascade with water flowing down a succession of wide-shallow steps built into the slope of the hill behind the great house; and even a small maze. The list of various features seemed almost endless.

Sarah was intrigued by an area labelled the "Cottage Garden and Sensory Garden" and so they agreed to separate for an hour and then meet up again at the section on the map marked for picnics. Jack took over the lunch bag, while the young couple went to investigate the maze before having a delightful time roaming the paths and walkways threading through the less formal part of the gardens.

"Years ago I remember coming with the family and having a splendid time with my sister and brother playing hide-and-seek around here! I think some of the more elderly visitors were rather shocked," Paul recalled with a chuckle.

"I bet children have played that game here for centuries," Hannah retorted. "Probably with anxious nursemaids scuttling around hoping nobody was going to get hurt!"

In the end, without the map to guide them, the two young people were a little late finding the picnic area. Sarah and Jack had already started eating. Sarah, of course, had made too many sandwiches, but her hungry son made short work of several.

It was nearly three-thirty in the afternoon when they returned to the main gardens; Sarah wanted a quick look at the Arboretum. This turned out to be part of the informal gardens that Hannah and Paul had already explored. They were quite happy, however, to follow on behind just enjoying Sarah's enthusiasm as she looked at some of the plants and shrubs and examining the labels.

About an hour later, they returned to the car tired but happy.

Paul's parents thought that they could enjoy his and Hannah's hospitality more if they delayed their meal out until the following evening. In fact, as they motored home for a welcome cup of tea, followed later by a simple supper, Sarah had a suggestion.

"As a retired member of the senior staff at the Leopold, I can get 35% off the cost of a meal in the restaurant. Last year, I took Jack for a nice dinner to celebrate our wedding anniversary. I can book a table when we get home if that idea appeals to you."

"That's a lovely idea!" Hannah said after looking at Paul for his approval. "It would also be nice to see where you used to work, but please don't go into autopilot and start inspecting bedrooms."

Sarah laughed. "As housekeeper, I had to spot check at least half the bedrooms every day and all the public rooms."

"How did you manage to bring up three children?" Hannah exclaimed.

"Well, I was only a humble chambermaid most of the time and finished at about two o'clock in the afternoon unless on late shift. After Sue was born, poor Jack had to hold the fort until his mother arrived to take over; fortunately his parents only lived half a mile away – in fact in the house we now have. Paul was born six years after Sue, but she soon became a surprisingly helpful child and would even do some of the housework after school. Mark is just over a year younger than Paul and so the pressure grew when we had two young boys to cope with. But we managed somehow!"

Sarah looked back over her shoulder at Paul with a loving smile. "All three of our children have turned out splendidly," she said and then added: "Of course, Hannah, don't forget that they were young adults by the time I was promoted and had greater responsibilities at work and often had to stay quite late in the evening. Sue had a secretarial job but was always home in time to cook the evening meal if necessary and the boys were either at college or university. Sue only got married and went to live in Haltwhistle about two years before I retired."

"My father ran two successful greengrocers in Sheffield for years and owned the larger one outright," Jack volunteered suddenly. "I managed the smaller shop until it could no longer survive the supermarket competition and had to close. That's why I became a taxi driver. We inherited my parents' old house, mortgage free, soon after my father died. My mother went downhill very quickly and only survived him by nine months. It was very sad."

Everyone became rather sombre and quiet for the rest of the journey and Hannah felt sorry she had unwittingly stirred up some painful memories.

Over a welcome cup of tea and a slice of Sarah's homemade cake, however, everyone was much more cheerful; the happiness of the day's outing had been restored.

After the meal that Hannah helped to prepare, Jack kindly suggested that she might like to 'phone her parents on the landline instead of wasting money using her mobile. It was the first time she had spoken to them since announcing her engagement. After a good chat, she was delighted when her parents suggested bringing Paul down to stay on the farm for a few days later in August.

"We must start planning immediately!" her mother said with some alarm when Hannah informed her that she wanted the wedding to be just before Christmas.

"We want a very simple affair!" Hannah told her firmly.

Paul and Hannah's last day in Sheffield went amazingly quickly. Jack, of course, had to work again, but the young couple took Sarah into the city centre to find a present for her birthday, due in a few weeks. Paul went to the bank to draw some cash so that Hannah could take his mother and help her choose an item of clothing.

Meanwhile, he relaxed in a café with a cup of coffee and a small notebook to begin planning his physics lessons for the new term; it would be the first time he had taught the second-year of the A-level course and his students would be those he had had during the previous two terms.

An hour later, the others joined him looking pleased with the result of their search. Sarah opened her carrier bag to give Paul a glimpse of her nice new blouse.

He continued his lesson planning during a quiet afternoon, feeling some urgency because he had been invited to join Hannah and her family on the farm during the last few days of August.

He did not stop until Jack came home for the inevitable cup of tea around the kitchen table. Meanwhile, Sarah and Hannah had both had showers and so everyone was ready to leave for the Leopold by seven o'clock.

The evening was a real success. Sarah was greeted like an old friend by several members of staff, including the senior of the two receptionists who came out from behind her counter to greet Sarah with a handshake that rapidly turned into a hug.

"The head waiter is looking forward to seeing you again," she exclaimed, "and when you get to the table you'll find that the manager has instructed him to put a celebratory bottle on ice. Don't worry; I made sure they remembered that it should have low alcohol content."

In the attractive restaurant, the head waiter, after profuse greetings, took them to one of the best tables where a waiter was waiting to help pull out the chairs and open a bottle of sparkling wine that he produced with a flourish from an ice bucket.

"All this is amazing," Hannah whispered to Paul. "Not only have I never been in such a nice hotel but Sarah's welcome has been overwhelming; she must have been a very highly regarded housekeeper."

"She was quite strict – having been brought up in the old school – but was always kind and patient, especially with new inexperienced staff," Paul said quietly.

After a very enjoyable meal, they had not long adjourned to the lounge for coffee when a distinguished-looking man in a smart suit came in and introduced himself as the duty manager.

"I'm a relative newcomer here," he said, "but the manager expressed his great admiration and respect for you before he left earlier and asked me to make sure that you are being well cared for this evening. We also hope the sparkling wine was to your taste."

The man looked both pleased and relieved when Sarah and Jack said how nice everything had been and asked him to convey the family's thanks to the manager for his kindness.

"I shall certainly do so," he promised and then looked at Hannah and Paul. "May I congratulate you on your engagement; I don't suppose you will be getting married in Sheffield – although you would be very welcome in this hotel – but I wish you all a very happy day when it comes."

CHAPTER 27

Paul and Hannah's last happy evening with his parents in Sheffield seemed to have softened some of the pain of the next day's departure. The morning passed quickly with Hannah spending time chatting to Sarah in the kitchen as they shared the job of ironing the washing that had been done on their arrival. Sarah then made sandwiches for the journey while the young couple packed their rucksacks.

"Everything fits in so much more neatly when the clothes are nicely ironed," Paul said with a cheeky glance at his fiancée.

"Huh! Don't expect this treatment when we're married. I only did so much because your mother seemed to expect it!" Hannah retorted, "Although I must say it's lovely to go back with almost everything nice and clean; not the way I usually return from holiday!"

Their parting from Paul's mother was rather emotional, but Hannah was left with the sense that she had made a really good friend in Sarah. After a short bus journey, it was not long before they were seated on the London train and looking rather sadly out of the window as the eastern edge of the Peak District disappeared behind them.

To help Hannah cheer up, Paul went to get some coffee and they began to think about the visit to her family later in August.

"I must spend at least a week putting some flesh on my lesson outlines for next term as soon as I get back to Basingstoke," Paul said.

"No problem," Hannah retorted, "my parents are not expecting us until the Tuesday before August Bank Holiday weekend: that's in about ten day's time. I suspect they want us to spend our week there as near as possible to the end of the school holidays so that we can help with harvesting! Anyway, there are hourly slow trains from

Waterloo to Exeter that stop at both Basingstoke and Sherborne. You can join me on the train at Basingstoke."

Just before the train arrived in St Pancras, Paul announced: "I'm determined to see you safely settled back in Tooting."

Although Hannah was inwardly delighted, she tried to object because of the delay it would cause him. However, he clinched the matter by saying: "I'd like to see where you live so that I can picture you during the lonely days ahead!"

Once in Tooting Broadway, they did a little shopping before walking to her top-floor studio flat.

"You're certainly right about it being tiny; it makes my flat look almost palatial!" Paul exclaimed.

"That's good," Hannah said as she put the kettle on, "because soon there'll be two of us living there. I'm looking forward to seeing it."

Over a cup of tea, they decided to meet only once during the ten days before the Dorset visit to give Paul some chance of finishing his work; Hannah would take a day trip to Basingstoke the following Wednesday.

After a simple meal that she quickly prepared, Paul took his reluctant departure and made his way sadly to Waterloo for the next train to Basingstoke. It felt strange to be on his own for the first time in nineteen days and the small quiet flat just emphasized his loneliness, especially after he had 'phoned Hannah to tell her that he had arrived safely.

After a cup of coffee and carefully stowing all his nicely washed and ironed clothes, he spent a long time praying for Hannah and all the family members and finally went to bed much happier.

Except for Sunday, when he went to his local Anglican church in the morning and a nearby Baptist church in the evening, Paul worked extremely hard until the time came to meet Hannah off the London train just before midday the following Wednesday.

They hugged for at least a minute before he guided her to a coffee shop where they could exchange news.

"My parents are really looking forward to next Tuesday," Hannah announced. "They've even booked us a meeting the same evening with the vicar of our village church so that we can arrange the wedding booking and the details that will be needed for the banns to be read both there and in the parish churches in Tooting and Basingstoke."

"I tried the Anglican church near my flat last Sunday morning and a Baptist church in the evening," Paul told her. "Of course, we'll need to try places together before we settle somewhere."

But Hannah was looking at him rather sheepishly. "What's wrong?" he said, with some concern.

"Reading between the lines, I think I know the reason why my father wants us to get the visit to the vicar out of the way; he's hoping we'll start working on Wednesday helping to harvest our broccoli! I may not have told you, but our farm is only a small one and specializes in organic vegetables, together with a small apple orchard and a few chickens."

"I'd be delighted to help, provided we can work together that is!" Paul said. "I love being out in the fresh air – and with you of course!" he added quickly.

Hannah relaxed and beamed at him. She squeezed his hand under the table. "I'll be alongside you all the time. After all, I'll be your boss and showing you how to it! I used to be able to harvest broccoli almost blindfold: it's one of our major crops."

Paul grinned at her. "And there I was thinking that your father was a gentleman farmer with lots of employees and living in an enormous farmhouse!"

"Rubbish! I'm sure I told you we only had one part-time farm hand. However, the house is quite large because it used to be part of a much larger farm. In fact, we only got our organic certification about five years ago; for over two years before that we were really struggling financially because we had a lower crop yield during the transition period – due to all the restrictions imposed – but our produce could not be sold as organic."

"Do you remember our first meal on the Pennine Way in Standedge?" Paul said, appearing to change the subject completely.

"How could I forget, especially when it was followed by your brilliant deduction about the dongle!" Hannah exclaimed.

"Well, while we were eating, I looked across at you and got the picture of a schoolgirl coming home from school and trying to juggle both her homework and jobs around the farm," he explained. "However, it was milking the cows that I imagined, not planting, harvesting or sorting vegetables; so I got that bit wrong."

Hannah laughed. "I've never milked a cow in my life, but you're right about the hard work. It was particularly difficult in my GCSE year as my results showed!"

"All this is another reason why I love you so," Paul said softly, but continued quickly to avoid getting distracted by her obvious pleasure. "Continuing the Standedge theme, however, I've got some lunch all ready to cook when we get to my flat; plenty of vegetables peeled, cut and ready for boiling and two thin lamb steaks that have been marinating in some cheap red wine overnight to help make sure they're tender! I'm determined to do better than the ones we had in that restaurant. I hope you can wait until about two o'clock before we eat?"

"Of course," Hannah replied. "It sounds delicious. Thank you for taking all this trouble."

Fifteen minutes later, they arrived at Paul's flat. Hannah was delighted by the size of the open-plan living area; even with a table and four chairs, a small settee and easy chair, a bookcase and a desk, there was still a reasonable amount of floor area.

"My whole flat could fit in here," she murmured.

But the bedroom was much less impressive; it was almost completely filled by the single bed and modest amount of bedroom furniture. There was, however, a decent built-in wardrobe with a mirror on one of its doors.

Paul could see her disappointment. "Most of the furniture comes with the flat except for my desk and computer. I'll ask the landlord to remove this single bed. If the chest of drawers goes in the living room, I think a standard double bed will just fit in here. It might be a good idea for us to choose one on the way back to the station; I can then order it fairly soon."

They worked together on the meal and Hannah was most complimentary when she started eating. "These steaks are delicious," she said. "I must remember the marinade trick."

They had such a good time together that the flat seemed very empty when Paul returned from seeing his fiancée off on the London train. Extremely hard work during the next few days, however, kept him occupied, buoyed up by their regular evening 'phone contact.

At 10:25 on Tuesday, Paul was standing, full of excitement, on the platform of Basingstoke station waiting for the Exeter train to arrive. He and Hannah had decided to book tickets on-line from London to Sherborne and specified the 9:50 from London Waterloo to obtain the best advanced fare available, returning a week later on a train shortly before midday.

Quite remarkably, it was appreciably cheaper for Paul to do this than obtain his tickets between Basingstoke and Sherborne because the advanced-fare discount was not available over the shorter distance. Not surprisingly, he wanted to accompany Hannah all the way back to her flat on the return journey anyway. He would just need to purchase a single ticket to Basingstoke when he returned home in the late evening.

They had agreed that Hannah would be as near as possible to the fifth carriage from the front and so he had positioned himself on the platform accordingly. The train was a few minutes late, but, at long last, he saw her waving through the window as it drew to a halt. The carriage was not very crowded and she had managed to save him a seat beside her.

She immediately launched into sharing the latest news.

"I told you earlier that my uncle is kindly meeting us at the station and driving us to the farm. Well, he has now offered to take us out for a meal beforehand so that he can have the chance to get acquainted before you stay with him the night before the wedding. He says he knows of a nice country-house hotel about two miles east of Sherborne where he may take us. Of course, I gratefully accepted the offer and then 'phoned my mother to say that we would arrive at the farm mid-afternoon."

She paused, now a little embarrassed. "I've been putting two and two together on the train. My uncle already knows that we hope to marry on the Sunday afternoon before Christmas and that my parents have invited Sarah and Jack to stay on at the farm for Christmas and expect us to join them on Christmas Eve – the Wednesday. Well, to my surprise, he ended our 'phone call last night by casually asking what we planned to do for the three nights beforehand! I simply said that we'd not thought about it yet but would obviously want to go somewhere fairly near. However, I'm now wondering if he's dangling this particular hotel in front of us for a reason; it would explain why he's not taking us to a restaurant in the town."

"I'll certainly pick up a brochure there," Paul said. "I'm determined to take you somewhere really nice and a country-house hotel might be ideal for the short time that we have available."

"But it's probably very expensive!" Hannah said with some concern.

"Ridiculously so for Christmas itself, but they probably have a really enticing rate for the few days just before: it must be a very slack time," was his reply.

CHAPTER 28

Hannah's uncle was waiting for them at entrance to Sherborne station. "This is my Uncle Ted," she said to Paul as she introduced them.

"Just call me Ted," a friendly-looking man in his mid-sixties said as he shook hands vigorously. "I'm so glad to have the opportunity to meet the fiancé of my favourite niece!"

Hannah laughed, "I'm your only niece!" Nevertheless, Paul could tell she was pleased with the compliment.

Ted shrugged as he led them to his car. "Well, I'm still very fond of you and want to wish you both a very happy life together. Rebecca, my sister, tells me that you're fixed up to see the vicar this evening. I very much hope he can manage a wedding on the Sunday afternoon just before Christmas; it must be a very busy time."

"We really hope so," Paul said. "It's the earliest date we can manage because Hannah needs to give a term's notice at her school. If we had to leave it until the beginning of January, there'd be no time for even a short honeymoon before the next term starts at my college."

It was not long before Ted had driven the short distance north through the town centre and joined the A30 going east towards Salisbury.

"Our train stopped in Salisbury fifty minutes ago. I hope we're not going all the way back there!" Hannah joked.

"The Grange Hotel is just over a mile along here and then a short distance up a narrow road on the left," Ted replied. "It's part of the Best Western hotel chain; very quiet and pleasant. I expect we'll have to eat in the bar at lunchtime but I can show you the very nice dining room. My wife and I have had dinner there several times; the last not long before she died. It was cancer; I expect Hannah told you, Paul?" Ted was suddenly silent with the painful recollection.

"Yes – I'm so very sorry!" Paul said quietly.

"At least the end came suddenly and she didn't suffer much," Ted said.

"Uncle," Hannah said. "You shouldn't be taking us to a place that stirs up unhappy memories."

"If you like it and decide it would be good for your very short honeymoon, then it will have been well worth it!" Ted said firmly. "I'll keep it a secret, of course!"

Hannah, sitting beside Paul on the back seat, looked at him with a smile that said, "I told you so!"

Part of the front of the hotel edged a narrow lane that seemed to lead to nowhere in particular. The Grange clearly functioned by reputation, not by attracting passing trade. Ted parked cautiously beside an expensive-looking Mercedes and they made their way to the attractive bar.

When Ted was younger, he and his wife had been keen walkers. He was therefore interested to hear about some of the young couple's experiences on the Pennine Way while they all enjoyed an excellent hot "dish of the day".

Afterwards, they had a pleasant walk in the attractive grounds at the rear of the building. Most of the public rooms had wide panoramic windows overlooking peaceful lawns dotted with mature trees. What were clearly the more expensive bedrooms on the upper two floors had the same splendid outlook.

Paul could see that Hannah was impressed; neither of them had stayed in a top-quality hotel before and he was determined to bring her here after the wedding even if the prices were high. Uncle Ted looked on smiling: his plan was working.

After Paul had collected a brochure giving details of the tariff for the coming autumn and winter months, Ted drove them for about four miles through attractive countryside until reaching the outskirts of a small village. Hannah took Paul's hand as they did several more twists and turns before pulling into a peaceful yard.

"We're home," she said. "It looks just the same as ever!"

Facing them across a paved yard was a large farmhouse, its rather shabby exterior considerably improved by a huge climbing rose carefully trained up and along wires attached to the wall.

Ted parked the car and the three of them approached the front door, welcomed by the delicate scent of a profusion of yellow roses.

The door opened before Hannah could ring the bell. A small wiry woman, her sun-tanned face creased in a beaming smile, stood there with her arms extended in welcome.

"There you are! I thought I heard the car!" she exclaimed as she exchanged an enormous hug with Hannah.

Ted then received the same treatment before the woman turned to Paul, now not quite sure whether she should hug him too.

"My mother, Rebecca," Hannah said quickly, although it was hardly necessary. "Mum, please meet Paul, my wonderful fiancé!"

Paul quickly took Rebecca's still partly extended hands in his and shook them warmly.

"I'm happy with hugs too," he said. "My mother was hugging Hannah within a few hours of our arrival and we'd only just met as complete strangers on the train to Sheffield. Anyway, it's great to meet you and very kind of you to invite me to visit with Hannah."

"Paul's looking forward to helping me pick the broccoli – I gather dad has left us a large section just ready to cut for the first time," Hannah said, realizing that her mother was rather in awe of the fact that Paul was a university graduate teaching A-level physics.

Paul's words and Hannah's intervention had done the trick. Rebecca found her voice again.

"I'm so glad you were able to come. The kettle's just boiled and I'll make the tea. Hannah will show you upstairs and then the living room when you're ready. I'll bring the tea tray in there."

"Mum, we're quite happy to come to the kitchen for tea!" Hannah exclaimed. "You go there with Ted now and I'll take Paul upstairs with our things."

Upstairs, she showed him where her parents' room was situated and her own single room opposite, next to the bathroom. Down a short corridor, they came to two sizeable doubles, the first with twin beds and the second with a double bed and a small en-suite with a rather ancient-looking shower. Hannah explained the arrangements.

"Mum has made up one of the single beds for you but says you're welcome to use the shower. Your parents will have the twin when they come for Christmas and your sister's family the double; a neighbour can lend us a cot for Toby. Then, of course, we'll have the double room when we return on Christmas Eve."

A few minutes later, Hannah took Paul downstairs to the homely farmhouse kitchen where Ted was already sitting at the big table sipping a cup of tea.

"Mum, I've told Paul that he can call you Becca, as most other people do. I hope that's OK?"

"Of course it is!" Becca said as she poured their tea. "Do try one of these little fairy cakes. A dear friend of mine made them in honour of your visit."

"You live in a lovely part of the country, Becca, it's so peaceful," Paul said. "My parents have a small house in a suburb of Sheffield and my father has to drive for hours, often in heavy traffic. He's a taxi driver, although hoping to retire in just over a year's time. For years I had to walk a couple of miles to college and then even further to university along drab streets and busy roads."

He smiled when he had another thought. "Sometimes at the weekend," he recalled, "my friends and I would travel a few miles into the Peak District just to get some real countryside and long hikes in fresh air."

"Mum, you should see some of the beautiful scenery in the Peaks and on the Pennine Way," Hannah exclaimed enthusiastically. "Paul and I had a lovely time and masses of exercise!"

She smiled warmly at her finance because she realized that he had deliberately mentioned his father's occupation to help her mother relax and not put him on some sort of academic pedestal.

Ted had been invited to stay for the evening meal and so he took Paul on a brief tour of the small farm while Hannah helped Becca in the kitchen. It was not long before they paused on the edge of a field of swedes and waved to Hannah's father and his farmhand hard at work near the centre.

"Welcome!" Hannah's father called across the intervening space. "I'll greet you properly when I come in and clean up!" He raised hands covered in muddy soil.

Ted and Paul acknowledged his greeting and walked on.

"I don't know how David manages to cope at the busy times of year," the former remarked. "His assistant Bert is only works part time normally, although he's coming every day at the moment, and the help my sister can give is fairly limited because she has the chickens to look after and the house to run. Occasionally, David's able to borrow a Romanian girl from a neighbouring farm: apparently she's excellent, especially at sorting and washing vegetables ready for market."

They returned to the house and Ted began to ask Paul about his work.

"I'd be really interested to hear how you try to encourage your students to carry on studying physics, mathematics, or engineering at university or technical college," he said.

"Before I retired about a year ago, I worked as an accountant – in fact the only accountant – in a small engineering company making electric pumps and other small electromagnetic devices. As our older engineers and factory technicians retired it became increasingly difficult to find well-qualified young people able to take their place."

Ted looked thoughtful. "I can only think of two reasons: first, schools may be tempted to improve their performance rating by encouraging pupils to opt for the easier subjects; secondly, many young people may be living for the "now" and regard science and engineering as boring and too analytical, demanding perseverance!"

Of course, Paul could not supply any easy answers to this conundrum but he did launch into a description of some of the interesting experimental and investigative projects that his physics department was trying out in the effort to make the subject more practically relevant to the students.

Ted was interested and asked so many perceptive questions that it was with some surprise that they heard Hannah's father's voice in the kitchen raised in affectionate greeting to his daughter.

When David came into the living-room with Hannah to greet his prospective son-in-law, he turned out to be small and wiry rather like his wife, although a couple of inches taller. He was very friendly and asked Paul several questions about his job and its prospects.

Although clearly fond of his daughter, he seemed rather dismissive of the fact that she had chosen to teach PE, especially as far away as London. Perhaps, thought Paul, it was because he was disappointed that she had not followed a career in farming.

Hannah disappeared back to the kitchen to help her mother dish up, and, a few minutes later, the men were called to the kitchen table. The meal went well, greatly helped by Ted who was adept at keeping up a lively conversation.

Hannah grinned broadly when Paul expressed his appreciation of a delicious concoction of mashed swedes.

"We grow so many swedes that mum has made this dish a speciality," Hannah told him. "She has more than one variation, so we never get tired of it. Very few people are privileged to have the recipe but she has promised to give it to me."

Becca looked pleased at all the compliments.

The meal finished with coffee or tea, after which the young couple disappeared upstairs for a few minutes to get ready to go to their eight o'clock meeting at the vicarage. It was less than half a mile away but Ted was going to drop them off on his way home.

Ted hugged Hannah and shook hands warmly with Paul as they thanked him for all he had done for them that day.

"It's been a pleasure," he said. "I hope to see you again before the big day, but, if not, then Paul and his brother are welcome to stay with me the night before and I will do all the necessary chauffeuring. Whatever you do, don't waste money on a limousine; I'll make sure my car is looking its best and has the traditional white ribbon!"

Four minutes later, they were waving goodbye to him at the vicarage gate.

The vicar turned out to be a grey-haired man of about seventy. When they looked rather surprised, he chuckled. "People my age are often put out to grass in a small parish, although I'm responsible for two churches in neighbouring villages. I've only been here for a year but I gather your parents have been faithful members of this congregation for thirty years or more."

"I came to junior church here until I was about thirteen," Hannah said.

The old man nodded understandingly. As he guided them into his study he said: "I gather from your parents that you'd like to be married on the Sunday before Christmas?"

"Yes, please," Hannah and Paul said, almost in unison.

"As it happens, I can just manage to fit you in. It would have to be at one o'clock, about an hour after the morning service, because we have a special children's service at 3 pm. However, the village hall is available for you during the afternoon at a modest charge if your parents would like to have a reception there. Do ask them to let me know as soon as possible. Rebecca told me that she and David had a tea dance for their wedding breakfast. I must say it sounds rather attractive to me, but you young people may have other ideas."

The vicar stopped abruptly and gave them a searching look. "Now down to business," he said firmly. "Tell me about yourselves and why you want to get married?"

Fortunately, there was a knock on the door at this moment and the vicar's wife came in with three cups of coffee on a tray.

"I thought you might like this. It's decaffeinated, bearing in mind the time of day, but we think it quite nice." She gave them a beaming smile and disappeared.

The interruption had enabled Paul to get over his surprise at what had appeared, on the surface, to be an odd question to ask.

"We're in love and want to make a lifelong commitment to each other, but there's more to it than that," he said slowly.

The vicar waited, with an encouraging look on his kindly face.

"Although we both went to church with our parents when we were young," Paul continued eventually, "the Christian faith had little meaning until very recently when we stayed with my elder sister and her husband in Haltwhistle after walking up the Pennine Way. We went to a talk given by a visiting speaker at their church and it totally changed our lives. The next day, we both asked Jesus to be our Saviour as we sat on a rock overlooking Hadrian's Wall.

"The man who spoke at that meeting had been totally transformed by the grace and power of God. In addition, he told us something afterwards he could not possibly have known unless it was revealed to him by God – he told us when and where Hannah and I first met and added that it was not a coincidence but part of God's plan for our lives!"

"We'd not told anyone about the circumstances of our first meeting," Hannah volunteered, "and so we were shaken to say the least! What really impacted us, though, was Peter's transformation from a dedicated Muslim jihadist to the loveliest Christian man you could possibly meet." She stopped abruptly, astonished to see a couple of tears on the old man's cheek.

"You've obviously had a very special experience," he said quietly. "It'll be a privilege to marry a young couple with a testimony like that! However, before I take a few details about where you live and so on, can you tell me a little more?"

So they gave him a brief summary of the main features of Peter's remarkable testimony, including his miraculous escape into Turkey. When they had finished, the elderly cleric, tears now forgotten, beamed at them: his face almost shining with joy.

"God is so gracious!" he exclaimed. "You'll never know how much your words have encouraged me."

Then he appeared to change the subject. "Will you be able to come to the service next Sunday morning; it'll be the first time your Banns are read?"

After glancing at Paul, who nodded, Hannah replied that they would love to come.

"Good!" the old man said. "Would you think and pray about the possibility of encouraging our small congregation by giving a short version of that amazing story? It can be edited to make it impossible for anybody to discover Peter's identity or where he lives – although I expect he uses various aliases for safety reasons."

The young couple sat stunned for a moment or two and then looked at each other. Although apprehensive, they both knew deep down that it was something God wanted them to do.

"Yes," Paul said. "We'll be glad to do it and will finish by declaring that it resulted in our decision to become Christians the following day."

"Thank you. There are people in our church who need to hear and understand that the Gospel really is Good News!" The old man looked relieved and delighted. "I'll just give a short sermon and then introduce you. Now I really must take down your details."

Hannah and Paul left twenty minutes later, armed with the forms that would enable them to get the Banns called in their parish churches.

Hannah's parents were pleased that everything had gone so well but slightly nonplussed by the fact that the young couple had been invited to speak after the sermon about their Christian experience. For them, churchgoing had been part of their lives since childhood and they were uncomfortable about being too vocal about their faith in God.

Everyone went to bed early because harvesting was normally underway by seven-thirty at this time of year.

So it was that, shortly after a good breakfast and dressed in their oldest clothes, David accompanied Hannah and Paul to the area of broccoli selected for them to harvest. To their surprise, they were joined by Burt and Maria, the Romanian girl borrowed temporarily from a neighbour. The reason became apparent as they approached a small field on the far side of the farm: a large rectangular strip along one side was covered by what looked like very thin gauze.

"I've tried an experiment this year," David said. "As you know, the pesticides that are allowed on organic crops are extremely limited. Last year I read an article about the use of fine-mesh gauze to keep pests out whilst still allowing the rain and sunlight to reach the plants. I've kept a regular check on progress and it looks promising, but the real proof will be as you two do the first cutting. We'll remove the cover now; all five of us need to spread out at intervals along one end of the sheet and gradually move forward along the gaps between the rows folding the sheet as we go."

It was not an easy job, even with five of them, because netting had to be released from the securing stakes at the same time. They eventually managed after well over half an hour.

David made sure his daughter remembered how to cut the main broccoli head before taking the other two workers back with him to carry on the heavy task of lifting swedes. Soon Hannah and Paul were alone in the field beside the handcart that would eventually transfer the vegetables to the sorting shed.

Hannah first showed Paul how to cut the broccoli. "Dad wants us to cut all the main heads, even if some are rather small, because we need to encourage the side heads to form. It's important to take a good length of stem below the head and cut it cleanly to avoid damaging the plant." she said, demonstrating the technique and making it look so easy. She then let him do several under close supervision.

"Take care, the knife is really sharp!" she warned as he fumbled at one point.

She took him to the cart; two canvas bags with stout straps were hanging on hooks at one end.

"These bags are for collecting the cut heads before depositing them in the cart," she said. "We'll work in adjacent rows but don't start chatting until you've really got the hang of it."

They shouldered the canvas bags and Paul walked over to the starting point. Before following him, Hannah reached into another bag she had brought with her from the farmhouse. Paul could see the top of a thermos flask poking out.

"It's a little early for our morning coffee!" he thought. When her hand emerged, however, she was holding a pair of gloves.

"It might be a good idea to wear these thin gardening gloves with finger protection until you get used to the job," she said. "I hope you don't find them too clumsy."

They started work. Not surprisingly, Hannah soon got some distance ahead of Paul, and so, after emptying her bag for the second time, she cut some broccoli heads in his row until he caught up. It was not long before he became more proficient and they had progressed well by the time she called a halt for a cup of coffee.

"This method of harvesting is not very efficient but at least we get to stand up and walk a short distance at fairly frequent intervals to relieve the strain on our backs!" she said. "Large fields on mass production farms are far more mechanized. A motorized container runs alongside a team of cutters and they simply toss the heads in; I guess some get damaged in the process."

Coffee finished, Hannah said: "I'll get you to help me move the cart closer to our new position."

Although it was hard work, Paul found that working in close proximity to his fiancée was a pleasure and he was quite surprised when she announced that it was lunchtime.

"We must take the cart to the packing shed on the way to the farmhouse," she said. "After lunch, Maria is going to deal with our morning's harvest. Dad and Burt will have to carry on with the swedes by themselves!"

Becca had prepared baked potatoes with melted cheese and salad for the five hungry workers, followed by a choice of fresh fruit. They all sat round the kitchen table and Paul was pleased to see that Burt and Maria were treated like one of the family.

The latter spoke quite good English and she told him that it was the second time she had come over from Romania during the summer months to work on a nearby farm. Although she usually had her evening meal with the farmer and his family, they let her live in a small granny annex.

Her employers were not church attendees themselves, Maria explained, but she was usually allowed Sunday as her day off because she liked to go to the Roman Catholic Church in Sherborne.

Hannah asked about Maria's family and then wished she had kept silent because tears came to the young woman's eyes as she spoke about her parents and two brothers and the rundown family farm.

"One of my brothers has to go out to work because the income from the farm is not enough," she said sadly. "That's one of the reasons I come to the UK, although I enjoy working here – everyone is so kind!"

Again Paul was moved to see Hannah reach over and give Maria's hand a gentle squeeze of understanding.

The next three days almost seemed to pass in a blur of hard work, excellent meals, short but happy evenings with Hannah's parents and refreshing sleep after work well done. By lunchtime on Saturday, they had finished harvesting the broccoli assigned to them and Burt and Maria were helping them restore the long sheets of gauze netting over the plants.

Becca had had to join Maria in the packing shed several times during the week. David was due to deliver a second load of individually wrapped broccoli to the local distributors early in the afternoon. He was also taking a couple of boxes of smaller heads to a large greengrocer in Sherborne where it would be sold loose by weight.

A small mountain of swedes was waiting to be cleaned and packed into crates. Paul found himself volunteered to help Burt, Maria and Hannah with this rather laborious task until they finally called it a day at seven-thirty. Burt hurried home to his longsuffering wife while Maria had been invited by Becca to stay on for her evening meal with the family.

Afterwards, Paul and Hannah, eager to stretch their legs after so much bending and crouching, accompanied Maria the short distance back to the farm where she lived. They were about to say goodnight and return, when Maria shyly invited them into her small lodgings. She was so obviously lonely that they agreed and a happy hour was spent chatting over a cup of hot chocolate.

During the conversation it somehow emerged that they were due to give a brief testimony at the morning service in the local church the following day. To their surprise, Maria asked if she could come with them and so it was agreed that they would make a slight detour on the way and collect her a few minutes after ten o'clock.

It was dark by the time Paul and Hannah left Maria. Fortunately, Hannah had had the foresight to bring a torch and the young couple strolled arm-in-arm along the quiet lane remembering the time that they had last walked by torchlight in Standedge.

CHAPTER 29

Becca, Maria, Hannah and Paul arrived at the little church in good time: David had decided that he must continue processing the swedes so that there would not be so much to do on Monday morning before they were collected by the wholesaler's lorry in the early afternoon.

The elderly vicar greeted them with a beaming smile. "I'm so glad to see you! I was rather concerned I might have scared you off by asking you to tell the congregation your story."

Maria was introduced to him and he shook hands warmly.

"You're very welcome to come any time you find getting to Sherborne difficult. In fact, I'll introduce you to my wife afterwards and perhaps she can arrange for you to visit us for coffee or a meal."

Hannah could see that Maria was impressed by his kindness.

There was no choir but the small congregation sang the well-known hymns with gusto, if not particularly tunefully. The scripture passages were read by a woman from the congregation, but the vicar did everything else – the beautiful liturgy, two lots of Banns, including Hannah and Paul's, and the prayers of intercession.

To the young couple, who were anticipating their turn rather anxiously, it seemed no time at all before the elderly man slowly climbed the steps to the ancient pulpit and surveyed the congregation with a beneficent smile. After he had given a short benediction, everyone sat down in anticipation. Clearly, the congregation had come to expect their priest to be relevant and interesting.

As it turned out, he was also dedicated to a clear presentation of the Gospel. He asked his audience to lay aside their possible misconceptions and reflect on what the Bible really taught about what Jesus had achieved for them on the Cross.

Hannah and Paul were, of course, unaccustomed to good sermons because they had paid little attention to what was being preached on their rare excursions to church. Now, however, it was different and they were so filled with awe at the love and mercy of

God revealed by the sacrifice that Jesus willingly made for mankind that they almost completely forgot their nervousness.

The congregation was rather surprised when the vicar drew his sermon to a close after less than twenty minutes and called for Paul and Hannah to come to the front.

"This dear young couple has just had their Banns called for the first time," he said. "But I discovered that they have a remarkable testimony about how they became Christians a few weeks ago. I've taken the liberty of asking them to share it with you."

He came down from the pulpit, guided Paul and Hannah to the lectern, smiled encouragingly at them and returned to his seat.

Paul spoke first and told Peter's story, finishing with the latter's message to them afterwards. His skill as a teacher enabled him to condense the episode without losing any of the most important points.

The congregation sat riveted in their seats and a small child on his mother's knee even stopped giving the occasional grizzle.

Hannah then took over and briefly described what had happened on Hadrian's Wall. She made a point of emphasizing the reassuring words from 2 Corinthians 5:17 that had seemed to shine out from the open Bible immediately after their prayer of commitment: "If anyone is in Christ Jesus, he is a new creation; the old has gone, the new has come!"

"So you see," Paul concluded, "it appears to us, at least, that we had an appointment with destiny – God's destiny – when we arrived at my sister's home unexpectedly early. We were just in time for something to eat before going with her and her husband to their little church in the town to hear this visiting speaker."

"And yet there's nothing special about us," Hannah added. "Jesus is more than ready to reveal himself to anyone humble enough to seek him. Thank you for listening to us so patiently."

She took Paul's hand and they were about to return to their seats when the vicar stopped them.

"You've heard a remarkable testimony this morning and I can see that many of you have been affected by it. I know we're running later than usual and the tea and coffee is getting cold at the back of the church! However, I feel that it would be right to ask Paul and Hannah to be in our prayer corner afterwards to allow people the opportunity to speak to them privately and receive prayer."

He looked around invitingly for a moment before concluding: "We'll miss out our final hymn and I'll close with a short prayer and blessing. Please stand."

Two minutes later, there was a general hubbub as most of the congregation either went over to the refreshment table or left the building.

Several people, however, still remained in their seats looking rather stunned. The vicar quietly approached a young couple sitting a few rows from the front and spoke a few words to them. After a moment he brought them over to Paul and Hannah and introduced them. "They'd like to speak to you," he said gently and left.

The young couple looked rather apprehensive as Paul drew up two chairs for them. "We know how you're feeling," Hannah said. "We were in the same position a month ago. How can we help?"

The girl looked uncomfortable but strangely hopeful as she shared some of the problems that she and her boyfriend faced.

"As we sat listening to you today we began to have a hope that God is not remote and disinterested but wants to take control and give us a direction in life," she concluded. "Would you please ask God to do for us what he has done for you?"

"We've only just set out on this journey of discovery ourselves," Paul assured her. "But the request needs to come from you; we can only support you by praying alongside you. The first step is to acknowledge that you have been living life your own way and your need to be forgiven. You only have to ask Jesus and he will forgive you and give you the guidance that you need. If you like, I'll pray and you can repeat each sentence quietly, but only if you agree with what I say because it needs to be a prayer from your heart."

Both the young people nodded in agreement, and so, step by step, Paul led them in a prayer of repentance and a request for Jesus to forgive them and take control of their lives.

Hannah then took over and asked God to fill them with his presence and go with them as they started a new life together. "Remember the biblical promise," she said. "The old has gone, the new has come!"

There were hugs all round as the two departed looking much happier than when they had come.

Paul and Hannah prayed briefly for two more people before they were free to go in search of Becca and Maria. The latter was now standing by the now empty coffee table waiting for them.

"Becca's gone to prepare the lunch but she's kindly invited me to eat with you," she said.

They found the vicar outside the church saying farewell to the last of the congregation and gave him a very brief report without disclosing any personal details about the people they had prayed with. He was delighted both with their talk and the result and profuse in his thanks.

"Your visit has been a real shot in the arm for this parish. I hope to see you again – apart from at your wedding, of course!"

They assured him they would come again whenever a visit to Hannah's parents included a Sunday, and, of course, over Christmas.

Back at the farm, the lunch, when it was eventually ready, was the most relaxed and enjoyable meal of the week so far. Even David managed to relax and talk about things other than farming because he had managed to make good progress with the swedes.

For the first time since they had arrived, Hannah and Paul were able to go for a proper walk in the afternoon without feeling guilty that there was work to be done. They decided to walk the two and a half miles into Sherborne and asked Maria if she would like to come with them.

"I'll treat you to tea and a cream scone," Paul said.

Maria accepted the offer with delight and it was a happy trio who walked into the town and did a brief tour before selecting a pleasant-looking teashop. Even though Hannah would have liked to have Paul to herself, she was glad they had invited Maria to come when she saw how much she was enjoying the outing and the very English experience of a cream tea.

They returned to the village shortly after six o'clock. Maria gave them both a shy hug of thanks before leaving them.

Becca and David had had a much-needed rest during the afternoon and were ready to spend quality time relaxing with their daughter and prospective son-in-law and discussing some of the details of the coming wedding. Becca had even prepared a simple cold supper that they shared in the large farmhouse living room around a cheerful open fire in the hearth.

Soon after ten o'clock on Tuesday morning, Uncle Ted arrived at the farm for a cup of coffee before taking Hannah and Paul to catch a train to London. David, Maria and Burt were hard at work harvesting another crop of vegetables but Becca stayed to bid them a fond farewell.

Paul accompanied Hannah all the way to Waterloo on his ticket because he wanted to see her safely to her studio flat and spend a few more hours with her before the hard work of lesson preparation recommenced. There was only a short time left before the new term began in earnest.

The little flat felt strange after the spacious farmhouse but Hannah soon unpacked and made a welcome meal with items purchased during their walk from Tooting Broadway.

They had just finished eating when her mobile 'phone rang.

"Tim here!" a cheerful voice said.

There was a pause as Hannah gave Paul a puzzled glance.

The voice tried again. "You know, Tim, the junior half of the Tony and Tim double act!"

"Oh, of course, I'm sorry to be so slow," Hannah replied. "Paul and I have just returned from helping with the harvest on my parents' farm. How are you?"

"Fine, I've just enjoyed a long weekend off for a change. Back to the grindstone tomorrow!" Tim said with some relief. "Do I gather that Paul is with you at the moment?"

Receiving an affirmative answer, he said: "That's good! Can you both spare me half an hour or so at six o'clock at the Café Nero opposite Tooting Broadway station? Tony has remembered his promise to put you in the picture as much as possible and thinks that I can do it more discreetly than he."

Paul gave Hannah a nod. "Fine, we'll see you there at six," Hannah said. "It's my treat!" Tim said as he signed off.

There was not much time before they needed to leave and so they cleared up the dirty dishes as quickly as possible. Reluctantly, Paul decided that he would have to go back to Waterloo after seeing Tim and so prepared to take his rucksack with him.

Their last few precious minutes alone were spent sitting together on Hannah's only comfortable chair; they would not see each other again until she came down to Basingstoke the following Sunday.

Tim was waiting for them just inside the entrance to the café.

"Sorry to be skulking inside instead of waiting to greet you like long lost friends at one of the outside tables, but, as you know, this is a completely unofficial contact," he said, shaking them both warmly by the hand.

After suggesting that they find a quiet table near the back of the café, he went to queue at the counter for three cups of coffee.

"I hope you had a good time on the Pennine Way and in Haltwhistle after all the excitement," he said, placing their drinks on the table; he had even thoughtfully provided two small packets of wafer biscuits to share.

Then he looked uncharacteristically shy for a moment. "You may think me completely mad," he said, "but I was praying for your safety as you went up the Pennine Way ahead of me."

Hannah gave a big grin. "We deduced that you might be a Christian when you wished us "Godspeed" as we left the café in Gargrave. Well, our good news is that we both became Christians after hearing an amazing speaker at Paul's sister's church in Haltwhistle."

"We'll give you a potted version of that testimony after you've revealed as much as you can about the dongle mystery!" Paul said.

Tim gave them a smile of real pleasure before launching into his tale.

"You two really came up trumps, not just as superb decoys but with the black car's registration number and that business card giving the address of the antiques shop in Mitcham," he said. "It meant we could arrange to keep both the shop and the hire garage in Derby under discrete observation. There was another benefit; our boss and another minion stayed fairly close to Horton and didn't follow the original plan of moving closer to the A1 trunk road ready to follow if the crooks made a getaway towards London."

He gave a quiet chuckle. "It was a very good job that they did, because, to our surprise, the gang split up. For some reason, the blond man was left in Horton and the other two took their car back to Derby about an hour after you two departed. This meant that our boss could leave the new man in Horton keeping an eye on the very distinctive blond man while the rest of us followed the dodgy antique dealer and his unpleasant assistant to Derby. Our boss wanted both of us to come with him because we knew those two by sight. In fact, Tony and I had to follow them on the train from Derby to London while our boss took the car. The tracking device was particularly helpful because we could follow their movements on the train without being seen and also as they moved through London."

Tim spent a moment or two sipping the excellent coffee and chewing a chocolate wafer biscuit.

"We followed them at a distance all the way to the Mitcham shop. After half an hour, the owner made a telephone call – our people were listening in by this time – and arranged to see a certain party using some sort of code. Then he left on foot, together with travel bag and attaché case, to go to his home less than a mile away. Shortly after, he was picked up by taxi and taken to another address where he spent about twenty minutes before returning home minus attaché case.

"Our people kept an eye on all the premises involved until six o'clock the next morning. I'm glad to say that Tony and I were allowed to go home for a bit of sleep. Not much, however, because we were involved in the raiding parties that swooped on all three places in the early morning.

"We arrested the antique dealer at home, the small dark man as soon as he turned up at the shop, and a foreign national together with the attaché case. Rather annoyingly the latter turned out to have diplomatic immunity, but at least he has been expelled from the UK.

"The shop was searched thoroughly and the two sales staff questioned. Later, we asked an expert in antiques, pictures in particular, to check on some of the items on sale but he only spotted one possibly fake picture and another that may be a stolen original; we're in the process of checking now."

Tim paused again, ostensibly to drink more coffee. It was obvious that he was now choosing his words with great care.

"We're still trying to discover the mole in the Ministry of Defence. Unfortunately, there are several people who work closely with the careless rule-breaker. Some have visited him at home and know the layout of his office.

"There's also a bit of a mystery about the blond-haired man. My boss discovered that he had been given the job of porter-cum-caretaker at the shop fairly recently; before that he was in prison. When asked why the man had been left in Horton, the antique dealer said that he had generously paid for him to have a week's holiday as a reward for all his hard work. Thus, when a report came in from the detective back in Horton that the man appeared to be enjoying walking in the hills, our boss decided that we could deal with him later and concentrate on the work in London first. Thankfully, the detective was recalled to help!"

Hannah and Paul exchanged a quick glance at this point. Tim was sharp enough to notice but continued on the same theme.

"After a week, our blond friend turned up at the Mitcham premises and didn't seem too surprised to see a police constable guarding the door. He nervously explained who he was, produced a key to the front door and asked if he could go up to his flat above the shop. The officer escorted him upstairs but contacted us on his radio. Tony was busy and so sent me over to ask some questions.

"I found out that he had heard about the arrests from one of the sales staff in the shop. He said that he had only recently become suspicious about the small dark-haired man, mainly because the latter was seldom on the premises and knew nothing about antiques. He hadn't liked to query why he had been ordered to meet the man and escort him back to the shop with the attaché case, or why a roundabout route was necessary, because he was frightened of loosing his job.

"He then surprised me by volunteering the information that he had been in prison until recently, making it hard to find honest work. I must say he really went up in my estimation at this point!"

Paul and Hannah found that Tim was now looking at them very intently as he continued. "Finally, he said something extremely surprising; he assured me that he was a completely reformed character after meeting two people in Horton who had helped him come to faith in God. He sounded completely sincere when he said that he had become a Christian and his past had been forgiven.

"Very unprofessionally, I must have shown my pleasure at this point because he asked to shake my hand as we parted. I said I would put in a good word for him and told him to stay on in the caretaker's flat until the future of the business had been decided, assuring him that, even if the place went into liquidation, he would be paid for guarding the stock until it could be sold off. I then wrote a brief report of the interview for Tony, being as positive as I could!"

Tim suddenly gave them an almost cheeky smile. "Those two people weren't you, by any chance?" he asked innocently.

Hannah smiled back. "Guilty as charged! We got back to Horton quicker than expected having taken the train part of the way – Paul wanted time to show me some of the Peak District before the end of our holiday.

"We had finished eating in the Golden Lion and were just having a cup of coffee, when, to my great surprise, I looked over to the other side of the room and saw Mike starring at us in amazement. He came over and sat down at our table. Within a minute or two, all his worries and fears came tumbling out. He said he'd started out by enjoying his enforced walking; in fact, he seemed rather pleased about it because he knew his boss had intended it to be a punishment. However, all this had been spoiled by the news from Mitcham and he was now afraid he would be arrested when he went back to collect his few possessions and the small amount of money he had saved from his wages. In our attempt to offer advice, we took him out to a quieter table in the garden and Paul got some liquid refreshment. Somehow, we began to share with him that his only hope was to place his life in the hands of God."

"In fact, we told him what had happened to us in Haltwhistle: the testimony we're about to share with you," Paul volunteered. "To cut a long story short, Mike asked us to help him pray to Jesus for forgiveness and so I led him in a prayer of commitment – the first time he has ever prayed in his life!"

"It was almost completely dark by that time, but it was wonderful to sense the Holy Spirit at work in that rough man," Hannah said softly. "I'm sure he's a changed character and I hope you can continue to put in a good word for him."

"Thank you for being so open with me," Tim replied. "I'll certainly do my best. But now let's hear your story!"

CHAPTER 30

Paul woke with a start; an elbow had dug him in the ribs.

He had been sleeping so heavily that it took him a few moments to become aware that he was in an unusually large bed. Then, with a surge of joy, he realized Hannah was lying beside him.

They had been married at one o'clock the previous afternoon – the Sunday before Christmas – at the little parish church in the Hannah's childhood village: a beautiful and simple ceremony conducted by the elderly vicar who had been so kind and understanding at their wedding interview four month's previously.

Hannah had looked wonderful in a modest white wedding dress attended by a single diminutive pageboy.

Young Toby was now much steadier on his feet than he had been in Haltwhistle but he still insisted on calling his new aunt, "Anna". Sue and Ian had brought him with them from Haltwhistle, together with Mark, who had first driven north from Skipton and left his little car in Haltwhistle so that he could spend Christmas with the family when they returned after two nights at the farmhouse.

Sarah and Jack had come down from Sheffield in the latter's taxi and they would be staying on at the farmhouse over the whole Christmas period. Hannah and Paul would join them next Wednesday, Christmas Eve, after their short three-night honeymoon.

Paul had been delighted that his good friend John, now completely recovered from his operation, had been able to drive over from Basingstoke with his wife for the day.

Apart from her parents and Uncle Ted, Hannah's family was almost non-existent. Her only other relative was her grandmother who lived in a pleasant retirement home five miles away and had been collected for the celebration by a friend of the family.

This unusual lack of relatives, however, had been amply counterbalanced by friendly villagers who had rallied round to support the marriage of the only daughter of two long-established and valued members of the community. Several had even taken it on themselves to organize the wedding breakfast buffet in the church hall.

Uncle Ted had come up trumps as a chauffeur. The previous day, he had driven Paul and Mark from his flat in Sherborne to the church before going to the farmhouse to collect Hannah. Then just before six o'clock in the evening, after the newly-weds had rather clumsily concluded their last dance, Ted had driven them off in a shower of confetti to the farm for Hannah to change before taking them to the country-house hotel where they were now staying for three nights.

Needless to say, the "tea dance" itself – the brain child of Hannah's mother and the vicar – had continued for at least two hours after the departure of the happy couple, enthusiastically and rather nostalgically supported by the older folk in the village.

As Paul lay there peacefully listening to Hannah's very gentle breathing, he could not help reflecting on the amazing things that had happened since their first meeting on the train to Sheffield the previous July.

Everything had appeared to happen so naturally: an intriguing mystery shared; the discovery of a common interest in walking; two rather shy young people finding themselves increasingly comfortable doing some serious hiking together.

Hannah's love of walking and amazing stamina had meant that they had reached Haltwhistle just in time for the most important meeting of their lives. If John had been his companion, they would have probably taken a day longer on the journey.

The God who loved them had worked all these things into his plan, culminating – at this stage, at least – in Peter's astonishing testimony and the private revelation afterward that their initial meeting on the train had been no accident. The specification of the precise day and place of the meeting – something that Peter could not possibly have known – had shaken Paul to the core. Even at that stage, he was beginning to realize that the God he had chosen to ignore all his life was actually interested in him. Peter's testimony may have left him on a knife edge of indecision but the personal message had tipped the balance; he, along with Hannah, had been ready to make a commitment.

He now also realized that the faithful prayers of his parents and sister over the years had played a large part; this side of heaven he would probably never know just how much. Suddenly, he was flooded with an intense feeling of gratitude and his eyes filled with tears as he thanked Jesus for them and asked that the Lord's blessing and protection would cover them and Ian and little Toby.

"Please open Mark's eyes as you have ours," he found himself whispering. "He feels particularly sad now after recently breaking up with yet another girlfriend. Although we are very close, it must be difficult for him to see his brother now happily married."

Hannah stirred and Paul waited for her to settle again before slipping as quietly as he could to the bathroom. He guessed she must have been out some time before him and was surprised to see that his watch indicated the time to be just on six o'clock; he must have been asleep longer than he realized. He managed to creep cautiously back to bed without rousing her and lay there much too alert and excited to sleep again.

Thanksgiving for the wonderful girl a few inches away flooded over him. There had been no sudden spark when they first met. Nevertheless, they had fallen deeply in love in the space of one week, albeit having been almost constant companions during that time. Also, he must not forget, God had planned for them to get married.

It had been so different with his only other serious girlfriend, Jayne. Her beauty had bowled him over and he had been totally astonished and delighted when she responded to his shy approach.

He was ashamed now, as a Christian, to have slept with her several times. The first time, she had shown no embarrassment about literally throwing off her clothes and almost literally jumping into bed with him. Needless to say, as a red-blooded male, he had responded eagerly, ready to allow her to show him anything that gave her sexual pleasure.

Of course, it did not take long for her to tire of him, especially as he was a hardworking scientist hoping to achieve a good degree and she did not seem to care about her history course. Although besotted, he had thankfully kept his feet on the ground and resisted her expectation to be given almost undivided attention. Fortunately, as it turned out, she had met someone else, more handsome, with deeper pockets and equally idle.

Tears came to Paul's eyes again as he silently voiced his thanks to God for forgiving his past and washing him clean. His biblical knowledge was still sadly lacking but he seemed to recall somewhere that God has promised to completely forget our sins when they have been forgiven. In our humanity, we may recall them with a sense of shame, but he will never bring the matter up again.

The previous evening now came vividly to Paul's memory. Of course, they needed a good shower soon after reaching their comfortable hotel room; the tea-dance had been surprisingly energetic! Thus, following a delicious but fairly frugal dinner and a cup of coffee in the attractive lounge, they had not needed long to prepare for bed.

After he gallantly carried Hannah over the threshold, she shyly asked him to use the bathroom first. Then, while she took her turn, he reduced the lighting to a single bedside lamp before climbing into the king-size bed and waiting for her to emerge.

It was not long before she did so. Glancing shyly at him, she sped modestly across the room and slipped quietly under the duvet beside him. Then she turned to him with a nervous smile.

Paul was almost overwhelmed by the intensity of his love for her; she looked so young, innocent and vulnerable. Her small sweet face, now without a trace of the rather mischievous demeanour that greatly appealed to him, was completely serious: just as it had been when they prayed together on Hadrian's Wall and were not quite sure if they were doing everything correctly.

"Hannah," he whispered. "I love you more than I can possibly describe. In fact, I love you so much it almost hurts!"

With that, he drew her slowly towards him and kissed her so tenderly that she began to cry gently.

Gradually, their passion increased and it was not long before they became so completely focussed on each other that their surroundings ceased to exist.

Afterwards, they could not bear to part; Paul just held his now sleepy wife tightly to him. In the end, however, one of his arms began to go to sleep and he gently eased her down beside him with her head resting against his chest. Her close presence was so wonderful that he imagined her being bathed in the love that seemed to emanate from every pore in his body.

Nevertheless, it was not long before they were both fast asleep.

The early morning recollection of their first lovemaking was totally delightful and Paul sank into a contented reverie in which he was completely aware of his surroundings but too lethargic to move a muscle. It was only when someone's alarm clock sounded faintly in an adjacent room that he looked at his wristwatch; it was 6:45 and Hannah still appeared to be asleep.

He was glad that she had had such a restful night after all the stress of getting ready for the wedding and he began to pray for her. Very soon, he was flooded with an intense sense of thanksgiving that God had brought such a wonderful girl into his life.

"From the bottom of my heart, Lord, I thank you for Hannah!" he breathed.

"Did you call my name?" a sleepy voice asked.

"I'm sorry! I was praying and must have spoken aloud without realizing it. In fact, I was thanking God for you."

A hand found his and gripped it tight.

A moment later, Hannah said: "Thank you for last night. I had no idea making love could be so wonderful!"

"You were amazing," Paul whispered in reply, "but I haven't even begun to show you how much I love you!"

"Show me..." The two simple words came with quiet longing.

He reached out in the darkness and drew her warm supple body towards him. Her mouth found his and then nothing else in the world mattered.

Eventually, he lifted her out of bed and carried her to the bathroom so that they could share the spacious cubicle for a shower before breakfast.

"I'm ravenous!" Hannah said in his ear. "But I mustn't get fat this week!"

"There's absolutely no chance of that," Paul replied with a happy laugh. "You'll always be slim and totally delectable!"

The End of the Beginning